THOSE ENDEARING YOUNG CHARMS

THOSE ENDEARING YOUNG CHARMS

Marion Chesney

Chivers Press • **G.K. Hall & Co.**
Bath, England **Waterville, Maine USA**

LP
Che

This Large Print edition is published by Chivers Press, England, and by G.K. Hall & Co., USA.

Published in 2002 in the U.K. by arrangement with the author c/o Lowenstein Associates.

Published in 2002 in the U.S. by arrangement with Lowenstein Associates, Inc.

U.K. Hardcover ISBN 0–7540–4746–6 (Chivers Large Print)
U.K. Softcover   ISBN 0–7540–4747–4 (Camden Large Print)
U.S. Softcover   ISBN 0–7838–9625–5 (Nightingale Series Edition)

The text of this Large Print edition is unabridged.
Other aspects of the book may vary from the original edition.

Set in 16 pt. New Times Roman.

Printed in Great Britain on acid-free paper.

British Library Cataloguing in Publication Data available

Library of Congress Cataloging-in-Publication Data

Chesney, Marion.
     Those endearing young charms / Marion Chesney.
        p. cm.
     ISBN 0–7838–9625–5 (lg. print : sc : alk. paper)
     1. Large type books. I. Title.
     PR6053.H4535 T47 2002
     823'.914—dc21   2001039796

The Flaxfield
by Stijn Streuvels

Translated by Peter Glassgold and André Lefevere

Sun & Moon Classics
Sun & Moon Press
Los Angeles

English translation copyright©, Peter Glassgold and André
Lefevere, 1988. Originally published as *De Vlaschaard*, in Dutch,
by Manteau in Belgium.

This book was produced with the cooperation of the
Foundation for the Promotion of the Translation of Dutch
Literary Works, and the Flemish Community, Flanders, Belgium.

Cover: *Boer Kerckhove* (Peasant Kerckhove), by Gustave Van
de Woestyne, 1910. From the collection of the Museum
Mx. J. Dhonlt-Dhaenens, Deurle, Belgium.

Library of Congress Cataloging in Publication Data
Streuvels, Stijn
    The Flaxfield.

I. Title
Sun & Moon Classics, number 3

FIRST EDITION

10   9   8   7   6   5   4   3   2   1

SUN & MOON CLASSICS
Sun & Moon Press
6148 Wilshire Blvd.
Los Angeles, California 90048

This translation is dedicated to Joost de Wit, with gratitude and affection.

Introduction

The Flaxfield (De Vlaschaard) is the most important novel written by the Flemish author Stijn Streuvels (the pen name of Frank Lateur), who lived from 1871 to 1969. Streuvels' extraordinarily long life and prolific writings assured him a leading place in the Flemish cultural revival that had begun in the 1890s under the inspired hand of his uncle, the poet Guido Gezelle (1830-99). The Flemish movement itself paralleled similar but better-known language-defined renascences, such as those in Ireland and Provence. Streuvels' novel of 1907 can surely be called a forgotten classic of world literature, even as its author has become largely forgotten beyond the limits of the Low Countries. This, however, was not always the case.

Born in the village of Heule, near Kortrijk, in West Flanders, Streuvels' formal education ended with two years of secondary school, after which he became a baker's apprentice and, eventually, a master baker himself. He began writing in the late 1890s, contributing to the Flemish nationalist periodical

Van Nu en Straks. After the success of his first book, *Lenteleven,* a collection of short stories, he devoted himself entirely to literary efforts, publishing during the next four decades at least one book a year. In 1905, he settled in Ingooigem—again near Kortrijk—where he was to remain the rest of his long days. His national and international fame reached its peak in the period between the two world wars, when his work was translated into French, German, Italian, and Russian, among other languages. Rosa Luxemburg counted *The Flaxfield* as one of her favorite novels.

Streuvels' earliest writing was heavily influenced by the great Russian and Scandinavian novelists of the time; though his formal schooling was limited, he was well read in several European languages. His intellectual outlook can be called one of enlightened fatalism, which saw the universe and all life-forms in it, humanity included, as ruled by the inexorable law of growth, flowering, and decay. Those who live according to that law live at peace with themselves; those who defy it—like farmer Vermeulen of *The Flaxfield*—will be broken by it. Childhood is the only grace period the law allows; once children achieve adulthood, they must take their places in the world—like Vermeulen's son, Louis—inevitably at the expense of those who came before.

Most of Streuvels' work is in the European naturalist tradition, and his chosen locale, as in *The Flaxfield*, is quite literally the fields of Flanders, the farming village of his native southwest Belgium in the years before the First World War. His language is appropriately regional, often archaic, and deliberately rough. The Dutch he wrote is a mixture of the dialect of his region, the standard language of Amsterdam, and his own literary idiolect: Streuvels' collected works, published in the early 1980s, provides a necessary glossary of his peculiar West Flemish.

Streuvels' naturalism is tempered, however, by intensely lyrical passages, not just when he is describing the countryside and the passage of the seasons—the most obvious expressions of his universal law—but also when he portrays his characters, transfiguring the crimped mortals of his fiction into beings of almost mythical dimensions. Though his work is set in the narrow stretch of land between the Lys and Scheldt rivers (Leie and Schelde in Dutch), those few square miles seem at times to epitomize the universe. Beneath the towering cumulus of the Flemish sky—a presence familiar to us in both traditional landscape painting and Van Gogh's hallucinatory canvases—doom takes on a perennial grandeur, in the weather, the soil, the very cycle of life.

The Flaxfield is built around the rhythm of the seasons, which in turn dictates the sowing, growing, flowering, and harvesting of the flax that is reflected in the novel's four narrative divisions. The action—more a symphonic, at times discordant unfolding—follows the course of the agricultural year in rural Flanders and the murderous rivalry that emerges between the ageing farmer Vermeulen, desperately hanging on to his *patria potestas,* and his ever more assertive son, Louis, as they contend over the cultivation of their most profitable and prestigious crop. Threaded through the narrative is Louis' growing sexual awareness and his attachment to the girl Schellebelle, one of the maids resident at the farm. Vermeulen's hypocritical rage over their puppy love opens a window on the social hierarchy of the region: the farmer's son must not throw himself away on a mere maid. At the same time, the situation provides Vermeulen with an excuse to exercise his full power against Louis: he will shunt his son aside, *contra naturam,* by setting him up on a neighboring farm. But nature—Vermeulen's ultimate antagonist—forestalls the farmer's manipulations and brings the novel to its brilliant, tragic end, with Louis lying in a coma, struck down by his father's hand, and the father himself broken, helpless, pitiful.

The Flaxfield is more than just a novel about the conflict of generations and erotic awakening or an allegorical meditation on the theme of eternal growth and decay—Streuvels was far too keen an observer of the common people and the land around him for that. In the most palpable sense, *The Flaxfield* is an amazingly accurate record of life in rural Flanders at the turn of this century, replete with folktales and folksongs now all but lost. Here are the farmhands and maids, the hawkers and the hired laborers. The Vermeulen family and the relatively well-to-do farmers stand for the only wealth that existed in the region between the Lys and the Scheldt in those preindustrial days, a culturally subversive wealth that would achieve higher status at the expense of its own traditions, its own language: Vermeulen's daughters are being educated in French and are unlikely to adapt once more to the rude life of the farm.

Streuvels' almost photographic observation; his rendering of regional speech; his detailed charting of Vermeulen's and Louis' emotions; his explosive lyricism, which lends a mythopoeic resonance to uneventful lives in an obscure corner of a then relatively backward country—this is the mix of ingredients that makes *The Flaxfield* the wonderfully unique novel it is. This eulogy must be tempered, however, by an apology: it is simply impossible for a translation to do full justice to a work of such complexity. Yet what we have managed to filter through into English of Streuvels' homely West Flemish will allow American readers to savor at last, after more than eighty years of inaccessibility, one of the lonely masterpieces of twentieth-century literature.

André Lefevere
Peter Glassgold

Sowing

I

The heavy gray sky weighed on the world. A thickness of accumulated fog, from far below up to the highest levels of the air, pressed down its harsh burden—an immovable sadness, a sorrow without hope or end. For days everything remained dull and dark. Then came the wind, unleashed unexpectedly, whipping up clouds of muddy rain that raked over the soil, slashing and scourging the fields. The flat land lay there bound by its close horizon, drenched with mist, useless, soaked through, solitary, left to the cruel elements without respite, like a wilderness at the dawn of the first day.

So the sullen winter dragged on, without a speck of clear light, in desperate monotony. Spring had already come into season, but everything remained locked up, blanketed with the darkness of long nights and days in between that were no days. What name could you put to it, the twilight that dribbled out from under the clouds, deadened by the thick cover—the dullness that without blush of morning or glow of evening separated the nights for a short span of time and plunged the world from one darkness into the next?

The air was full of dampness. Fog and spray floated in ragged whorls before the wind, and in it the crows turned and wheeled their wings, black as mortal sin, shrieking utter gloom in wild cries over the land.

Vermeulen stood watching it through the window.

"Springtime!" the farmer mocked bitterly. "More like the darkness come Advent!" An unspeakable boredom tormented him. He twisted round and round without purpose, fretting at the almighty elements he could not overpower and which kept him locked up in that huge stuffy kitchen where he wandered about with his fists in his pants pockets, like a caged bear, from the window to the fire and from the fire to the window. Every day brought the farmer a new disillusionment. In the morning he got out of his warm nest with reluctance, tired of lying around and angry because he could not wait there, in the drowse of sleep, for the coming of the clear weather.

That winter lasts four months Vermeulen tolerated well enough: those were the months for starting the stored seed, for thriving after the hardship of the summer labor. But that there was no break yet, no opening in the sky after four months! Not a bit of consolation, nor a trace of life when the time had come, the sowing season when the task of the spring work began to press, when the farmer's year should otherwise have started. . . . And still all was mud and slush, and ever new clouds of moisture came sailing through the air. . . . And that there was nothing you could do about it! All curses were powerless, and you just had to swallow your gall!

"Having to eat your heart out like this! The land's soaked through like a swamp, it gets wetter all the time, the draining ditches are spilling over with mud, and that smothering fog. . . . Last year the job was all done and forgotten, and we had a good sowing wind: the flax was already up."

His wife, who was used to hearing the farmer rant, had learned to be patient: she no longer listened. It was only from habitual indulgence that she added, indifferent and resigned:

"What can we do about it? It'll get better. Summer's never failed to come yet." And the farmer's trustful wife thought it neither necessary nor desirable to look up from her work and cast an eye outside, so certain was she of the fixed course of the seasons. She left her husband to his hopeless ennui.

Yes, what could they do about it, and what could the poor small farmers do, except wait and submit to the idea that though March might be treacherous April had never failed them yet? Be patient and submit! It was all right for the womenfolk to chatter on so, but think of all the time going to waste!

"You've never been too late with the harvest yet," she went on. "Are you going to get all jumpy again and run around with ants in your pants? What help is that?"

Vermeulen decided not to open his mouth again

and to hold in his sour temper.

He stood by the window once more, unthinking and unseeing, and pushed his fists even deeper into his pants pockets. The windows, they were deceptive breathing holes, the only things linking people with the world that existed outdoors: sight only, without the good blast of the wind and the draft of the open air. You could lean against these and stand and stare until your own breath fogged up the view and everything became obscured and indistinguishable. Still, Vermeulen was drawn to those peepholes, and his angry nature forced him to watch the ugliness outside.

He was resigned enough. Does an old farmer lack resignation? Who knew better than himself that summer had to come? That the east was full of beautiful days! But why then didn't they come on time? Why didn't that heavy damned fog crack open and the grayness lift? The craggy farmer tortured himself like this since he could only stand there fidgeting helplessly and move nothing in the sky. From one end of the year to the other, the obstinate attack and the equal push back continues; always he must fight and hold on, only in the end to stand in meek expectation and let the mindless powers lord it over his work, over his property and goods.

But that will not stop an old farmer from grumbling about his troubles time and again, constrained and surly as he paces back and forth underneath the black ceiling—five months running between four walls, having to breathe in the stuffy

air of the hearth. It will not stop him from getting
sick of looking at the same tiresome things through
that peephole of a window—the outside immersed in
the tedium of sullen darkness. In great lungfuls he
has always sniffed in the free refreshing air; his eyes
are used to taking in the whole valley, lying open
and bare as if in front of a wide window—the
immeasurable expanse of living green glowing in
the splendor of the sun. And now the land is all one
full swamp of mud; the view stretches no further
than a bowshot, and you cannot distinguish a man
from a woman. Roads and canals have been
transformed into runnels, and where five trees stand
nested together, they look like a wall, a cloud, a
formless pit of blue smoke, or some other unshapen
thing. Houses and gardens lie submerged in
smothered heaps in the damp, and you cannot make
out door from window or roof from chimney. For five
long months, the sky weighs down on the world like
a heavy blanket, with no breathing hole, no light, no
brightness, no sun, no moon. Cut off from all traffic,
everyone is left on their own, cast away on the farm,
surrounded as on an island on all sides with mire,
mud, and submerged land. And when you have
counted the days for five months and jumped from
one chair to another, with your shins burned by the
hearth and a crick in your back because of the cold
drafts; when the hour of deliverance is there and the
weather ought to change but does *not* change. . . .
When you are ready to start on the job, and you feel
your hands itch, wanting to grip and heave and

push and dig—just to get on with the work! . . . Yet
storm and rain keep up regularly, and March hangs
on like an old winter rat. . . . A farmer, of course, is
ever a store of resignation, but the damned boredom,
that sticks in his craw; begrudging and irritable, he
finds everything gets in his way, and life does not
seem worth even a kick from his heavy-shod feet.
Wouldn't you begin to wonder if after all there was
something out of whack with the sun? or if
somewhere a cog has jumped the catches of the great
wheelwork, and the days turn senselessly now
without moving the axles that are supposed to raise
the sun to its height and power?

Vermeulen certainly knew better: it was the same
every year, but a man does not become more
reasonable with age, he develops whims and quirks
worse than a widowed hag. His heart was set on
work today; with all his might and desire, the farmer
now at once wanted to pound open the fog, to have
a break in the sky, to make a gap and see the
blue—oh! the level blue, the depth of the sky! It
gnawed at him, and like a child he longed to go out
in the fields—as if this were the first and last year of
farming left to him. It played before his mind like a
distant happiness: motion, the land, coming alive,
labor, himself bellowing out his orders over the fields,
watching the horses pull, the ploughshare tearing
through packed soil, the hands at work everywhere,
the color of their clothing, their gestures, the sound
of their voices, the bustle far and wide throughout
the valley—feeling growth in the air, the mild, fertile

air with a refreshing wind out of the south, and the sunlight, the warmth, the scintillating brightness over the plain, the greening of a new spring!

Vermeulen saw it in his imagination as a memory from a dim past, unreal—something that was gone forever and never would return again: a beautiful dream remembered after waking. For in his sober mood, he viewed things otherwise: before him, the land was blanketed, soaked, soft as a quagmire. And suddenly, he felt it: the terror of his humanity small and puny, drowned in the presence of an awesome power. It seemed as though the farmers had lost forever all mastery of their fields, that there was no live bond left between mankind and nature—the land lying so cruelly forsaken, dead and drab, colorless and flat, as if it were congealed water or a sinkhole in which houses and gardens lay stranded like shapeless barges on the verge of rot. All the toil and all the diligent activity of the autumn work now seemed a ridiculous effort, a stupid children's game done for nothing, and of which nothing, not a trace, would remain, no more than the black crow leaves a streak in the air where it wings by. The seed must surely lie rotting in the haze. And of the repeated ploughing and harrowing and furrowing, there was not the tiniest crease left on the ground: the rains had filled in everything and turned it into mush. Nowhere in the entire vicinity was there a hint of approaching greenery—the fields lay covered with water, and the slender shoots of rye lay stuck together and beaten into the leached and muddy soil, churned up and washed out. People had in turn put their expectation and their hope on the old and the new moon, but it was all women's talk . . .

Vermeulen turned his head away in disgust, so as not to see the landscape any longer. In his clogs, he shambled over to another window and gazed out over the yard. At least here the farming was going on. The girl was slopping the hogs; two of them wallowed in the wet earth and rotting straw, snuffling in the filth. The cowherd stood singing by the feed grinder. A groom was throwing fresh bundles of straw down through the window of the loft. From the barn came the steady thudding of flails: the wheels were humming in the scutching room, and you could hear the shudder at regular intervals, each time flax came through the swingles. Everything flowed on in peaceful activity, as it had all winter, in daily recurrence. Jan, the old groom, hauled scraped beetroots to the stables. Louis, the farmer's son, young Vermeulen, strode around the yard with his boots on—purposely, it seemed, through dirt and muck, from here to there, in and out of the sheds; but now he ran after one of the girls. Laughing in her loose-fitting blouse with its sleeves rolled up, she took the yeastpot to the bakehouse, where the chimney puffed energetically.

Louis was every inch the sturdy young farmer, very much the man, his legs slender in his boots and his body firm beneath his clothes—a youth with ruddy face and alert eyes. Not sensitive to the bad weather, he walked about cheerfully, without boredom or irritation. He was in the glory of his twenty years, unmarried, free on his father's domain, intimate with all its workings, because he had been born and raised there, had grown up with it—in his whole look, he was like a young thoroughbred that understands no limits to its strength and splendor. He was the new force, the robust sound, the rising power, spreading forth unperturbed the abundant flowering of his life, going his own way on the great farm, next to the old farmer, the chief, the authority, the almighty personified: his father.

"What does he want with that girl in the bakehouse?" Vermeulen growled, dissatisfied.

His wife went on peeling the potatoes, as if not a word had been spoken.

Vermeulen let the matter drop, pretending he had been talking to himself, and went to sit by the hearth. He pried the ashes out of his pipe and filled it again.

Besides the bad weather and the rudeness of the season, there was something else that irritated the farmer and made him short. The long winter and the aggravation of sitting there useless—that came from outside and worried him in his helplessness, with ever new frustration at the delayed emergence. That would pass; with a little patience, it would get better: spring would surely set in, he knew that, and the dismal feeling would soon be forgotten. But the other thing struck deeper, an incessant uneasiness he carried in his innards: for he saw no improving it, he knew himself even more powerless here than against the elements.

Vermeulen sat there, the weight of his wide body filling out the whole chair; his heavy face withdrawn, knees pulled up and arms in his lap, he puffed on his old, well-smoked pipe. In the hearth, flames twisted upward from the wood chips at his feet. He was aware of himself sitting there: he was the totality of the great enterprise, the keeper of that teeming activity; in his mind were the laws and the business arrangements for the whole farming year and the prospect for many years to come. Whatever commands he had lay in his imagination like a smooth, wide road, and he held infallibly both the means and the end in his powerful grasp. Aside from the broad outlines of the foreseeable plan, he held just as firmly the small matters of each passing day. To the farthest corners of the yard, barn, and stables, he knew the condition of everything that stirred and was alive. He knew every farmhand, every maid as if they were his own children, and he was the first to notice when something was amiss with any animal in his stables, likewise with the minute particulars of each piece of equipment: he saw it, even if it was only the arm of a swingle about to break or a nut come loose. Vermeulen was aware his strong will gave order to that whole enterprise, all the work and activity, and kept it going and in repair; everything there followed one course, forced to it by his own inner vision. The farm was a world of its own—all those who lived in the vicinity found their subsistence there: whoever had worked it in summer could fatten up there in winter; when everything lay frozen over, with no work anywhere, the house with its many roofs offered a secure shelter for all those in need. The farmer reigned like a king whose presence inspires awe everywhere—all falls silent when he appears. Vermeulen had received this authority from his father, and he knew how to keep the upper hand: with a tough will and a hard fist. Not only on the farm but in the entire province, he was known as a steadfast farmer, more influential than anyone else the whole region wide. It was he who gave advice, surly and gruff, imposing his opinion on other farmers; he who maintained the old customs and traditions, who farmed following fixed usage—for whom the others waited in order to start and plan their work, their harvest, and other tasks: "Vermeulen's doing it, Vermeulen isn't doing it" acted as a signal in the district that found response, making an impression everywhere.

He did not ask how or from where that prestige had been attached to him or why and with what right he was allowed to exercise it. He understood himself to be the strongest, the most knowing, and he knew how to bend all the others beneath his headstrong will. That was the way it was and the way it would remain.

And yet the uneasiness gnawed at him from within. He did not dare think of it, he tried to push it away—and yet: the end of his concern and the beginning of another's stewardship lay in his mind as destiny. Time had booted and hammered his

brain . . . so many summers, so many winters—so
often he had seen the sowing, the harvest, the wheels
of the round year come and go. His step had grown
heavy under the weight of his body, his scalp showed
through his hair, and the features of his face were
now as though carved in stone, lined with deep
grooves in the weathered brown skin, like the bark of
an old tree. Age had increased his authority: he
could feel himself stand firmer, his voice had a
graver tone, and giving orders came off more easily
for him now that he had become the old, important
farmer who knows better than anyone else, simply
because he *is* older and has seen more. His
pronouncements were always sharp, and what made
others tremble with its very recklessness he discussed
with a conviction that seemed to him in accord with
his long experience.

It was whenever Vermeulen saw his son—until
recently just a runny-nose kid, now a handy lad with
firm, supple limbs and a cocky stance; Louis who
went everywhere, come rain come shine, strutting
around the yard as if it were his very own—whenever
he saw his son busy, or thought about him, there
came into his mind the image of the ancient tree
that has reached its full growth, overshadowing
everything with its broad crown, but from whose
roots has sprouted a shoot that will grow next to the
old trunk and in time become a tree in its own right,
overgrowing the old trunk and obstructing the wide
crown, until they together fall into conflict and fight
each other for the clearest space beneath the sky.

That is when the old one must give way, Vermeulen concluded, since it has given up all its life's juices to the young shoot.

The farmer thought of his son. There was no malice in his thoughts, since the boy excited no fear or anxiety in him. Up to now, Louis had been agreeable and easygoing, a wild stripling without opinions or presumptions of his own with respect to the farm's management—and later on, Vermeulen would certainly show him the way, if it appeared necessary. The simple realization that there was a will, a consciousness growing up alongside him had Vermeulen worried—the sinewy fighter felt as if power was slipping away from him and that sooner or later he would have to struggle to remain on top. He saw it coming as of necessity: as the children grew bigger, he would have to exert himself all the more to keep that rising power in check which threatened his rule. However he turned the matter over in his mind, the tree stood doomed in the general course of things—he felt authority slipping from his grasp, like water through his fingers—the fate weighed upon him. Barbele herself, his wife, with whom in the past his life had been so intimately intertwined, now seemed to turn away from him, a stranger: she acted without him; she had her own will and her own word, even in matters of the farm; and behind his back, she complained about the farmer to the laborers—he knew it . . . and with his daughters she did just as she pleased.

The two girls were in boarding school, and it

always made him bitter to see how those bluestockings were growing away from their father and the farm, becoming young ladies instead of farmers' wives. He simply let things pass now, but once they'd had enough of it and stayed home, he would quickly strip away the silliness and affected aping; he would see to it then for sure that they got into the farmwork. But already he anticipated the time of their homecoming as a great disturbance: by now, those two had moved away from him as well, and he would never again have them under the power of his hand.

He said nothing, because words were no use, and looked fruitlessly for ways to change things. In the past, when the children were all small, he had never thought it would turn out like this; he lived then without suspicion, supreme in the full realization of his rule. But that beautiful time had flown away, and you could expect many more things to change.

Vermeulen tried to calm himself.

"I'm not old yet," he thought, "and it's a hard punch that knocks me down!" But that was only false comfort. "We'll just have to wait," he concluded, "and see how they aim to take my authority away from me. Wait, like for the weather to break."

Without his noticing it, darkness had fallen, and the flames of the hearth lit up the kitchen.

And so the day passed like all the others, and once again evening came much too soon.

After dinner, when the men sat around the hearth and the women were done banging the pots, there was more talk about the same things as yesterday: complaints about the bad weather and the late winter, stories told of floods and accidents . . .

Then, in the middle of the lamentation and whining over the reluctant season, like someone unaware and under the delusion that tomorrow the sun will rise, Louis dropped his cheerful voice among them—a signal of joy, clear in the stuffy kitchen still damp with the reek of wet clothes.

"Father, where're we sowing the flax this year?" he shouted out loud.

Vermeulen made a defensive gesture with his shoulders and replied to that inopportune question as if to a little boy:

"The seed's all right where it is, so let it be. What's all your talk now about sowing?"

But his wife lifted her head from her mending and, looking over her glasses:

"Seems to me," she said, "that it's really not too soon, since it's the middle of March already. Isn't this just the time to talk about sowing?"

"Pour your seed in the brook, it'll lie there dry as on the ground," Vermeulen said irritably.

"The weather changes quickly, and before we get started, we certainly *can* talk about where it's going to be sowed," his wife insisted.

"It could stay dry for six weeks straight and more, and you still couldn't take a team out to plough."

"Six weeks is a mite much," a groom asserted. "If the wind picks up, it can dry out pretty fierce in a few days. And also the sun can help some."

"The days are getting longer all the time . . ." Louis put in.

"And March must give twelve days of summer . . ."

"April showers answer for that," Vermeulen scoffed.

From then on, he bothered himself with the conversation no further, remaining alone in his harsh gloominess, much like the winter itself the others wanted not to think of anymore. The younger people longed for spring: they looked forward to the beautiful days, could feel them approaching, and knew that sowing time drew near and with it the start of the great excitement of the new farming year. They began to settle things among themselves—the laborers with the farmer's wife and the young farmer—arranging the entire use of Vermeulen's eighty hectares of cultivated land, while the old farmer sat by, just as though it did not concern him anymore, pretending not to hear.

There were two large plots available for growing flax. For twelve years, that crop had not been cultivated on them; last summer, one had yielded potatoes and the other sugar beets, neither of which would suck the soil too dry or impoverish it, and the ground had remained cleared and fertile to reap a beautiful field of flax. One lay in the base of the valley on the east side of Vermeulen's holdings, the other on the height of a slope to the north, protected by a small grove of oak—a lovely field, round as a belly, with a soil of heavy clay. Before the winter, they had both been ploughed under and prepared and especially manured; it only remained now to choose between the high field and the low, the heavy soil or the light.

"If you could know in advance if the summer was going to be dry or wet . . ." Poortere, the old farmhand, ventured.

"I'd risk going up to the high field," a scutcher said. "Flax that's been well manured can stand drought better than the damp. And the soil there's ideal for a flaxfield; in clay you usually get a fat heavy boll and thin stalks."

"If only the weather's with us," the farmer's wife said.

"In the clay? Then you can wait for sowing until May!" Louis asserted. "And if drought follows after that, you can forget about the flaxfield until another six weeks go by!"

"Who says it's going to be dry?" Vermeulen suddenly shouted from his corner.

He did not speak another word of conversation all evening; he let the others babble on and show off their high learning—but then it already stood firm in his mind: the flax would be sown on the high field.

II

The young people sized up the time right: March continued, but with no more lies.

All in one morning, while everyone still lay asleep, a new wind had risen up: it came riding over the hills from the east, the heavy clouds drifted apart before its breath, and the day then turned clear, fog and rotten vapors entirely dispersed. The blue of the sky came through, and that morning the sun showed its glad face for the first time.

"A calm before a storm!" the old folk shouted. "There's still more to come!" And they pointed north, where the malignance massed in the sky, a dark mountainous heap, ready to lash out with hail and snowstorms that would fast put out the sun's false glow.

"April fool!" And indeed it hailed and snowed just like on Christmas day at the onset of winter. But the harm was short-lived now and of little account: the clouds broke again, clearness prevailed, and the fog was swept away for good. Now the countryside lay open once more in its diversity, bright and plain as far as the eye could see, with the sloping lines of hill and valley intersecting where trees stood along the roads in ranks, the windmills square on their foundations, farms and houses spread everywhere. It was the first good day of the year, and it very quickly brought joy and a new feeling for life to everyone. But the very next day the weather began to turn, the whole northern part of the sky loomed black, and with a sudden change thick snowflakes were whirling around. Yet they fell as though on hot stone, melting even as they drew near the ground, and as soon as a cloud was wrung dry the sun fought through again, and a sweeping wind chased what was left of the murk to more distant regions.

For days afterward, the struggle among the contending elements continued: first came hail and wintry chill, then it would clear again, the sun between storms thrusting its lances through the clouds. There was movement and life in the sky, and that cheered everyone's heart once more: winter had been vanquished, spring was coming on, it was drying.

Here and there a farmer, elated, put his horses to the plough and drove them to the field.

"Let 'em drown," Vermeulen grumbled. With his clogs on he made the rounds, wading through mush, puddles, and courses of mud to check the condition of the soil. He followed the paths so long as they were passable, and on higher ground he marched along on the other side of the ditch where people had completely leveled the edges of the fields with their trampling; the roads themselves were useless, full of pools of water and driven through with deep cart tracks. The drains could not swallow it all, the ditches and brooks fed in the water so heavily. With his spade, the farmer made trenches here and there and let the water loose. He took a few steps on each of his fields to feel the firmness of the earth. The high field still lay in readiness for winter, ploughed with cruel deep furrows from end to end, turned over, sliced in straight lines, broken and bumpy. But by now the great rains and the winter weather had washed and rounded the gnarled surface, so that the whole field was knobbed in vertebral chunks, like the incoming wave of a choppy sea that has hardened suddenly and lies still. Vermeulen pushed on it with both feet at once, but the wet clay stuck like a mass of rising dough. It squished under the heavy weight of his steps, and he had trouble getting his clogs out.

Vermeulen walked farther on to look at the meadows and the corn that had been sown in the fall as well. Then he went on home, but said nothing about what he had seen.

In the meantime, Louis had been out scouting in another direction, and he too brought back his own thoughts. And now, in his elated, impetuous way, the young fellow at once told how the land lay—in his experience, work should start immediately. He supposed he was old enough by now to put a word in, and without giving way to his father he gave his opinion.

"The soil's firm," he said, "and it's past the time. The lower field's ready, lucky we drained it last year—it sure took some cost, but now it's really a powder-dry seedbed, and it'll be a great field for flax—twelve years without flax! No danger of blight to the crop. . . . The farmers from all over will want to come and see it! We'll go open it, Father?" Louis asked cheerfully, in high spirits.

Vermeulen looked at his son with eyebrows raised, and:

"Get a cart of beets to the bulls' stables," he said, and turned his back to him without another word. Though he shouted further from over his shoulder:

"Jan and Poortere can start strewing waste slag iron around the meadow! Hey, you!" he yelled to another groom. "Over to Zaveleinde with the team of blacks and the manure-spreader!"

Vermeulen gave out orders all around, and when everyone had started work, he went himself wherever he thought it might be necessary.

For the first time in his life, Louis looked at the farmer with an angry glance and felt sorry he was not his own master and could not do as he saw fit. Now, for the first time, it appeared to him that his father's head was too large, his body too heavy and wide, and that his legs, like huge pestles, stood firmly planted in the earth. Louis saw how ugly his father was, and the discovery made him start, not so much because of the ugliness itself but that he had all at once taken on the expression and form of a stranger: puffed up in his swollen flesh, with the testy

obstinacy of a fattened bull, resentful and gruff . . .
hateful. Vermeulen indeed stood there like a tree,
immovable, implacable, unapproachable, with his
thick tawny hide—a supreme being, a tyrant who
holds all the authority, the entire management of
the work, the running of the farm locked in his head,
for himself alone, and maintains his power with
jealous fervor. And now, for the first time, Louis had
looked at his father not like a submissive boy, having
come to the realization that he was just as tall and
could measure himself against him, head to head.

As a boy, Louis had grown up with an unlimited
admiration for his father, convinced that he was the
best farmer in the world, with an absolute knowledge
of all things. When Father said it, it was the truth;
what Father did was right. A word from Father's
mouth was always the final, conclusive verdict, no
matter what was being argued about. The farmers in
the entire district followed Vermeulen's advice, and
his influence in the village was as great as his
authority on his own farm. Often while Vermeulen
was talking with the farmers about raising cattle or
crops, Louis had watched his father's face, admiring
those resolute pronouncements and observing how
opponents always had to give in and bow to his
father's supreme omniscience. That same stout
resolution on his father's face he now disliked, and
he thought again of a bull shaking its horns.

But Louis was a boy no more. Now that he himself
lived the life of a farmer, his guileless mind had
become firmer; he saw things through his own eyes;

and he had heard people talk, left and right, who were, it seemed to him, also intelligent and yet thought otherwise from his father. He kept gaining new experience from what he observed and saw happening around him; he tied insights and results together and from them spun opinions which he kept to himself as his own found property. From working with them all day, he learned the make-up of the air and soil, the life cycle of crops and animals; he sought out what might be of advantage or disadvantage to the business. Moreover, he discovered technical books in which all the information about rural commerce was recorded and examined with utmost precision, and good profit could be drawn from them by whoever wanted to apply his studies with a little understanding. And so Louis made the discovery by himself—and the disappointment of it pained him—that he as a boy had suffered under a false illusion for so long. For now the young farmer knew that his father—even if he *was* farmer Vermeulen—could not by himself hold that most precious information stored in his mind, no matter what he claimed or how he imposed the pretense on others. And worse: there existed a higher form of agriculture which his father, with his unschooled and old-fashioned notions, could not reach. The boy discovered that everyone has his own insight into things and that obstinacy and pedantry usually come from arrogance, rather than from sound and properly gained knowledge. His childlike trust in his father had been broken.

Yet the disappointment that came from this realization did not go deep with the young farmer's son. Louis, in his twentieth year, felt too exuberant to brood over these things now, to start keeping the account books, hunting for the last red cent among debits and credits! He'd wash his hands of it and leave the management and responsibility of the farm to his father: what did it matter to him? He himself wanted to live life to the full, free and easy, and let things be. Father was and would remain the boss, mother generously doled out the drinking money—all was for the best. But occasionally, a thought rose up in him unexpectedly, and with no harmful intent of inflicting his own opinion, his youthful recklessness would collide with his father's headstrong conceit, when it ran contrary to the obvious truth. Reluctantly, against his better judgment, he would have to carry out something that he himself wanted to do differently—albeit he was constrained and disgusted. Then two or three blunt words would fall; the son would give in—but for a few days afterward they both would sulk, each on his own side maintaining a stubborn silence. It mostly occurred over important work arrangements or the buying and selling of horses or cattle. But it sometimes seemed as if the old man deliberately acted to provoke his son, to force him into submission. Louis then felt a violent urge, a rebelliousness that wanted to burst out—he suppressed it and bridled his mood, but the resentment lingered on, growing into a persistent aversion to the

coarse heavy figure of his father. Slowly there came
on him a craving to stand on his own feet, to act
independently, as well as a sense of spite, even
repugnance toward the work that, against his will,
he had to do "like so" and no other way. The
farmyard seemed to have become too small for the
two of them, and they avoided each other—even if
there was outward peace, they no longer looked each
other in the eye. But Vermeulen's authority stood so
firm and deeply rooted of old that up to now none of
this growing disagreement had ever come out, in
word or deed. It smoldered in the young man's heart,
but he did not dare think of giving his resentment
shape or form—he would not risk standing up to his
father with an opinion of his own. The lad made
himself agreeable most of the time as well, doing as
he was told; he tried to be indifferent to it all, taking
the lighter side of things. And so Vermeulen had not
yet been able to notice any opposition, and the only
reason for his uneasiness was merely this: the sight
of the vigorous young figure of his son, with the
certainty that the boy would grow over his head and
not remain so good-natured. The farmer foresaw
that a will and intention would clash with a will and
intention of his own; before long, he would no more
be sole master—he sensed the upsurge of power next
to his own and the unavoidable struggle.

The weather remained on the good side now, and
at every opportunity the subject of work and sowing
came up. Louis had pressed his opinion and views on
his mother, and she dared come right out for it, since

it was her conviction as well: the flax should be sown on the newly opened and drained field.

"Why else did we go to all that expense and trouble to lay in those metal drainpipes?" she asked.

Vermeulen looked up, raising his eyebrows high, and stared at his wife in mock amazement. Deadly calm, he flung it in her face:

"That's where we sow the oats, Wife. That's how it's supposed to be." And that pronouncement came off as a matter of necessity, with no more fuss. Vermeulen proved and enlarged upon the advantage of the site and the fitness of the soil. They flooded him with words and arguments on all sides, but the farmer deemed it ill-fitting to prattle on about it further. The flax would stand on the high field: that was fixed firmly in the very depths of his heart. Vermeulen acted out of unconscious intuition; the decision had been made without deliberate will—already he could see the crop growing—and once made fast, no further consideration could change it in any way. He foresaw no fear of drought. The clay would yield a heavy, fine crop, and the low fields were unsuitable. Why or how that conviction had come to him he did not explore. A farmer who begins to hesitate and falter, Vermeulen thought, is a farmer who falls back and goes under.

"Nobody's to know the plans for the farm or meddle with its running! Remain the boss by yourself! Stand firm on your two feet and . . . never hesitate! When they won't go along, force 'em, that's how it's got to be done! Then only the powers in heaven can knock it out of your clutches, that and nothing else!" Yet secretly, in the depths of his heart, there was also a delight in frustrating, holding his own against everyone else's opinion—that by itself was reason enough to stand by his resolve.

Spring held at last to its lovely course; the snow- and hailstorms were no more than a few freak interruptions of the warm April days. Green unfolded everywhere; the soil dried quickly under the watch of the red moon, while here and there, as if by arrangement, the farmers went out to tackle the fields with plough and breaker and harrow. People rapidly forgot their peevishness and boredom, for the sky was blue, the horizon had widened, and a new and loud joy in life thrived on the farmsteads everywhere. The cows lowed to be let out, the hens cackled, and the cocks were full of fire. The time had come for the spring season's work to begin once more, just like the year before, though without a sense of repetition. Sturdy teams pulled up and down through the fields; on both slopes of the valley, from top to bottom, each farmer worked his own land, and the appearance of the whole region changed in almost no time.

Instead of the waste and desert solitude of winter, life everywhere now was caught up and moving in bustling activity. Before your eyes, the fields took on an altered look. The manure had been ploughed in and the deep furrows already drawn. Just let the wind shift and sweeten now, and spring is here!

Early one morning, when the promise of lovely

weather hung in the air, Vermeulen sent his two
grooms to the low field, each with a team; and Louis,
happy as a lark at getting on with the work, felt no
unwillingness or reluctance—he drove the cart
himself, and on the very field where he had wanted
to plant the flax, he now went to sow oats, glad at
heart.

For a whole two hours, the young lad walked up
and down the sloping field. With a firm step and a
wide flourish, he scattered the oats around in full
handfuls, in strips as wide as he could throw. This
now was an easy business; he could do it carelessly,
having started his apprentice time with it the year
before. He gazed after the teams of horses that
passed by him and listened to the farmers chatting.
He inhaled the mild air with full lungs and let the
caressing wind play through his hair. Spring did him
good and, working, he felt a new strength awaken in
his young limbs: happiness, a zest for life, and a wild
recklessness welled up in him, exultation of the new
season danced in his blood. His arm swung and the
oats fell like shining gold dust before his feet. He let
his gaze wander over the wide fields, higher up the
slope, and there saw other farmers—old friends,
neighbors sowing like he was: arms full, and
strutting, with their necks proud and straight.

"It's flax they're sowing," he guessed, and his
jealousy awoke, since they were busy in front of him
with that wonderful task while he was still walking
there with oats in his sowing apron.

Each time Ivo or Jan asked him while passing by,

"When's the farmer going to sow his linseed?" he had to shrug his shoulders and, smiling, shout without breaking step:

"In May, boys, in May, when the cherry trees are in bloom!"

"Used to be Vermeulen was always the first," one of the grooms remarked.

"What if they waited for him now!" the other laughed under his breath.

The old man was getting unpredictable. The grooms knew it—and all the people working at the farm, but with his son they pretended not to know. Louis felt uneasy and ashamed around the others, and it angered him that he could give no reason for this stubborn delay. He himself waited and longed for the sowing as if for a state occasion. Sowing the flax was the weightiest act of the entire year, and for the second time in his life it would be entrusted to him. He was proud of that and eager, too, since the past year had turned out so well.

Flax is held in the highest regard, the most precious and choice produce a farmer can bring in. Its success makes the farming year profitable, and the crop builds each grower's reputation from when it's still in the field until long after it has been stored and delivered. For he is known by his harvest of flax and through it wins honor among his fellow villagers. This same crop for Louis was the spring and summer season itself, just about the only reason for the horses to go out to the field and the farming to be done.

Why was his father not now, as before, first and foremost among the farmers, the one who gave the signal for the whole region to start the work?

By evening, when the sowing apron had been shaken out and the roller was going over the field for the last time, Vermeulen came by to see if the men had done the job carefully. He had one groom replough a furrow and weed out one edge of the field. The young sower was tired but unsubdued: he stood and looked contentedly over the finished work, and when the groom's mistakes were repaired, he walked home with his father, next to the empty cart, through the beautiful spring evening.

They spoke a few words about tomorrow's work, quiet and satisfied, overtaken by the calm surroundings of the day's tranquil end.

"Sobrie sowed his linseed yesterday, and . . . Duitschave's beginning to plough already too," Louis said. "If the weather stays like this, they'll even be done sowing this week . . ."

"Let 'em," Vermeulen said calmly, "there's still filth in the air, and we've got time . . ."

They spoke no further word, and each remained with his own thoughts. The young farmer searched the sky for wherever that filth might indeed be and wondered how his father could know it was there.

The wind had thrown open the overcast sky, dotting it with flecks of cloud as though dappled by milkwort, with nowhere a trace of murky weather. The blue had never been so soft nor the clouds so serene—and what a glow in the west where the sun hovered low, clear as an eye!

Coming to the pasture, Vermeulen veered off the lane to check the grazing and look after the young cows and the calves that had been put out on the meadow just yesterday.

Louis led his horse to the stable. He bit his lips in disgust and came to the dinner table without a word.

That same evening, the farmer's wife again tried to pressure him about getting on with the flax, but Vermeulen replied curtly that managing the fields was beyond her grasp: it lay in his charge.

"Am I the farmer here or what?" he shouted harshly all at once, and after that remained sitting in his corner with nothing further to say. He stretched his legs toward the fire like someone quiet and firm in his resolve, the boss who means to show it.

What everyone considered and explained as an aging farmer's pigheadedness was Vermeulen's prudence and care to be certain to lay in a good crop. To obtain the best linseed, he had made inquiries on his own, asking around without telling any of the household about his plans. Where other farmers were content with ordinary stuff, like "rose seed" or "second throw," he wanted only the choicest grade-A "Riga," straight from the barrel. He had searched for a long time and, finding the right kind at last, had written away for it immediately . . . had waited for an answer, and just now had first received news that the seed had been sent on from Russia . . . only it did not come. He exercised patience and was silent—kept his anxiety hidden behind the fixed severity of his features, although he had to exert all his bodily strength to keep silence and not burst. For he more than anyone suffered from the delay, feeling hurt by the postponement, since he was not first, before the other farmers. His wife reproached him for being hardheaded and sitting around; his son looked at him suspiciously, like you would an old man beginning to dodder. And still the seed did not arrive. "It'll come," he grumbled under his breath, while outwardly he remained the man who has his reasons and knows what he is waiting for. "And if it doesn't come, we just won't sow any flax," he mused . . . "or could be it's the high field that's cursed."

But the linseed did come. One morning the postman brought the yellow slip, the notice that the merchandise was at the station. Vermeulen had been watching for the mail for weeks, and finally, his patience waning, had begun to suspect the postman of causing the delay; more than once he had been seized by a desire to snatch the mail sack away and smash him over the head with it . . . but now at last he had brought the news. Which was why Vermeulen examined the date before he signed his name. He then sent a cowherd with horse and cart to unload the freight.

"You start on the high field tomorrow," he said to Louis in passing.

III

The signal had been given at last. It rang in Louis'
ears, a shout of joy echoing through the air, bringing
delight to his heart. Why there had been so long a
delay, why the signal had been given now and not
earlier, did not matter to him. He was bursting with
energy, like a wound spring. Now just to get going!

"Jan, Ivo! The horses! You up front with the
breaker, Ivo behind with the roller. I'll take the
harrow." The young man's orders boomed out, loud
and rousing as a battle cry. The high field had to be
broken open and turned over.

"It'll be no joke in that clay," Jan said, and he
immediately teamed the three strongest horses
together. He laid the collars on the harness and lifted
the link of the long trace into the hook of the heavy
harrow.

"Gee up!" Three circlets of bells jingled on the
horses' necks, and their sleek bodies pulled across the
yard with a dancing step toward the field.

Jan was the older, a warmhearted groom whose
only pleasure was his work and only relaxation his

horses. He was anxious about them, as if they were his own, looking after them like children on show for all to see, at any time, these three gray mares from Brabant—short-built draughthorses with solid hips, strong legs, and coats glossy and pure as silk. They were his honor and his pride—they were his life. He did not speak in other terms; other ideas or desires never troubled his mind. The horses and his work—they were enough for him. Let the gawkers come and look where he had passed by: there was no groom in those parts who could draw a furrow as straight or work the field as smooth. That he knew.

The team was already stepping over the shoulder of the road. The groom halted at the top of the field to look it over before setting in to work.

"It'll take a few days to get this clay softened up," Jan thought, stamping open a clod of turf with his foot. "We'll see."

Joining action to word, he pushed the tail of the harrow down, and the seven sharp teeth touched the soil. At a signal, the three horses started up: their heavy bodies braced themselves as one and pulled the traces taut. The colossus rolled forward, the earth ripping open under each steel-pointed tip. And there behind, where the wheels had passed, lay seven open furrows.

All winter long the field had been lying exposed in its raw state. The heavy rains, the wind, the frost had hammered it by turns and made the clay soft and giving under the spade. This morning the top layer was still flecked with white, lightly frozen, and now the gnarled, fistlike clods were turned over by the violence of the heaving teeth. The team went slowly up and down, first along the edge of the plot of land, round as a belly, and then again a second track next to the first; and so, bit by bit, with patience and perseverance, the surface would be dug up and rent apart. Jan's left hand pushed at the tail end of the harness, and with his right he guided the lead horse where he wanted the team. The whole body of this countryman was bent over his work, his neck stretched forward in the path of the drive. His feet stamped firmly on the bumpy ground, and the whole while not once did he look up and around from his work. At each end of the field, he lifted the cutters out of the soil with the lever—and then the groom's sure horse sense told him his team would turn around and start a fresh path without useless shouting.

In the afternoon came Ivo, the second groom, with another pair of horses hitched to the heaviest roller, and Louis followed him with his half-bred Holland dray dragging the lighter harrow and disk plough.

As they fell upon the work together, it looked like a regular assault. The teams crossed paths again and again, each in its own gait. Jan's harrow lifted, and the cruel cutters tore open the ground in deep gullies. And Ivo's heavy iron roller drove over them to flatten the loosened clods under its weight. Louis then led his smart, light prancer in their tracks to rake up the leveled soil again with his harrow's sharp wooden teeth.

Each team went its own way, the horses pulling diligently and turning sharply at the borders of the field on the grooms' commands. There was a continual coming and going: breaking, flattening, raking. And when the whole length of the field had been worked over like this, from top to bottom, the same thing had to be done, left to right, to its breadth, until gully, track, and raking all crisscrossed. After a while, Louis switched to the disk plough, and now he stood like a skipper on his ship, limber and light on his feet, his body yielding, on the slant back of the harnessed rigging that was being dragged along with regular jolts, leaving coiled and zigzag designs in the soil.

The men went on all day long, each behind his team, back and forth the same way. The fresh, mild spring wind caressed their faces, and there on the heights, in their strange isolation, they walked the lofty plateau and had a commanding view of the whole valley lying open before them. They themselves and their horses stood there like giants, outlined against the pale gray sky in their heavy labor, for all the world to see.

Spring hung in the air, the birds proclaimed it everywhere, and the first green was dusted over the oak grove, over the crowns of the wide-branched trees that hemmed the field, like living powder scattered over the whole expanse in a single throw. The earth gave off pleasant smells, and the soil held under foot with satisfying firmness. The countryfolk felt it glorious to walk about at the onset of the

young year. None thought that this was merely a
rebeginning, doing again what they had already
been doing for so many years—a labor that turns
and turns without end. They had yearned for it for so
long, as for a new life they would enjoy again to the
full. The air was clean and good to breathe in;
everything seemed new and just created—the shining young green in bud everywhere. All who stood
there felt the impact: the awakening fresh flowing
strength, a new love of life in their hearts. Growth
quivered in the soil, brewed and seethed, burst out
all over, and the sap that would make the seed
germinate gleamed in the purple sheen of the
turned-over slices of earth. The air had been swept
clean, made clear as an eye, the mild wind that blew
over coming from a region where nothing had
breathed or touched it before. Spring was like a great
joy come to delight the world for the first time. How
luxurious and at ease people felt as the beautiful
days lengthened and turned calmer, advancing in a
gradual, firm, stately march toward the regal
splendor of summer. It was nearing, and they would
overtake it one day soon. The countryfolk now had
to take care they were ready with their work when
the time came.

The grooms stayed on the job until late in the
evening, and you could certainly see a
transformation where they had been. The knots of
earth had been made smaller and crushed fine. They
had made the heavy clay flat, light, and loose, so
that the surface lay raked and spread wide, with

winding little furrows from the disk plough.
Tomorrow they would go on to make the soil finer
still.

That first heavy day, the horses and the grooms
were weary from the field and exhausted; the work
weighed like lead in their tired limbs, but their mood
was high, and at the dinner table they talked and
laughed together with the young hands and the
girls. The grooms had brought back the country air
in their clothes, and the girls who now sniffed it also
felt the desire in their blood to start work outside in
the open. They thought of the work that was waiting
for them, their eyes gleaming with anticipation of
the fun, and they listened like little birds to hear
something about the conditions in the field. For the
new season brought animal spirits to their limbs and
tickled their desire to laugh, free and easy, the joy in
their young hearts. They had heard the lowing and
bellowing of the cattle that had been let loose; in
their turn, they felt like imitating the foolish
gamboling of the fillies and heifers. But the grooms,
who had tasted too much of the air outside, were
quickly seized and already overwhelmed by the heat
in the kitchen, falling asleep in their chairs. Louis
was the first to shake off his boots and wish the
company good night. The others went too, each to
his own bed, to find their well-deserved, salutary rest.

The new year had set in, and for six months, day
after day, with no pause and no mercy, the heavy
labor would continue. Early in the morning, before it
was light, the horses were given their feed and stood

groomed and ready to go. Jan hitched them to the lighter harrow, and Ivo took the roller to the high field. Louis followed with the costly seed in the cart. It was as if they were riding to a fair or going somewhere to celebrate a happy event. Recklessness and satisfaction both lay on the grooms' faces, and Louis stood high on the cart, legs wide apart, like a hero about to work his miraculous powers.

On the field, they rolled and harrowed and harrowed again, as long and often as it took to make the unruly clay so tame and fine that the whole surface would lie smooth and powdery like a toboggan slide and feel light as a cushion under the feet. Suddenly, before they were ready, Vermeulen broke into view. Leaning on his spade, he stopped at the far end and surveyed his field. It was he who would speak the final word and say that it was enough.

Then Louis made like a priest about to say Mass: he tied on his long white linen sowing apron and crossed himself at his chest. He secured the straps above his shoulders and filled his lap with linseed. With his hand, he burrowed in the rich, glistening powder, letting it run through his fingers like water for the pleasure of its soft caress. The grooms and the old farmer stood still, anticipating the sight of the first, beginning step. Louis traced a second cross, in all seriousness and simplicity. And then without hesitation or show, with a smile on his face but emotion in his heart, he did take his first step. At the same instant his fingers plunged into his lap, and with a wide, dignified sweep he made the first throw, the seed flying around the sower in a full circle, fine as invisible pollen. Not with whole handfuls as for rye, wheat, or oats—coarse stuff requiring less attention—but ever so lightly, tenderly, with the tips of the fingers: each throw scarcely a pinch, the powdery seed floating in the breathless air. The sower walked with a powerful stride, as if setting out for a long journey, his head high and his arm moving in steady time with each step. And after each throw he drew his arm close, scooping seed out of his lap and swinging out once more.

Vermeulen stood at the far end of the field and watched. The whole region lay open before him in its expanse, filling his eyes, but they saw nothing but the striking sower who stood tall and alone on the flat land. He saw the firm step, the legs lifted high, and the full frame, tall, slender, supple as a young branch, the arm swinging ceaselessly on the broad angular shoulders of that young, strong body. A smile broke out on his closed lips: he recognized none other than himself in the young sower—his youth, the cheerful, lively lad of years ago, who walks through life firm and undaunted, as over the field he goes, chin out, eyes bold, and . . . sowing. Vermeulen too had once been such a man, before stoutness had aged him and the years had made him gruff and crotchety. His double stood there before him in a sudden revelation, so vividly portrayed in the youth who was sowing. For the first time Vermeulen realized how very like his child is a

father; he knew now that a son is nothing else than
the continuation, the recovering of a father's spent
life . . . a shoot off the old tree. The thought made
him chuckle, then grit his teeth. The old, sinewy
fighter stood there on his own field, the sky high
above his head, the space wide around him. He felt
knocked around by the great elements, dragged into
the whirlpool of some savage sea, a mere trunk
without arms or legs to defend itself, floating
powerless, then sinking along with all else that
perishes. His youth was gone. Time had gnawed and
eaten away at his life. And now he saw that lad
there starting his own youth afresh, inheriting
everything the old man had fought a lifetime to
conquer. Never before had it stood before his eyes so
tangibly, the inescapable destiny: the old man
slipping, giving way, while the other rides right over
his head to lay ahold of life. Vermeulen had
supposed his son would remain a child forever, a
mischievous kid, never serious, with nothing but
play on his mind. But look at him now walking
there: so slender and firm of limb, so tall of frame! It
was his own shape, his own strength and pride
Vermeulen now sensed beyond himself—stolen from
him through his own fault. There was no going back
now: that second Vermeulen, the son, had enough
vitality to keep growing and make his living without
any help from the old one. He felt regret, like a
greedy miser who would swallow up all his wealth so
nobody else might enjoy it; he foresaw how his own
power would shrink, gradually and later completely,

before that other power which had sprung from him.
But it was fixed firm in his mind: he would not give
an inch so long as his legs would carry him. And
even if paralyzed he had to sit glaring in the corner
by the hearth, he would still have his voice to bellow
out orders. Whoever wanted to eat his bread and was
not obedient to his will he would have beaten and
kicked out. Vermeulen gnashed his teeth in spite;
anger gripped him by the throat; deep down he
raged in resistance against implacable fate—but this
violence leveled off, rushing out like a wave on the
open beach, rising and falling in turn. Last year had
been the first that the strange sower had taken his
work from him—why, only two years ago he himself
had walked with that same step, and now it was
gone, irrevocably. His legs failed him—he stood no
longer so firm on the knotty earth which all his life
he had crushed under his heavy heel. He would be
just an onlooker from now on, the gentleman farmer
who makes the rounds giving orders and no longer
joins in the work because he has become too fat and
worn out—because he can no longer manage what is
child's play to the younger ones. Vermeulen foresaw
the time when he would sit driveling, an old shortwinded grumbler with loose teeth, letting life go on
around him, unable to take part in it any
longer—like a stranger in his own home, watching in
a haze whatever happens, waiting for death.

And briskly the sower went his way, resolute and
conscious of his youthful energy, intent on what he
was doing and nothing else. He sowed without care

or design, in clear delight. As the sun comes in its time, so the sower came: spring was near, the air and the soil rich and ready to receive the seed and make it grow. That put his heart at ease, and he sowed with an eagerness to do his work well, free of worry and care over what had to be done with the crop later. He went up and down without a break, not to waste time by stopping, in fear that the still air would begin to stir, making his task more difficult. Alongside where he walked, the two teams of horses passed, with no audible thudding of hoofs. Softly, as on a cushion, slowly, gingerly they followed back and forth, pressing the seed smooth into the soil after the sower had gone.

That full activity on a single field, all working together at one and the same splendid venture, enthused the young farmer, and there on the high land he felt as if he were the noble performer of a great deed: he who brings the dead land to life! He looked forward to the beautiful crop in its growth and bloom, with the heat and light of summer above it: the flaxfield would be a showpiece all season long for the whole region, that very region that now opened before his eyes. Each time he walked downhill, the land lay spread like the surface of a table. Irregular fields crossed on the downward slope, fully settled with farms and houses. Farther away, a broad belt blended into a hill along the entire length of the horizon, bordered above the by blue veil of fir trees and below, at the foot, by the silent river, visible from here, which pleasantly followed the course of its meandering bed. And when the sower turned uphill, the edge of his own sowing-land was a black line against the sky, his father standing at the far end, framed by the light—a man hewn of stone, with one shoulder raised, leaning his heavy body on his spade.

The lad was proud of his father, proud that he, as his son, as his prince, was allowed to help farm the largest and most prosperous spread in the area.

He walked downhill and looked over the valley; he walked uphill and saw the big man against the light, his hat low down on his head, his face in shadow . . . and his legs did not weary, nor did his arm feel lame from its hefty swinging.

Already the sun was setting, and in the little oak grove, the soft cooing of birds settling down to sleep had begun. Night dew was starting to form on the low fields, and it grew dark in the distance. There were still the ends and edges left to do, as well as a corner to make level for the horses to turn. After that the lad, still in his long white sowing apron, came and stood next to his father, his open hands hanging down, face aglow with the exertion, and eyes radiant with happiness.

"It's all in there," he said, his heart's pride shining through his strapping frame.

Vermeulen stood self-contained and nodded yes. The hard eyes of the burly man, though, did not look at his son but surveyed the flaxfield for something still more to do before they left. He fixed his gaze on the two grooms, who were taking their final turn with harrow and roller.

"In my day we did that manually, and no horse was allowed to put a hoof on the field. . . . That's all changed now," he said, without looking at anybody. He then took his spade and poked here and there for a bit of soil from a furrow, sifting it open over the sowing-land. The sun, grazing the horizon, glistened over the soft contours of the round-bellied high field in a wash of glowing red, then thrust its golden fins high up through the clouds and went under. The sheen faded from the land, but the same red hue remained, blossoming all over the broken clouds in the west. Then this too disappeared, and at the close of the beautiful and mild day of sowing, there now trembled a pearl-gray sky in even stillness—a blessing and an augury of good growth.

Yes, the seed was in, and from now on a strange power would hang over that choice piece of land. There was nothing more the farmer could do: friendly or hostile elements would rule over it, and if all went well, a good crop would flourish before six weeks were gone—a sea of the finest green, a rich yield for the farmer. Unless pestilence or the plague struck and brought destruction.

Vermeulen was willing to admit his helplessness now, and on either side of the flaxfield he hammered a cross into the loose soil with the back of his spade, to warn off the evil powers, bad weather, and birds. And then suddenly, as if it was finished business and entirely indifferent to him, he turned his back on it. On the way home, he gave Jan and Ivo their orders for the next day.

"Tomorrow you can start deep ploughing the ten-acre field. And clear the beetfield."

The work was finished here—the flaxfield could be left to wait now—but that was no reason to dawdle. On a farm with such a spread and such a crew of workers, you always had to keep order, and Vermeulen carried the arrangements, with all their attendant cares and the disposal of the work, in his massive head. As shepherd and supreme providence amid that great mill of production and consumption, he went about his actions solely according to laws that he alone knew, and of which no one else had a grasp or notion. The hands waited for his orders as for a supreme injunction, and meekly they did what they had just been told, knowing the complexities of life would follow their courses and everything fit together properly.

And so without rest or halt the days would go by—each hour filled with work, and everyone given his own job to do.

Legs wide apart, Louis stood whistling on the empty cart and drove to the yard in the same way he had left it that morning. Ivo and Jan, weary and exhausted, walked together through the dusk, behind five horses crowded next to each other, filling the whole path. From far off in a different direction, they saw the cowherd driving home across the landscape with a cart full of feed—a load piled high of bright yellow, rich and fresh, moving festively over the gray evening countryside. It gleamed like a flame, a radiance trailing across the sky in the tracks where that immense bushel of deep yellow flowers slid past. The horses whinnied at each other, their neighs sounding like sharp laughter over the field. Louis felt these things more than he saw them, and the silence of the evening together with the memory of that glorious day filled his heart with unutterable pleasure.

Behind him he heard the grooms reckoning how long the work would last. One said:

"We'll have ourselves a good pipe when it's all over."

The pipe meant a breathing spell, the reward they promised themselves with the prospect of each finished job. "Anxious for work, anxious for rest, that was their life," the young farmer mused. And he experienced it himself, how in the morning he had been filled with eagerness and excitement to begin sowing, and how he felt such enjoyment now that it was done . . . and how tomorrow's work already beckoned, how the continual activity, the working of the land filled his whole life . . . The lad did not yet suspect that difficulties of any kind could trouble a man's inner calm.

The next day, Jan set to work on the ten acres with equal industry and spirit. For years in succession now, the old fellow had gone through the same round of recurrent business on Vermeulen's land. He had become worn and stiff with pushing and dragging through the cold, rain, and great heat. On a plot nearby, Ivo—a newcomer who had everything

before him and not much in his past—was spreading
manure. Both grooms worked on adjacent
ploughland, separated only by an open expanse of
crystal-clear air. Their work occupied all their
thoughts and desires; they lived out a humdrum
existence in constant longing for something new that
always turned out the same. The farmer was their
provider, their security; he arranged their lives and
bore the responsibility for everything. Here in the
great hustle and bustle of the farm, they walked free
from care. They lived with their horses, with their
implements, and while busy on the land, while the
weather and the seasons rolled over their backs, their
own fate was forgotten, along with their private
misfortunes and family burdens. From that
perspective, personal interests, fear and joy in one's
own life, seemed of little account. Here they had the
smell of the pungent earth at first hand, and they
sniffed the good decay of the spread manure and the
damp of the rich soil they walked on. They went
confidently from one plot of land to another, sure
that their work had been done well and need not
fear the light of day. Their thoughts did not penetrate
the deeper essence of the things of life; they had no
insight into the hidden connections among differing
circumstances. A few simple joys, or the unexpected
heavy blows that fell upon themselves or those near
to them, were the only felt stirrings of their spirit.
They accepted life itself without reflecting on the
meaning of the continual flux, reassured by the
illusion that they controlled the very things that

swept them along and into which they would sink, as ciphers, the way they had emerged. Inwardly, they carried the conviction that they did their duty, and in this plain virtue of the heart lived the hope of a better existence waiting for them in the hereafter.

Once the big tireless horses, the grooms, and the sower were gone, the field again lay deserted in deep solitude, along with the others on which as yet no foot had been set. But with the crack of day a flock of starlings swooped down upon it, hopping about brisk and eager, pulling up anything they could. And hardly had the sun shown its face than there were the doves, sparrows, larks, wagtails, tits, and other birds—whatever passed by through the air left off its flight. Flapping their wings, the doves flew up in whirls and landed again with a rustle a bit farther away on the loose soil. Sparrows and starlings, each to one side, pecked at the ground with their beaks and dragged up what they liked, seeds or worms, beetles or grubs. With quick movements, they rooted over the entire surface of the fresh flaxfield. Would that foul brood even leave a single little seed to sprout? And was the cross at the corner powerless against the ruin of that mean-tempered swarm? Was there nobody to drive them away?

Not a soul came near. Silence and solitude lay over the field—a calm, wonderful rest in anticipation of the life that would awaken there but was now still deep in sleep. The pure air hung above it, the dew and the mellowness of growing season, and the sun baked it through down to the lower layers.

The great elements are left to their work now. Meantime, grooms and farmhands are busy elsewhere, while the farmer remains fully at peace; for he has entrusted his flaxfield to the care of the supreme master who reigns over the eternal course of things and orders them on high.

Weeding

I

Spring came like a fair, altogether a delight to everyone; and the countryfolk settled into it from the first, as if the bad days had never been. They were not conscious, these people, of what was changing or happening around them, but they enjoyed the new life, the luxuriant growth in the fine spring season. They celebrated their feast of the sun, without wondering over their own high-spirited gladness and that of the whole countryside—for spring had been expected: it came every year, surely, at the set time.

Palm Sunday! The Easter sun!

The walk to church, to High Mass, was like a triumphal march of green. Farmers and their wives, farmhands and maids, old and young, all carried their spray of evergreen—not hiding it but holding the branch high, pleased, even proud, with so great a size and such color.

And after the service, when the Easter greenery was shared out in every house, they brought cuttings from the sacred palm outside and planted one at the head of every field.

In the course of that week, or shortly before, the miracle of moment had taken place in the fields: the seed had come to life, the tender young greenery peeping out above the dead land. As if by magic, the barren nakedness of the dry and doughy earth was covered. Every crop lay in solid color, like new finery, across the wide expanse of plain, but the opening leaves of the fodder outshone all around, over the wide fleece of green, in swathes and patches of billowy gold.

The miracle excited no general surprise, since it had to happen and had never yet failed. But it pleased the farmers right enough, and they were especially curious to check just how the crops were coming up, how they were growing. Throughout the entire countryside, that alone was the happening of great and serious interest; people spoke of nothing else, and after lunch, anyone who had sown anything could be seen walking on the pathways among the fields. They had a look at their own crops first, though they also wanted to inspect their neighbors'. There was talk at the taverns in the evening about the progress and growth, and when farmer met farmer, the first question after their "Good day" was: "How's the flaxfield?" They were most concerned and preoccupied with the flax, which was worth more than all the other work of the farm. What had been done in autumn and spring now lay open to judgment, for all eyes to see; each farmer's reputation was appraised publicly according to the state of his crops in the field. What countryfolk sometimes dared cover up on other occasions could not now be hidden or denied. Everyone was free to hand down an opinion—the evidence stood along the roadside—and the know-it-alls readily declared where too little or too much had been done to the land and what would be the matter with the produce at harvest time.

Legijn's and Duitschave's flaxfields were the best in the neighborhood; Verschaeve's was better still, Veroken's too thin.

"That's what he gets with his chemicals!" the farmers mocked. But Veroken let them be:

"We'll wait till the weather changes," he said, "and when the others fall through, *then* we'll talk."

Sobrie had sowed too soon: the soil was congealed, and the crop would be lost. Vermeulen's lot was a fiasco. The farmers passed sentence, with bold predictions, as though they held the weather and the growing in their hands and it was already designated who would be number one this year and who had better pull up his crop without waiting . . . and plant beets on his flaxfield. Yet the farmers were far from unanimous in their pronouncements, and the failure of a crop was in fact sometimes explained by two wholly contradictory causes. One man ascribed it to the poorness of the soil, another insisted it had been sown too thinly or not been ploughed in deep enough, since the field was too gravelly, or too compacted. Or it might have been that late cold spell and the heavy rains. . . . But everybody stuck to his opinion and stood by his verdict.

Though predictions differed over the many flaxfields, everyone had to concede that Verschaeve would have first licks this year and be top man . . . and that Vermeulen's large lot *was* a fiasco—just as well yank it up right now.

However, no one said a word to Vermeulen himself about his mistake, overawed by the fierce farmer. Among themselves, the men speculated about what the failure of such a field amounted to in lost manure and seed, but they kept quiet when he was around.

He knew very well himself what the situation was on his high field. His wife, who had gone out for a long walk in the afternoon, knew it too before she came home. And Louis, in the late morning, having gone to plant the shoots of palm, had met the grooms on the way back from there. That evening, then, there was heated discussion around the hearth touching on all the flaxfields in the area. They were in general agreement over the luck of Verschaeve's crop.

"All the same consistency," Poortere said, "fat and fresh like it's supposed to be, and not a stalk infected!" And the old farmhand, who had worked Vermeulen's land for half a century, savored the deep-felt pleasure of it.

"For all the flax I've watched grow," he mused, "I've never seen the like."

"Smooth as silk, not too thick, not too thin," one groom confirmed. "If the weather's right, it'll really be something!" The others kept silent, not answering—tension weighing on everyone's mind because of what they knew and dared not say.

Vermeulen sat and smoked, harrumphing now and then, but not speaking.

There was regret on Louis' face, but it was the farmer's wife, in her frank openheartedness, who said straight out what the others felt obliged to suppress.

"Seems to me ours is sowed a little thin."

A contemptuous sneer formed on Vermeulen's face. "Didn't they see it was blighted, didn't they know? And . . . but what's the use in worrying," the farmer thought. He cleared his throat and was silent.

But Louis, who had done the sowing, was old enough to know how much seed had been scattered; he knew it was pointless to answer his mother's naive statement.

"It's too wet, ma'am," Jan, the groom, asserted. "The water can't seep through the clay—the seed'll rot in the ground, all clogged and muddy, and with the cold spell too, it'll have gotten even worse."

"More the fault of all the grasshoppers' eating away the stalks," a farmhand maintained. "The grasshoppers *are* there, I've caught 'em with my own hands."

It was bad no matter what the cause, and no one could make it better. Everyone felt dejected, bewildered before the fact; and then conversation ceased, too, no one able to find a word to fill the huge gap. And the boss, the owner whom it touched most closely, Vermeulen, sat there staring cross-eyed at the smoke from his pipe. Now that everything seemed to have been said, he got up to go out and, his hand on the latch of the backdoor, he jeered over his shoulder, growling:

"Insulting! Silly predictions, weather wizards' blather! Wait, I tell you, wait! What are you all talking about crops and growing? What can you do about it? Wait, give it time to come up! Wait till you see what the weather'll do, and *then* say who'll have the best flax!"

He stamped across the threshold in his heavy clogs and shut the door behind him without further word.

"'Come up!'" Louis mocked, biting back the rest, unintelligible, between his teeth.

Without daring to say it, mother and son were ready to blame the farmer's pigheadedness, for which he had now been punished—for against all reason, he had forced his own will. They were deeply convinced there would never be a crop, or perhaps a very sorry one. They were not thinking of the labor or expense. But Louis's honor was injured before all the farmers in the area: the stupid deed was known, when it could have been so different and so much better, if he had only been able to follow his own judgment.

Fortunately, it was not always Sunday, and during the week you had no time to fret. The failed flaxfield weighed on the mind, a gnawing uneasiness, but it lay a fair ways from the yard, and no one went up to look at it, because the rest of the farming demanded

the business of the full workday. Beets were sown,
potatoes planted, and above the fields and work the
glorious sun shone in its steady course in the
beneficent first warmth of spring, moving toward
summer.

The young women and others on the farm who
had stayed inside no longer had to sniff the open air
on the clothes of the grooms coming back from the
field. Indeed, they were out in it themselves—their
time had also come—racking up the compost heaps
with pitchfork and trident and spreading the mulch
over the ground. This was their first job, and after
that long confinement, they now felt the free wind
blowing through their clothes; they could see open
space before their eager eyes at last and let loose
their ringing laughter at will. There they stood
together, a whole bevy of lively girls spoiling for
mischief. For digging into the fertilizer was only a
foretaste of the cheerful activity that would come
later in summer, when they would go out to rack the
hay. Everything they saw was new and fresh, and
how pleasant it was with the wind round about,
amid the luxuriant greenery, seeing your own gay
clothes flashing with the play of the living sun! It
was a fair, but of all too short a duration: their
nimble arms had much too quickly strewn the mulch
heaps around. A few had to stay and pick weeds
where furrows had been drawn on unfinished
ground; others might go to the young clover to snip
the couch grass—but hardly a moment, and they
had to be inside again, waiting. . . . Now that they

had had a taste of it and liked it, there was no
holding them back: desire played through their
minds, and they regaled each other with the
marvelous pleasures of the impending weeding time.

But desire had not seized the young women
alone—whoever now moved about on the land and
worked it fell under its spell, entranced by the
unfathomable miracle, ever old and always new,
which remains the great event of the year: the
awakening, all things coming to life from the realm
of the dead. The land, the air, the water proclaimed
it: new greenery sprang up everywhere and
proliferated under the sun's laughter and caress,
frolicking on tree and hedge, on bush and shrub—a
thousand colors to dress the whole world in splendor
and finery. The birds come now, all warbling
resolutely; the blood of beasts is in ferment, and they
shake off their sluggishness and stir with new
strength.

To the deep sense of their own return to life, people
add the further pleasure of watching the wealth and
abundance of their crops grow and prosper, the
results of their work take on form and shape.
Anxious to see the promise wax to a full yield,
curious about the outcome of their labor, they all
hurry while there is still time to get everything ready,
preparing to take advantage of the remaining fallow
ground. Now, or never, is there delight in farming
life.

Vermeulen had shared in that pleasure every year,
but spring now was ruined for him. He bore in his

mind a mortifying dread over the crop that had gone bad, the one lying nearest to his heart. Rage overthrew his quiet thoughts; he had to hold back his anger, pacing his fields a sullen man. He was used to holding his head high and showing the fruits of his labor to whoever he met—but not now. He was consumed with dismay: everyone knew that it was not Barbele nor his son nor his hired hands who did the real farming on the place, but he himself—the responsibility was his alone. Day in and day out, Vermeulen ranged over his domain, walking amid all the bustle of the new work—but without pleasure, because that damned flaxfield ravaged his soul. If only it was a general catastrophe over the whole region! If only it wasn't just him! He could see and hear how things stood with Sobrie, Verschaeve, and the others; he knew how they'd sing about it, mocking—the know-it-alls! And yet, he was convinced in his heart that the flax would be successful—there was no reason why not. Or else, just what *was* supposed to be the matter with it, and why wouldn't it take? It was the best seed. He knew the land like the pockets of his pants, and it had been worked and cared for under his own eyes. If he could only lay the blame on someone—"I'd kick 'em in the teeth!" And he felt like stamping and kicking his foot.

On the sly, but not without Vermeulen's notice, his wife had turned to religious expedients. She had gone to pray to Saint Benedict; she lit candles in the bedroom in the farmer's absence; and she had

Hantje, the pilgrim, exorcise the bewitched flaxfield. Vermeulen scorned such inanities: as a farmer, he chose not to give himself up as lost—if with good seed, in good soil well manured, the crop still did not take, he would not have it done through magic, or with spells either. The grasshoppers had turned up of themselves; they would have to be off again the same way. He did not believe you could get rid of them by occult or any other means. The one probable cause was the wet weather and cold spell after the sowing, that was why the crop came out so thin and so irregular. But that too was not sufficient reason--it hammered palpably through his head, and at times he wished the whole field would sink into the earth, so that the farmers in the area would not know him for his failed crop. It was the first time that would happen to him, and he saw it as the greatest possible disgrace to his farm and his own good name. If violence from the heavens utterly destroys his flaxfield, a farmer accommodates himself to it; but if he sows a crop that will not grow, it attaches directly to his reputation.

The flax was no longer mentioned in the house. It was obvious that everyone was preoccupied with it; yet, avoiding each other, no one spoke about it. Everyone felt guilty for the misfortune that had struck the field, as if it were a punishment for a private offense. Vermeulen's face pretended great indifference, and no trace of uneasiness could be sensed from his actions—the flax was an afterthought, forgotten in the wide stream of farm life. But he concealed three frown lines under his hatbrim or the peak of his cap, and whenever he had the chance, he turned his steps to the high field and crept stealthily up the road, irritated to find himself there again watching for a change. In his fear and uncertainty, he felt drawn to it like a murderer to his victim. He had scarcely left it when his doubts arose: Was it really that bad? Had he had a good enough look? And then again, time after time as he approached the field, he began to believe magic *had* been at work, a spell cast over his eyes—and he expected to see it all growing healthily. But there always was the same disillusionment! Good God! what a difference from other years, when, proud and cheerful, he had been able to draw himself up and announce: "I'm just going for a look at the flax!" When he was able to claim at every opportunity that he had produced the finest crop in the district. How whoever he ran into he would get to look at the flax, and how flattering it sounded to him when an acquaintance would say: "But Vermeulen, how do you manage it? We do everything we can and still never get such a fine crop!" How often had he had his game scolding the farmers for their stupidity.

Now he had to creep away on the sly and keep an eye out for someone in the neighborhood spying on him. He approached with fear in his bones, yet as soon as he arrived, his face went dark, his lower lip drooped, and he felt spite and anger rise in him again at the first view of his field. It was really a pitiful sight, the thin, faded stalks standing in bunches, far apart and irregular, in so sad a hue, worn and dreary, of rampant sickness. What kind of clumsy idiot had come here messing around, stupidly trying to brutalize the land? Who had been here—afterward—to ruin the seed, murder it, make it rot and decompose? If only it had not been laid out and furrowed under the farmer's very eyes, so he could blame his son or one of the grooms—how much pleasure he would have gotten cursing and swearing, throwing the dumbbell off the farm with one kick of his heavy clogs! But now he did not know who to blame. The idea had been his and no one else's; his headstrong will alone had forced it through in spite of both his wife and his son. Would he now have to admit that they were right and had a greater understanding of the business? Would he have to take it as a sign that he was growing old and coming into his dotage? Did he no longer have a sense for soil and crops? He now faced his son as a superfluous invalid who cannot any longer handle the ordinary things of life, who bungles everything with his foolish obstinacy. From whom had he heard it just lately? Who had actually said it, that the oats on the low land were doing so well, the oats where the "young farmer" had wanted to sow the flax? Was that just to torment him? If anyone dared to say another word about it, he would break their neck!

"And I won't give myself up for lost yet because of such a little thing," Vermeulen roared. But just the damned luck it had to happen like this to the flaxfield: his son had proved right, and they would secretly have their field day because "Old Pighead" had been chastened.

Vermeulen stood swearing, all alone on the field. He walked over its entire length with a heavy step—but could not find a single good side to the lot. The curse lay over the whole ground. Strips here and there, plain and barren as the sand by the sea. A vague misgiving roused a suspicion in the farmer, but he shook his head, no:

"It can't be his fault," Vermeulen grumbled. He did not consider Louis capable of ruining the crop out of spite; besides, how could he have?

"I was standing right by there when he was sowing, wasn't I?"

He remembered the trim sower's fierce stride and how it had pained and tortured him to see the lad so strong and lithe, how he had grown jealous of his son's youth: he could not himself start that fine life over again. No, there was another reason: the trouble had to be with the soil, with that damned loamy soil that would not soak up the water—that clay lying there in its doughy impermeability, heavy as mush, fermenting and bubbling like cake batter. The linseed had to rot there, in such a mess, and perish from cold. In the urge to know all at once the ultimate cause of his distress, the farmer squatted close to the ground, digging his fingers into the earth and bringing a handful of muck up to his face. He squeezed it, looking to find seeds, to discover germs of life. He flung the stuff back to the ground again and wiped his hand on his pants; but a few steps farther, he scooped out another fistful of mud from a completely barren spot, where not a single shoot of flax had come up. He poked it open with his finger in the palm of his hand, sifting through it like a gold digger would, anxious to find something of value. Then, all at once, his clouded face brightened with satisfaction. He picked up a tiny seed with the nails of his coarse fingers and put it between his front teeth. And as he nibbled it warily, it seemed as though he stood listening for an inner sound. He tasted and swallowed it while his fingers dug hurriedly through the clayey lump to find other seeds. He nibbled in this way on three or four more, after having examined them carefully or broken them open on his thumbnail. With a violent sweep of his hand, he threw the earth away, chuckling joyfully over the happy surprise, a few grunted swear words added. He walked on, off the field, and as he walked contentment so stirred his heart that his eyes began to mellow with tears.

"It's alive, it's alive, it's alive!" The phrase danced through his head, like the full, excited cry of a bird echoes through the air.

"It's just dormant now, it'll shoot up! It's alive, it's alive!"

The discovery had quashed his pent-up rage; his joy, his gratitude, bubbled up like water through a crack in a thick crust of ice—emotion surged within so powerfully that he was overwhelmed by it. He turned his glance to heaven in an uncontrolled impulse, a feeling of thankfulness to the Lord of All shining from his eyes—he did not put it into words.

Vermeulen had not expected this, having been so convinced up to now that he had been wrong and . . .

The afternoon sun was shining softly, in so lustrous a gold, quiet and warm—in a few days, that very sun with its heat would make his backward linseed sprout. . . . Vermeulen was saved: what he had considered lost would not be lost at all.

He now saw the great order so clearly: the powerful, tremendous urge toward life and perfection; how all things, even the smallest, follow their own ways and laws to reach wherever they had to go. Look, all around everything was green and growing, everything—for the time had come and the order had been given. He felt the fructifying air, he breathed it in; he could smell it, touch it with his whole body. The uncertainty and the fear that had tormented him, it seemed so premature and without cause. How could he have been so stupid as to doubt? How could the thought ever have entered his head that the flaxfield was cursed, that it would remain as barren as a layer of stone? The growth was an exultation all around, and the seed he had imagined dead was simply sleeping—it would shoot up! It would become a field of two or three stages of growth, but a field all the same of living flax—and the disgrace of having to pull it up was now gone. What a comfort to the proud heart of the tough countryman! What a joy to know his responsibility to his workfolk was now assured! Yes, he was the old but ever steady Vermeulen, the best farmer in the region!

"Let 'em run, the speed demons. We'll see in a couple of months who gets there first!"

As he neared the farm, Vermeulen checked his happy frame of mind, and the usual solemn expression appeared on his face. He was quietly biding his time now for somebody to pipe up about the flax. Meanwhile, he remained close-mouthed, though he had his retort prepared. In his arrogance, he knew he was the strongest—he stood high once more in his own esteem.

Now he walked his farm again on his solid legs, his mind settled and at ease, his belly thrust out and lips crimped, carrying the certainty that everything was in order, and he no longer cared to think of his fear. He did catch a word now and then behind his back, but never enough to seize on to vent his heart at the mocker. He simply waited, following the course of the weather; he would see the miracle happen yet on the bewitched field.

II

Spring still wavered back and forth, the cold rains falling too heavily for the young crops. There was moping and complaining among people who had supposed summer was already begun; yet now they put all their hope on the holy days leading into Ascension—after that, they expected that growth and warm weather would set in for good.

When the season turns, Heaven's blessing is invoked over the fruits of the earth and its protection is asked for the new harvest. Heavy rains, fierce drought, thunderstorms, hail or excessive heat, and other disasters must be averted from the fields: it is all in God's hands, whatever grows outside stands exposed to the violence of the skies—the farmers know it well. Which is why they put their trust in those days of public supplication and every one of them continues gravely performing his acts of devotion and penance.

As if it were Sunday, they come to church now early in the morning, whereas during the week it is usually quiet and deserted in the village square.

They come: the men and boys in their clogs and
everyday clothes, the dirt still sticking to their pants;
the women cloaked in black mantles; the worn-out
wraps of the girls white and blue or of faded colors.
The church is packed, just as on a feast day. The
procession begins after Mass. But not like at the mid-
harvest festival; they walk in all simplicity, without
pomp and finery, for this is a supplication and not a
celebration. The altar boys, miniature priests in
white robes, carry a cross between two shining
copper candelabra. The priest follows in his purple
cope; he bears the cross with the imbedded relic, the
sun's rays glinting off all its facets of wrought silver
and gold. The sexton carries the book. The village
policeman keeps the young boys in line, holding
back the noisy and excited ones pushing to be first. A
heavy throng of parishioners bursts through the
gates: farmers, workmen, rich and poor, all as a
group—their heads uncovered, they move into the
glaring light of the forecourt where the procession
starts. The dark crowd of women follows, girls and
little children among them—bright patches mingled
in with the black of the mantles. The farmers' wives
are there, their daughters, and the countrywomen
from the shantytown; whoever can get away from
home follows in the procession. The shining white
vestments of the priest and the acolytes, the piercing
glitter of the copper candelabra—and the entire head
of the procession is gone, winding out of view. The
line narrows in the lane between the cloister and the
rectory until it reaches the end of the way to the

church. There it abruptly spreads out wide over the village square, but narrows again in the shadows of the small street behind the houses there, the singing of the priest and sexton echoing ever louder against the exterior walls.

Then all at once, like a heavy torrent of light, the procession streams open over the broad dirt road where the boundless fields lie in the fresh sun-bright mist of the May morning. The land flattens out wide to the left and right, without ditch or fencepost, and over the entire expanse, the dew glistens on the young greenery. Lying enclosed in a horizon of blue vapor, the valley can be taken in at a glance; the air is mild and calm; not a single sound is heard in the distance. A multitude of feet shuffle through the sand, and at the head of the procession, the priest and his sexton chant their long litany, every verse of which drifts off into thin space. The sun reflects off the white surplices and strikes sparks on every curve of the copper candelabra. The cross rises aloft, opening up and pointing the way; the host of pilgrims follows in a train along the sandy path winding through the fields. Larks continually soar and dip, whistle and twitter, while the name of every saint in paradise is invoked with an unceasing *Ora pro nobis*. Finches warble, sparrows peep, all the birds of the air celebrate a feast in the sun, while below every complaint and calamity that must be warded off from the village follows aloud in long succession, ever punctuated by the three words, *Libera nos Domine*. Zealously the two voices chant in the

selfsame rhythm, answering each other in turn at
the same pitch, amid the piping of the birds—and
the large crowd of people walks behind in silence,
seeming to listen, humble and attentive. The whole
procession prays together, each one after the needs
and the desires of his heart. But while they mutter
the prayers, their attention is constantly diverted by
outward appearances. The eyes look left and right
across the fields along the road. The countryman
observes how the crop is growing, thinking besides of
the farmer or tenant who has been working here.
Thought follows thought, and gradually leads to
musings over matters of business, of housekeeping,
of life. And each time another crop or plot of land
comes into view, the train of thought changes. The
farmers and tenants along whose fields the
procession skirts feel more concerned. Their minds
are busy way in advance, and on approaching their
property, they nudge their neighbor at the elbow and
whisper a few little words:
    "What do you say? Nice flax!"
    A slight nod of the head, a little smile, mean much
at that moment and say everything; there is envy in
it at times, for pride runs deep in many farmers. But
the owner now, with the other pilgrims, has passed
his field, without remembering that this was the
propitious moment for him with all his might to
implore a blessing for his land. Or then again, he
looks at another farmer's crop and appraises its
condition and growth with pleasure or with envy,
depending on whether it belongs to a friend or rival,

softly sharing his opinion with the man walking
next to him. Many turn their heads back along the
cart track to look at the group that follows,
measuring at a glance the long procession that
lingers behind at the bend of the road. The sight of
all those bare heads and subdued faces calls for
introspection once more; the praying is resumed with
set purpose and attention paid to the priest's
chanting. But those who hardly ever come around
this way will spot something soon enough that will
draw them away from their devotions: a felled tree,
new work on one or another of the houses, a span of
horses in the field . . . and without realizing it, they
have again left their prayers far behind. Wherever
people are at work as the procession walks past, they
hold still, take off their caps, and stand quietly until
the line disappears.

Now it moves past Veroken's yard and Lamon's
mill, through Duitschave's field and along
Verschaeve's meadow. They will take another route
tomorrow: past Verschaeve's yard, over to
Kapellekouter. And on the third day: along the
heights through Vermeulen's fields and Sobrie's
ploughland, and the Vinckenbosch wood. . . . They
tread the major roads of the village three days in
succession—every quarter has its turn in the general
blessing of the crops. And for three days in a row,
they look at the fields and judge them. Every farmer
receives an overall impression, formulating his
opinion about the way the lands of the entire village
have been worked and their condition—and each

knows how the others have fared and what they will lay in at harvest time.

Leaving the soft sandy road, the procession reaches the cobbled paving of the village's main street, and the noise rises of clopping shoes, as more and more pilgrims turn the corner, their feet scraping against the stones. The singing of the priest and sexton takes on an altered sound amid the houses and is drowned in the rush and rattle of hammering footsteps when the procession reaches the village square. The first among them have already been seated in the church quite a while, but others still come, vanishing straightaway into the opening of the dark portal. The women, covered with dust, walk quickly to move up to the front rows. When all of the long tail has moved inside through the church's black maw, all at once a solemn stillness descends, and the priest gives his blessing with the holy relic over the silent crowd. And then, immediately, the people burst forth overflowing from the church, altogether in a tumult to be away and outside. The crowd flows open on the church square, swelling steadily with newcomers going their own way, out of the village in all directions. They will be at work immediately, without a break. Duty done, a pure trust cheers them, for the morning already gives promise of a splendid summery day.

Vermeulen had walked through the fields with the procession for two days in a row; praying with the crowd, he had peered left and right and seen a good many fields and much flax finer than his. But he had nursed no grudge—his mind was at ease. And the third day, when the pilgrimage was to be made through his own land, he was back in the procession; without trembling, his heart not pounding, the farmer approached his high field. He purposely looked elsewhere, yet all the while he listened intently around him to catch a word or a phrase about his abortive crop. Everyone had seen it now, and it would be bandied all over what had happened to Vermeulen's flax, but:

"They'll stand and gape all the more later," he mused.

The farmer's wife had put all her trust and her last hope in the blessing of the procession of the cross; the rest she left in God's hands. And in fact, her expectations were not cheated. For at a stroke, there began a succession of beautiful days ushering in summer, and the crops took root under your very eyes.

It was clear then that the wailing and crying had been premature, that the work would not really be lost. The sultry warmth of the sun chased away all evil: languishing crops revived and shot up in sturdy growth; failing flax ready to be pulled up improved so unbelievably that it seemed a miracle. While the first growth had stood but two inches high, the bare patches now and the seed that had appeared bad began to germinate, coming up thick as dust and soon covering the soil. The farming year was retrieved once more, and summer would yet put everything in order.

"What do you say now?" Vermeulen started in, having waited to speak for so long. "If I'd listened to you, the flaxfield would've been pulled up!"

Barbele had at first looked at it, dumbfounded, as a miracle, and she ascribed the deliverance to the procession's blessing:

"It's begun to get better, since then," she insisted.

"A little slowdown, and you're screaming and shouting and giving yourself up for lost," Vermeulen said. "I never doubted a moment that it would be a good field."

"It'll make a field all right, but in any case not good flax," Barbele commented.

"Not good? Who says so? And why not?"

"It's grown in two or three spurts," his wife goaded him. "Anyone can see that."

"It'll fill out. It's filling out. Within a month, it'll be smooth as a pond," the farmer asserted.

"And it'll have caught up with the other fields that came up first," his wife mocked. "We know all about 'filling out'! Just look at Sobrie's flax and Legijn's—why do you always want to go against the well-known truth? *Those* are flaxfields. We're bringing up the rear in every way this year, and we better not brag. They're weeding Legijn's flax already, and ours is still coming up."

Vermeulen felt the ridicule, and since the woman still as always wanted to put the blame on him, she was herself at fault with the farmer. With that, the joy of his discovery was at once quashed, and his fury quickly came again to the surface. He mimicked

her words, and without further cause—one thing
adding to another—he began to shout abuse: he
dredged up everything that for a long time had been
weighing on his mind. In his rush to come out with
it, he choked on his words, going purple in the face
and losing his breath. True or false, he spilled it out
as it came to him: the workhands were difficult and
no good, through her fault; she and that worse than
nothing of a son were trying to play the boss on the
farm . . .

"And those two smart daughters of yours!" he
shouted. "I don't know them anymore! You're
turning them into regular snots, it's a disgrace to an
honest farmer."

The girls' attitude and the way they behaved
crushed him the most, and it did him good to have
the opportunity just this once to spit out his
displeasure. Louise and Anna had been home for
three weeks during the Easter holidays, and for three
weeks long, the farmer had had to suffer and let pass
things that irritated him and went against his grain.
He had been cantankerous, angrily grinding his
teeth, but had held in his resentment and let matters
go, because he could find no point of attack.

He had given in reluctantly in the first place to his
wife's deep wish. With grudging consent, he had let
the two girls go off to boarding school. She had won
him over with her arguments: times had changed
over the past forty years, and it was a man's duty to
give his children a proper education, to maintain his
standing among those other farmers who also sent

their children away. . . . Yet he had never dared to
think it would go so far, that it would come to this.
They were grown up now, old enough and
thoroughly able to help out on the farm. But just
send your children away, and you can't tell how
you'll get them back. Vermeulen no longer
recognized his own daughters; he was embarrassed
to open his mouth in their presence. They sat there
laced up from top to toe in black. Their entire
manner, their gestures, their walk, and even their
tiny smiles were studied. The wild farmkids were
gone, and they now fussed for whole days with their
own little things—stuff and nonsense: the farmer
could make no sense of it whatsoever. Farmhands,
maids, livestock, stables . . . it was as if it were none
of their concern, not in existence. All their activity
took place in the best room, the one normally closed
off as a holy of holies and opened only once a year,
at the time of the village fair—there they received the
friends who came to visit. With these good-for-
nothings—all of the same ilk, too haughty and stuck
up to talk to the farmer or his wife—they would go
off together for little walks, under umbrellas, to the
meadow or grove. For hours on end, they would sit
like princesses in the garden arbor, whispering
secrets, wasting good time. A toad would frighten
them, and they would shriek with fear if they saw a
spider. At every meal, for three long weeks, those
cloddish damsels sat by themselves at a small table,
picking at a bowl of their own, and when they
deigned to direct a word to their parents, it was only

to point out what ought to be changed and had to be done once they settled back here at home for good! "Once"! For now it seemed that this famous education was not even close to completed! And their mother simply gave in every time, letting it pass; clucked over and pampered them, whispering, flattering—and held the farmer beyond the pale, telling him only what she wanted known.

He was fed up with the whole goddamn thing—he would crush it under his heels.

"They weren't even once in the stable! But then how could they really, dainty little things, with such teeny-weeny shoes on their feet and lace on their skirts? Why aren't there clogs ready for the girls when they come home, or have their footsies become too delicate for 'em? They're not my daughters!" Vermeulen roared. "They're really ashamed to be from the farm? Good. I'm happy not to see them anymore, they can stay out of my sight forever. Just make sure you've got a baron ready for each of 'em when they've got their learning. Now they're away again—work's starting, but it's got to be done by outsiders—and instead of getting their help, you even have to work to get junk ready for those little snots. And did you hear what they're planning for here, once they come home? Turn the whole farm upside down and renovate everything—parties and music all day! Just prancing and gorging and getting fat! . . ."

"Now, now," his wife soothed, "when they come home, they'll start working just like all the other farmers' daughters—you'll see. It's not that bad—you always yell too loud. Are you going to let your children out in the world with no manners or without an education? You're half a century behind in everything."

But there was no way to make Vermeulen see reason or to hold him in check. He was deeply offended—his daughters had badly confused him with their studied deportment.

"I can see them already hauling buckets of milk across the yard," he sneered.

"There will certainly be other work for them to do," his wife said.

But now Vermeulen opened his eyes wide:

"Other work?" he shouted. "Sure. Toying with ribbons and bows? How could you think that we'd allow such fakery here? They have to *work*, goddamn it, like I saw it in my family and you did in yours!"

"Mm-hmm . . . and you'd be the first to not let them . . . Look at Veroken's daughters and Sobrie's," the farmer's wife said, standing squarely before him. "What's more, you can do as you want with Louis, he's yours. But the girls are mine! And I'm keeping Louise and Anna in the house!"

"Then put 'em in a glass case between two candlesticks!" the farmer roared. "But everyone who lives on my farm works: 'your' daughters go to the fields with the others, and they'll go to the stable and wherever there's work."

With that, he walked out of the kitchen and slammed the door behind him. He made the rounds of the yard, giving the farmhands and the cowherds a taste of his bad temper. He raged inside: it wouldn't happen, he'd teach them a lesson for sure. . . . But deep down, Vermeulen saw a thing so atrocious, so unassailable, that he gave himself up for lost in advance, in spite of his stubborn resolve to hold out and force his will. He knew how cunning the women were and at one in their intentions . . . and he put all determination to rest and waited for the inevitable to come. Like with his son, so it would be with his daughters: they too had grown away from him—standing against their father with minds and inclinations of their own—and his hand could not keep them under control, no matter how he raged. Yet he could not accustom himself to the thought of having to yield one day and suffer a will or authority alongside his—he would never resign himself to that. "When I'm dead, they can do what they want, but not before!" was his conclusion.

In maintaining his control over his grown son, Vermeulen outwardly showed himself resolute and strong; but behind the steadfastness of his harsh bearing, under the bark of his wrinkled forehead, in the depths of his heart he concealed his sorrow that matters were taking such a turn. Resentment, rage, and repugnance had come rushing up and now burst out in a storm; he had rashly put the blame on Barbele, without rhyme or reason. Then whose fault was it? It was going on all around him; he had his part in it himself, as had others, as had time—everything conspired to drive his children from him. In half a lifetime, he had seen so much around him change and take on a new appearance. The sturdy farmer was aware now that he stood alone. He felt himself being dragged into a whirl of innovations, of things he knew were evil and which he had to detest. He had already abandoned one part of his own nature, and now the other threatened to escape him as well. Bitterness gnawed at his conscience each time he had to admit he had accepted some of the newness, but there was no other way. His harsh disposition and his rich farmer's pride stood pitted against each other, fighting for the upper hand. Was he supposed to watch grovelers and scroungers stand up and crow and do more than himself? Small farmers with nothing at all raised the devil and started acting "grand," and would he shame his daughters among those who were less than their equals? Pigheaded Vermeulen wanted his daughters to be like brood mares, sturdy horseflesh—the whole show, in true Old Flemish fashion: ready little workers with their hearts on their lips and their souls in their eyes, laughing in fun, giving all they'd got, doing their share of labor alongside the strongest of men. On the other side stood the lordly farmer who wished to be first and foremost in all things, above the heads of his peers, and who upheld his lofty position. With their luxurious youth and beauty, his daughters had to be the absolute glory of the farm; exquisitely dressed, they were to be praised as creatures of wonder throughout the district.

But the ordinary, everyday Vermeulen was not

even conscious of this inner struggle with his double. Only when Barbele laid these contradictions before his eyes, when he was trapped by his own arguments, did he not know what he wanted or what was best. He would look for a way out by exploding in anger, seeing no end to the matter except by stamping his heavy clogs. Those were Vermeulen's worst moods. But once in the fields, alone with himself and matters of the farm on his mind, pondering serious and important business, all his uneasiness over these petty trifles seemed of little account. He then began to feel obliging, ready to see reason and give in. The large enterprise that spread around him brought peace back to his heart, and he regretted losing his temper and lashing out. He admired Barbele again for her gentle nature. He bore no grudge over their quarrels. Nevertheless, he would never humiliate himself and ask for forgiveness: he simply forgot all about them, and when he came home, he would ask, with the usual manner of the preoccupied farmer: "Have you seen to the women yet about the weeding? The flax has taken hold, we've got to get on it quickly."

Vermeulen did not bother much about the women's work on the farm, letting Barbele arrange it all. He avoided mixing with women and girls—that sex lived in a world of its own, of which he had no understanding. He went to inspect only when their work was finished, thundering over it, of course, as he found necessary.

And so, the next Sunday the farmer's wife made it

her job to ask for all the women and the girls she could get. First she went to those who lived on the property belonging to the farm, and then she visited all the shacks and shanty settlements of the weavers and swinglers and one-cow farmers where women and girls could be spared.

"The bigger the group, the sooner it's done," she thought, "and all in one push."

She did not find too many to ask: most of them were already working for other farmers, while some, only just laid off, had promised themselves elsewhere. But promises were lightly broken as soon as talk went around of going to Vermeulen; everybody knew that for food and wages, it was better than anyplace else. The young people above all appreciated it, since the farmer's wife tolerated pranks and good fun.

And so Barbele got just as many women and girls to weed as she wanted.

III

They turned up from all over one Monday morning at the crack of day, the girls looking fresh and scrubbed clean in their freshly washed summer blouses—pale blue, pink, of striped, dappled, or flowered cotton—their skirts shortened and underclothes dark. They waved their broad-brimmed straw hats or carried their light clogs by hand, walking boldly on bare feet. Their hair pale, brown, or blonde as wheat, they came together and stood huddled in the large farmyard, the quick tongues of their voices shrill and crowing all at once. Some were almost fresh from their first Communion, hardly grown out of their girlish frocks, and drew back from the others and timidly looked around. There were lanky, overgrown girls, wise and sober as the morning dew, taking part in the trek from one flaxfield to another for the first time; half-grown girls with a slender looseness still in their limbs and guilelessness on their pale faces; virginal girls from the congregation, with wonder ever in their eyes, who did not know how to carry themselves in their

diffident, coy modesty. And girls too with full round
limbs, firm bodies under their tight cotton jackets,
with hips ample as churns; precocious girls, playful
as fillies, firm fleshed, with cheeks like apples and
glancing eyes, skittish, wild, defiant, always ready
for a laugh; others shy as sparrows, with arms
crossed in a bashful gesture over their all too
beautiful breasts. Married women were there among
them too, with babies in their arms. Thin, withered
women with voices sharp as knives, which carried
over all the high-pitched words; widows with the
misery of life on their faces, emaciated through
slaving for the farmers by day and at home by night,
in order to scratch out a living; and many an old
crone come whining, with a burlap sack for under
her knees, stiff with rheumatism and bent over with
the heat.

Young and old, whoever could even barely get
around had come, and they stood there clustered
together in a dense pack, the whole yard full. They
chatted on while waiting for coffee, the youngest
playing ball and cavorting, others whispering
confidentially in small cliques—a motley swarm,
each different from the next, yet all the same as a
whole. As soon as the door to the house opened, the
crowd stormed inside, those who could sprinting to
be first at the bench by the table, there to gulp down
the hot coffee and the high stacks of bread and
butter until there was nothing left. And bang! the
women bubbled outside again, one after the other,
waving their aprons over their shoulders, their straw

hats or clogs in their hands—romping and playing and whirling forward, with a great din of voices, through the gate, across the bridge over the canal embankment, along the lane on their way to the flaxfield.

That first day Louis, somewhat against his inclination, led the whole troop to work. Once arrived, he stood there aimlessly and watched how the weeders arranged themselves in pairs, and in a long line made their way for the first time to the far end of the field. They crawled forward on their knees; their bodies, bent over, rested on the left arm, stretched out as if on the wing of a chair, while the right hand alone worked, pulling up the weeds among the stalks of flax. Louis stayed at a distance behind the line, and having nothing to do except look out over the bent backs of the weeders, he realized that for the first time he was overseeing a crew of workfolk.

After a hesitant silence at the beginning, the weeders got into their work and acted as though they no longer knew the young farmer was standing behind the line. Loud babbling broke out in three or four places, and where two or more friends were grouped together, the talk was confidential or whispered. Louis paid no attention. He had plenty to look at where he stood, and a gladness stole into his senses that beautiful May morning, as he felt how calm it was all around, near and far, and how that calmness matched the inner contentment of his heart.

The morning fog had steadily lifted under the sun, and dewdrops trembled on the small stalks all over the field, a cascade of pearls scattered over ground lacquered with green. The sparkling hurt the young farmer's eyes. Farther off, on the low land, a living red glow of mist floated where trees and houses sat in the sun-bright haze. Threads of cobwebs drifted like woven spun silk over the freshly ploughed fields, and where the sun shone upon it, the whole area stirred like churning water. The air was clear on the heights, and the white and red of houses and farms stood out against the marked-off pastures in untouched purity. The young man daydreamed without following his thoughts; under the spell of the morning's beauty, he had the splendor of the green vista before him and the joyous blue of the sky above his head. . . . Yet, tired of gazing out, he no longer watched anything and turned inward, moved as he was by a desire for something intangible, a longing for something he could not name but which filled his whole being with a feeling of quiet sorrow and sweet yearning. He heard the glad cry of the larks, rising and falling in turn, the happy babble and chatter of the weeders. The echoing song of the blackbirds struck him as a call to go and lie down awhile over there in the good shade of the grove. Without a sound, he walked off across the flaxfield and left the weeders to their work.

Only one girl in the group had noticed Louis going away, and she glanced furtively over her shoulder to where the young farmer had vanished into the grove. As if a cloud had moved in front of the sun, the brightness around faded before her eyes. There was no one else among the whole gathering who so yearned and looked forward to the coming opportunity in the flaxfield as this girl had, and she viewed the morning when she could go out for the first time as the most fortunate moment in her life.

Rieneke had been but a child until lately, dressed in all the simplicity and charm she had brought with her from home. During the early years of her service, she had remained unnoticed in lonely isolation on the meadows and among the sheds; none of the people on the farm paid any attention to the high-spirited child, even though she was forever making merry all by herself, morning to night, hopping around the world and singing. Just fifteen years old, she had in a short time grown to the fullness and form of a girl of twenty: robust, with strong legs, round hips, an ample body, and slender limbs, with a sunny face and a head of hair light as wheat, always loose in a tangle of curls, and under it her blue eyes glittering like jewels. The flushed pink skin of her cheeks was delicate as the down of unpicked peaches, and the sun could not tan it whatsoever. Between tender-fleshed lips, two rows of ivory-white teeth forever sparkled, for all to see; her laughter and the ringing of her happy voice echoed ceaselessly over the yard.

Because of her unshakable good cheer and resounding laughter and song, she had picked up the pretty nickname of Schellebelle, "jingle bell."

Schellebelle delighted everyone with her

merriment; whoever met her called out a nice word to her, even if only to receive a still nicer reply. Quick with her hands, into everything, never tired and always eager for work, she took on the duties of a full-fledged stable maid. Vrouw Vermeulen was especially fond of her because of her helpfulness, and if something needed to be done, she would call for Schellebelle.

No one would allow that there could be something else in the girl's head, that deeper in her mind, beyond her laughter and merriment, an original idea lay brooding—they were aware only of her open, frank, healthy, spirited nature. But she was not so foolish as to tell everything she knew and felt.

Lately, the other girls had told Schellebelle so many stories about what goes on among the weeders in a flaxfield that she had been whole nights without sleep. Her heart was as pure as the May morning itself, and the least thing suggested to her, even remotely, for fun and novelty, rang in her like bells sounding a feast, and she would come aflame immediately with effusive satisfaction and enthusiasm. Without being able to guess what was actually going to happen, she had counted the days, and filled with all sorts of expectations, the first hour of her happiness had struck at last: the whole merry parade of girls had come, and she had marched along in high spirits, arm in arm with two of her comrades. And so she now sat between Marietje Verlinde and Fientje Vandoorn, the three of them in quiet conversation.

Everything had started off perfectly that morning: warm weather, just the right kind for weeding; the expanse of field open before their eyes . . . but that Louis would come along to the field—that was something Schellebelle had not expected or even thought about, and it made her happiness complete. She told no one—but she felt pleasantly content whenever she knew the farmer's son was nearby. She did not try to explain why this was so—had never even admitted it to herself: she simply felt drawn to him and surrendered to the urge with all the guilelessness of her soul.

And so it seemed as if something had gone into eclipse around her when Louis went away. But no sooner did the group realize that they were alone than the laughter and shouting rose up louder along the whole line, one woman striking up the first flax song in a wavering voice that sounded like a lament over the field:

A young knight would awandering go . . .

The new girls listened with close attention, in fear of losing a single word of the tale, which they took as a true happening. The long-winded story unfolded over an endless number of stanzas, punctuated by an ever-recurring dirgelike refrain. The knight, in quest of love and finding it nowhere, went roaming in the fields, and there a maiden was working amid "the early flax." He was enchanted at once by the fresh, lovely girl and was so delighted with her beauty that he promised her riches, gold, and money for her favors. He implored her: Let him just rest beside her in the early flax for one short hour. To which the girl, arch and scornful, would say "nay" and "nay" again after each new promise and appeal.

Schellebelle saw the girl sitting there as plainly as if it were she herself, and she knew as well the gentleman who came asking for her.

> O gallant knight so fair and fine
> After my love are you asking?
> You see I'm but a farming girl
> With no time for gallivanting.

The courtly knight promised her in succession: a gown of rich satin, a comb of reddish gold, slippers of pure crystal. . . .

But cool and roguish came the mocking reply:

> You tempt me not, O noble sir,
> A maiden born for working.

The song went on, telling of ever-renewed advances and harsher rebuffs, until the knight left off at last in sorrow, and with his farewell a stern moral was thrown at his back, to ring in his ears for a long time to come:

> Beware, you maidens, young men of grief
> From town with love come roving:

With boasting false and embraces sure
The girls in the flax enticing.

Schellebelle was enchanted, pleasure and
excitement shining in her eyes. How good to sit here
and listen! Who was going to sing another one? It
was not long before a piercing voice rose up at the
other end of the line, and a woman sang something
of the same kind but heartier and more robust in
tempo. The seducer did not fare any better, the
maiden he spoke to cracking right back at him:

O my good baron, you fret so in vain.
I scorn both your love and your gold.
I'm a good farmgirl, upright of heart—
To hell with your treasures untold.

It continued the whole morning, everyone singing
her song—those of the women as old as the hills,
while the girls sang newly learned lyrics of wooing
and love. There were rhymed stories of murder,
misfortune, or cruel happenings that had taken
place in the vicinity, and other, mischievous things
in a light tripping measure, burlesques and amorous
ballads. But Dille Verwee drew the most applause
with a song she had made up herself, and which told
her own story: how she had come to know Aloïs, how
they had gotten married, how he had left for France,
and the letter he had written to his wife in which it
said that he had taken up with another, leaving her
to sit—

in woe and distress, hunger and terror,
moaning and fearful of death

After that came Wantje's turn—Wantje the old
crone, who was taking part in the trek through the
flaxfields for the sixty-fifth time. She sang "her"
song, the same as always, about Genoveva of
Brabant.

To the down-to-earth yet lively girl who had never
heard anything but cowherd's songs, all this was a
sudden revelation—a new world that lay open to her
as if by magic; things she did not know existed
except for a vague feeling in her own heart were now
represented all at once, made clear in words: the
language of love and life's many dangers, the
goings-on between young men and women. It
danced and sang in and around her, rustling in her
ears along with the chirping of birds in the glorious
sunshine. Desire was awakening, and she wanted to
know more, much more about those things.

At noon, when the bell rang, the whole crew
straightened right up, everyone taking her own heap
of weeds in her apron and carrying it to the draining
ditch. The younger ones frisked and bounded off the
field, while the old women moved sedately behind,
slow and easy through the lane to the yard.
Schellebelle walked arm in arm with Marietje
Verlinde and Fientje Vandoorn, one of them singing
to the step and sway of their slender young bodies:

Joe, Joe, Joe—

Now there's a fine lad truly.
For him the girls all yearn.
He is so cute, so strong, so fast,
And don't he like the girls the best!

All three together repeated the refrain in ringing
voice, just for the pleasure of the wonderful sound.

Two long tables had been arranged in the kitchen
with platters full of potatoes and tureens of porridge,
and the farmhands and the weeders took their places
quickly. The noise and chattering here was no less
than in the field, the grooms and the other big shots
helping it along some by teasing the women and
girls, laughing at them, each trying to crow louder
than the rest.

Just as soon as the noon meal was finished, they
all went outside and wandered around the yard
looking for a good place to sleep away the midday
break in comfort. Some—the troublemakers—hadn't
sense enough to rest; they ran here and there,
crawling over wagons and carts and in and out of
every door, going to the orchard or the grass along
the embankment to toss a ball, scuffle, laze around,
or make a little mischief together.

The bell rang their summons at a quarter to two.
The entire bunch was allowed inside for coffee, and
from there they headed back to the field. This time
Vermeulen went along as overseer. With a wicker
basket on his arm and his broad sun hat on his
head, he followed the rollicking herd. Once at the
flaxfield, he walked over the swathe where the

weeders had passed. He watched how they positioned themselves and were working; and when to his mind it was well under way, he took his place in the middle, behind the weeders, set the basket on the ground next to him, and pulled out from it his great family Bible. There, in the blistering sun on the open field, he began to read, slowly and word for word:

"Joseph, being seventeen years old, was feeding the flock with his brethren; and the lad was with the sons of Bilhah, and with the sons of Zilpah, his father's wives; and Joseph brought unto his father their evil report . . ."

The sentences flowed together, one after another, in stately procession, and the wonderful tale grew steadily, with the gravity of an all-important world-event.

Straight ahead gleamed the fleecy green carpet of the large flaxfield with its surrounding acres, running down wide to the depths of the valley and up again in a sharp incline to the higher hill where everything lay misted in a rich blue. Here the weeders sat, tiny dots enveloped in the expanse of the valley, on the high crest of ground round as a belly, with nothing above them but the sky stretched in a wide dome of joyous azure and sunlight. With their faces bowed to the earth and backs bent, they crawled forward on their knees, looking for weeds between stalks of flax. The farmer, behind them, followed in their tracks, step by step, while the Bible story unfolded in all its solemn dignity: the hatred among brothers grew, and the oppression of innocence stood pictured as an appalling monstrosity in the courts of time.

The lovely May sun glistened on the young greenery, the birds in the thicket proclaimed their delight; the afternoon quiet seemed the same as on all other days, but it was as if the sun threw off a stronger light here and a more sacred stillness hung in the air round about where they all knelt listening in fearful anticipation of what was going to happen—so solemn did the farmer's voice sound in the silence. The weeders no longer made out words or were aware that it was Vermeulen who stood behind them reading something from a book; they only had to lift their heads—they were so carried away—to see the events of the "Twelve Brothers" acted out over there on the rise of one of the far hills, in the brilliance of the afternoon sun. So crystal clear was the space, everything in it pure and translucent—so deeply, intimately interwoven with and framed by the mood of the story.

When Vermeulen came to a stop and was silent, there was relief at first, many a girl loosing a sigh, and a quiet murmur of admiration went down the entire line. A few raised their heads good-naturedly and looked up, rubbing their eyes in an unconscious gesture, as if to wipe away their amazement.

Then Krako the crippled cowherd appeared on the sandpath with his wagonload of coffee and sliced bread and butter for the late afternoon "vespers." The chattering started up again, the noise breaking the reverential calm of before. Light-footed, the young girls skipped across the field to the wagon and there flocked together in a circle, each jostling for her share, now falling all at once on the food. Vermeulen then took up his basket and Bible and left, his wife coming to relieve him. Following old custom, they said the Paternoster out loud together, and afterward the singing and storytelling resumed. The weeders sat working in the field until the day was entirely over and the evening prayer-bell rang in the village. And after supper, some went home while others stayed at the farm, where they found a place to sleep.

So, too, the next days passed during the weeding season, and Schellebelle and her friends lived at constant play without keeping track of the time or figuring on its ending. They basked in the open sunshine on the flaxfield, and knowing every nook and cranny on the farm, in those places together they revealed the fervor of their hearts. From one hour to the next, the inexperienced girls learned something new that ever and again widened their outlook, disturbing their young minds and giving them fresh matters for anxious reflection over what yet was lurking in the mysterious life around them. The country love songs, the dangers to deceived or trusting girls; love unhappy, rejected, repressed; love in its thousandfold expressions—this was what excited and entranced them. In between were tales of murder and other yarns with robbers and ghosts, specters and ogres, that made their hearts thump and their blood run cold.

Netje Kyvere was at it right now, and terror hushed her voice in the telling—how her father, who was a trapper, was lying in wait one night along the water's edge where he knew an otter nested. And having found the animal's tracks and lain there so long he could hardly move his stiffened joints, he heard something coming closer, thump, thump, on heavy feet and made out a shape he had never been able to name or describe: smaller than a donkey but bigger than a dog—and it came up in front of him where he lay and plunged down into the water. Afterward, he heard the werewolf walked there . . .

Another woman, Triene, followed with hers: about this man who went out at night to catch eels in the Scheldt; how he dropped his hook into the gloom and could not get it out again with a single yank—how he kept pulling all night until, all in a sweat, he finally got it, along with a corpse he had fished up at the end of his line. How he felt a drop of sweat form at the root of every hair, and how he came home physically ill and three days later was dead.

Pauline told even a better one: about three girls who were binding corn at harvest time and talking together, complaining about hard times and that they had no money to buy clothes. Then suddenly a sharp-looking gentleman stood there before them and gave one of the three a gold coin, on condition that the first thing she bound up in the morning would be his. But that evening, the girl told about the adventure to her mother, a wise woman who made her daughter go to the field in the middle of the night, with no clothes on, and bind a sheaf there with straw rope. And indeed, barely had the sheaf been bound when it flared up like sulfur and flew high into the air. "You see," the mother then said to her daughter, "if you'd just tied on your apron first, the devil would've packed you off to hell. You can go spend your gold coin now, it can't do any harm." Then Tale Kok told about a young girl who had to stay home alone and watch the house and how a gentleman came in who asked for a hair from her head. But the clever thing promptly pulled a hair out of a whisk broom and gave it to him, the gentleman. And he was scarcely out of the house when the whisk broom began to dance, and danced out of doors, without anybody ever seeing it again.

And to prove that the devil roams the countryside in the flesh, Zenia told how two drunks were reeling along and they ran into a man who they invited to come drink with them. How they got angry because the man would not join them, shouting loudly and defiantly into the darkness of the evening: "We'll go drinking with the devil then!" They actually did come across someone else who would go along, and taking their new pal by the arm, they staggered on. At the first sign they saw, they went in and asked for a drink. But standing in the light, they noticed for the first time who they had by the arm: a blackened, slovenly woman with hanging hair, two horse's legs, and a tail sticking out from under her skirt. They sobered at once, reciting the Gospel of St. John, and the horror vanished.

And so one followed after another. The evil that looms, thriving, along the roadsides and streets was offered in all its shapes and guises, a warning to inexperienced girls, a caution to be wary of the company they kept, of strange gentlemen above all. The girls listened avidly: a delightful fear made their bodies tingle all over, and they forever craved more such things.

On other days, the conversation of the older women ran on about matters that interested the girls even more, but this was usually whispered softly and did not carry farther than three or four who were side by side, so that the others could catch half a word with difficulty and had to guess the rest. As it were in a school for gossip, with its several little rooms, were secret things laid bare; unknown village scandals, news about events that had been kept hidden, ran here like wildfire from one woman to the next, whispered into the ear and detailed until there was no more left of the secret except a certain secretiveness on the face and in the gestures with which it was told. Things the girls had never heard of or suspected—things that startled their imaginations and all at once gave them a whole other insight into no end of people and circumstances and relationships they had never considered—were picked apart here bit by bit and commented upon. With relish and waspish pleasure, with the intention of stirring up trouble, they cited forgotten situations, dredging up events from the past, out of the depths of oblivion, once more laying bare that shameful ugliness of life over which time had spread a recent appearance of gentility. Here on the flaxfield, in the quiet of the warm afternoon, the secret business of people's lives was raked over—a revelation for the growing youngsters, who in this way learned for the first time about what really goes on between adults. Those stories drawn from the experiences of married or older women made the girls' hearts throb with emotion and started a revolution in their young imaginations.

And so, with alternating silence and noise, bursts of laughter and reserve, with prayers, singing, backbiting, and tales, the weeders went on with their work in the flaxfield from one May day to the next. Through constant repetition, the same things recurring again and again, each part of the day acquired its special prospect, bringing with it variety and always new diversion. In the sober morning hours, with the dew glistening like pearls of sun in the supernatural dream world above the lowland mist, ballads echoed clearly of Faith Eternal, Love with Jealousy, Love with Sorrow, Love with Joy in Love. And all the while, the young farmer, who had come along to the field as supervisor, stood listening. Little by little, he appeared to take more interest in the gossip and chatter that arose from the group and even threw in a word to tease one girl or another.

Around noon, the hazy distances took on a new sharpness, the shores of the phantom island where the weeders sat in isolation expanding more and more, and they became aware again of their firm connection with the surroundings and the real condition of things. The talk then mounted and the voices of the singers soared, resounding far and wide. As the heat started to become more oppressive, a stillness and quiet set in. Then the old farmer dominated the whole area with his presence, the tales from the Bible again looming large in their imaginations. After Joseph appeared Moses, the awesome colossus and world ruler who traveled through the desert with a host of forty thousand men and drew a channel through the sand just like the river down there cutting its bed through the valley. After that, the horrors of the Book of Job were declaimed. In the rarefied air, unconfined by walls, the words sounded like a voice come from afar, prophesying the end of the world.

Silence fell again after vespers, when the sun dipped behind the ridges of the hills and, under the crystal-clear sky, everything began to shine in warmer hue and more brilliant color.

Then Barbele or the senior among them stood on the field by the women and recited the Hail Marys in her simple voice, ever repeating the same prayer that was to bring blessings to the land. Quiet contentment settled over the hearts of the weeders, all of them together affected by the charged emotion quivering through the fine atmosphere at evening's fall.

So each and every day was passed in the

enjoyment of the fair season, in the festive appearance with which all of nature was adorned. Not a one of them thought about the work or the weeding itself—that was the farmer's business—they came in the morning and left in the evening, without care or understanding or consideration of food and wages. Work starts with the gray of dawn, ends with the toll of the prayer-bell, and the Lord God does not alter the length of His days—beyond that was easy to figure: five stivers a day for the grown women, three for those in short skirts. For the rest, everyone was expected to work steadily and diligently, going about on her knees, and to keep in line and be responsible for the weeds in her own path.

The flaxfield had to be gone over like this up and down, weeded, cleaned, purified. Thistles, dropwort, cattails, madder, mayweed, garden grass, dewberries, shepherd's purse, and flax rust—whatever counted as weeds was known to the weeders: their hands had to pick over the stalks and soil like a head of hair afflicted with boils—and not a trace of malignance could remain. But the weeders had the time: the days had not been reckoned up, and it would be a long while yet before the stalks were fully grown and would be damaged by being crawled over. Everything alike passed over the weeders: they bore the heat of the sun on their bent backs and straw hats—they protected themselves from cold, rain, hail, and wind with worn-out men's clothing and burlap sacks over their heads.

They looked on the flaxfield afterward as their own. Through living together as a group day by day, there evolved a solidarity that grew into a sense of belonging, a spirit of mutual trust—they made up an intimate circle that no stranger could enter or gain any knowledge of, and no outsider was initiated into their practices. Moreover, the group was divided further into several cliques; where like to like joined together, they imparted to one another the joys and secrets of the heart. For all the exuberant cavorting and shouting and outward merriment, there was nevertheless a deeper side to their thoughts and actions, a prevailing mood of mutual understanding, which could only be observed, however, at certain moments. Tenderness lay in a fleeting gesture, a look, a smile during a game; when throwing an arm around one another's shoulders or in the whispering of a word, they unconsciously spoke a language expressive of their most delicate emotions; no "stranger" could make anything of it, though they did not know this and did not intend it. It happened that three or four of them would burst out laughing at the table simply by looking at each other; others communicated their secrets with the exchange of a wink. For days on end, something would be going on among a few friends without anyone on the farm becoming aware of their carryings-on. Affairs of the heart and mind were conveyed in a special way, and with a single word the whole of their innermost lives lay open and bared to whoever was allowed to look in.

Without knowing what was happening or changing inside her, Schellebelle was affected most strongly by the new circumstances. Until now, she had always been alone with her cows; never having followed her own feelings or thoughts, she was far from understanding how things were in someone else's heart and what went on with other girls. It seemed as if the joy of life was being revealed to her now for the first time. So much that was new had entered her mind all at once, all jumbled together and knocking around in a confused, crazy whirl. The singing of the ballads hummed constantly in her ears; every so often, she recalled something of the old women's darker arguments, and then in the midst of the daybright sunshine, an air of mystery and enchantment would reign over field and path because of all the things she had picked up from the tales. And from her younger friends, she got to hear all kinds of important information she would never otherwise have thought about. What she looked upon before as extraordinary and exceptional, a rare feeling pertaining only to her own person—what she had grudgingly kept covered out of a sense of shame—turned out to be a very common thing, one that everyone experiences and suffers from in youth. She learned now that all the girls, no matter who, liked to watch the boys, that a good many picked out one and went around with him in public. What "going around" was, was not yet clear to Schellebelle, but it certainly had to be the embodiment of supreme happiness.

Her friends had made her believe, moreover, that a girl was not tied to a fellow—that you are allowed to get out of it, for whatever the reason, and start the fun all over again with someone else—until you found the chosen one, your sweetheart, and began to go together and think of marrying. It inevitably had to end in marriage, her knowledge stretched so far but no farther—whatever else Schellebelle had heard about it hung tangled in a ball she could not unravel. She had not given out to the whisperers how it was with her, with her own love. But when they teased her about Louis and it was claimed out loud that he had his eye on her, always standing around talking to her and visibly going weak in the knees when he looked at her . . . she burst into riotous laughter and ran away to think about it and savor it in silence. She blushed with happiness and shame at the same time—she feared the idea of her secret being discussed by others in public, while simultaneously it struck her as the unexpected realization of an all too wondrous joy. And in her innocence, she wished it were true, for she felt annoyed now because maybe it was said only to tease her. Great and endless were the pleasure and joy! The beautiful summer days were filled with delight from beginning to end, and how wide was the space resounding with the bright laughter and song! In the center where all the light was shining, himself enveloped in a lustrous glow, stood the young farmer with his face, his eyes, and his strong, lean body—and wherever Louis turned to walk, the light followed like a breath of pure happiness.

In the beginning, Louis had moved through it with
indifference, standing there and looking at them just
the way a farmer's son looks at lesser folk. But later
on, through mixing with the group, the strange
creatures had become more familiar to him; he
found enjoyment there, and it satisfied him day after
day to see and hear the liveliness, that self-assured,
heedless merriment on the farm. At length, he
became aware of a deep richness among these lowly
young women, he perceived a sort of special quality
in the swaying motion of the girls' slender half-
formed bodies. . . . And he longed now for the
approach of mealtime each day, to see the whole
warm nest of them ranging over the yard and in the
kitchen. In between working hours, the silence that
weighed round about the farm felt more oppressive
than at other times; ever and again he wanted to
hear that silly chattering of delicate voices, those
exuberant trills of laughter. He feasted his eyes on
those healthy, full-fleshed girls, always taking fresh
pleasure in making them blush with his compelling
gaze. But in that motley crew there was one who
especially attracted him, and she seemed to notice it
every time he tested her glance: the girl who had
lived on the farm for so long and who people called
Schellebelle—now for the first time, he really saw her
working, and he was struck by her immediately. He
saw her busy among the others, heard her ringing
voice above all the rest, and observed how her eyes
shone whenever she looked up. It amazed him, and

he did not know how it was possible he had not noticed earlier that she was beautiful, so well shaped and so quick. Suppleness and strength infused her form from top to toe, and the pale rose of her curly head stood out from the brown or blonde hair of the other girls. It particularly excited the young farmer to be able to make Schellebelle blush, but no matter how his stare insisted, her two blue eyes kept gazing back into his without shyness, until he felt the pressure himself in return and had to look elsewhere. "Bright eyes," he muttered in silence, "I'll get you all right!" Then she was lost in the group again; he could still make out the color of her curly hair; he followed the pale blue of the seamed blouse that stretched over her body, creasing with the motion of her supple limbs in her elastic step. But even when she had disappeared entirely and he stood on the field working and thinking, he could make the reddish-blonde roguish thing come into his mind more easily than all the others there, vividly in her clothing and movement. He found it more and more attractive each morning to go out with the weeders to the flaxfield. There, alone as overseer of the troop of women, he listened now to the songs and stories and helped as well when one or another was teased about her going with a boy in secret. But always, in every conversation, it was his intention to catch Schellebelle's eyes.

To himself, he considered this carrying-on with meaner folk as an indulgence on his part, a temporary game that did not go deep and left his

mind wholly at ease the other hours of the day. Yet
sometimes, while he was hard at work, it played on
his senses like a ray of light: he could hear the sound
of the voices and see the riot of color, and then a hint
of affection would well up too, along with a touch of
melancholy, because he stood much too high in life
to go around openly with those pretty girls. But that
too was soon again forgotten, and he remained
Vermeulen's only son—the future master of the farm.
He had revealed his interest in the girls no further
than he intended; if in his dealings with them, he let
slip a smile, a small word of flattery, or a joke, it was
not serious on his part—they themselves knew that
best. But those clever gossips with their peering eyes
had looked further into his actions and knew more
about them and had seen deeper into him than his
conscious intention would allow—and all that had
eluded him. It also happened, without his
knowledge, that while he was busy they watched the
direction of his eyes, whispering the name
Schellebelle behind his back. That remained muted,
but secretly well known among a limited set of
friends—some of whom found mocking amusement
in it, while others, too innocent, were jealous of
Schellebelle. It became a children's game among the
intimate circle, but when the farmer's son was
around, they hardly dared give themselves away to
their overseer with a wink from one to another.

Louis would leave the field toward noon, in his
usual way, considering himself relieved of it until the
following day. And so his mind, clearly unruffled

and calm, remained occupied with other things.

So matters went, on and on, until an unexpected event abruptly brought about a great and complete change.

It was shortly before noon. Schellebelle, whose turn it was as third stable maid, had come back earlier from the field to tend to the work in the sheds. Louis was walking idly around the yard, waiting for the bell to ring for the noonday meal, when suddenly he saw the lovely girl coming out of the dairy with a bucket in each hand. He remained standing under the eaves in the doorway of the cowshed, in the expectation that she would have to walk straight into him to go and do the milking. It seemed as if the golden sun were shining right across the rosy flesh of her face and bare arms, as if her head of curly reddish-blonde hair were a blaze sending out flames more intense than the sunlight through which she was walking. Louis did not stir and watched her coming. Without scheming, moved simply by what struck his eyes as a miraculous beauty, he decided to stay in the doorway where she had to pass. Though not understanding that something could happen here that would cause a scandal or which ought not be known, he nevertheless first looked around to see if anyone was in the shed who would spy on his actions. The girl came suddenly into the shadow of the eaves out of the sun's glaring light and walked toward the shed without hesitation, so that at the last moment Louis had to give way to let her through. But at the very instant the girl passed by him, his eyes looked imprudently at what aroused him most in the juicy young thing. And again at that instant, lust boiled through his entire body, blood driving like fire to his brain. Before he knew it or could think about it, his hands grabbed the flesh of the girl's plump arms, and he hurriedly pressed a kiss to her round cheek. As soon as it happened, he let go and fell back a step. Regretting what he had done, he felt contempt for himself, since this was no bold conquest, no lightning seizure, just the overtaking of a girl unable to defend herself, who was completely in his power. With the feeling of regret came something akin to compassion, for he had done the girl harm—and he wanted to make it up again to her.

"You know, you're getting to be a real looker," he said in a flattering voice, more to excuse himself than to give a reason for his move.

Schellebelle had squirmed out of his grip like a fish and had jumped far backward three steps. In her shock and surprise, she had held down a scream, and she stood there now, flaming red with emotion, a shy twinkle in her eyes. The hint of a pout on her lips expressed bashfulness, or certainly compassionate entreaty, but the full admission, the wonder of an intense happiness, shone, glowed in her radiant glance. A second thought made her look over anxiously at the cows. Then, knowing it could do no harm, she let go her full, rolling laugh until it echoed through the shed, and turned her back, twirling, as she walked away in triumph, the two copper buckets that shone in the semidarkness like two gleaming pails of light. Guileless self-satisfaction, pride in the treasure of her youth and her trim healthy body expressed themselves in the supple sway of her step as she strode on without looking back. She began milking the cow at the far end, and when she looked toward the clear light of the open door to laugh at Louis once more, he was already gone.

Instead of spending the noon break with the others, joking around and smoking a pipe, Louis went and looked for a place to rest in the hay, and there he basked for two full hours in the happiness of what had happened to him. And at work that whole afternoon, he did not dismiss the alluring image from his mind; he was obsessed by the longing to return to the flaxfield with the group the next day. It was not only Schellebelle now but all the young weeders, with their singing and chattering, their playfulness and joy in life—the flaxfield itself, with what belonged on and around it, that caused the delightful feeling that overwhelmed him with happiness. He joked and laughed with each and every one, but whenever his glance met Schellebelle's bold, frank blue eyes, he once again felt it as a caress of his very soul, and it set him at ease because he thought he read in it a token of their secret understanding. He owed her gratitude and thanks for her silence about what he had done to her in an ill-considered moment.

And then, without looking for the cause or reason,

the longing rose in him for the end of the weeding time. . . . He wanted to be rid of that bustling commotion on the farm, so as to watch the reddish-blonde girl go on her usual round . . . and to have her to himself alone.

"If things drag on," he had already remarked to his mother, "it'll be full grown. The flax is getting too long to crawl over."

But then, it was nearly coming to an end, and on Saturday evening that same week, the weeders were allowed to come get their money from the farmer's wife. She paid them off one by one, saying, "So, till the harvest, right girls?"

Quiet restored, the old routine started up again, with their own regular people on the farm doing the summer's work.

Schellebelle more than anyone had longed for the end of what she had first taken for a fair, a time of wonder in her life. For now she knew that the thing the girls had teased her about was true. She still felt that first kiss burning on her cheek. Ever since that great joy, that intense happiness flaming continually in her mind, ballads or stories could no longer tempt her; solitude was now dearer to her than any sound. She laughed and sang at work, but to hear her own voice and to give vent to her heart's exaltation.

Amid the cares of the busy summer's work, there was not much time for Louis to think of matters of the heart, and yet now and again he was overcome by a wistfulness that seemed to spring from an indistinct yearning for something he could not name—from a surfeit of all he had enjoyed—a mixture of pleasure and pain, like that first morning in May on the high field. Remembering the happiness that had been revealed to him on the flaxfield, and which had passed, brought nostalgia to his heart. And again and again, the face came to his mind of that pretty good-for-nothing with the reddish-blonde hair and the fair skin the sun had not tanned; he could hear her laughter tinkling like a bell through the rarefied air. And if he happened to see the girl herself walking across the yard, he received a vision of the flaxfield: an even fleece with slender, delicate stalks, filled with blue flowers . . . in the atmosphere of an earthly paradise.

He did not kiss the enticing girl again, appearing no longer to play up to her, no more than to the other girls on the farm, inasmuch as he kept a hold on his dignity and did not wish to stand ashamed before his father. But he dreamed to himself, brooding how everything had changed around him—how there were things he only now was first beginning to grasp. Tracing back, he became aware of how rashly he had lived up till then, without knowing what lay dormant in him and around him; how he, the cheery, open lad of twenty, was yet restrained about a lot of things, shy and timorous as a boy in his first pair of trousers. He pondered the reasons and found the origin was in the awe in which he held his father, the fear he had of displeasing his kindly mother, as well as the urging of his own nature—a deep sense of worth his parents had cultivated in him. Louis sometimes compared his own conduct with that of other farmers' sons he knew; he was aware of how they carried on all the time—making every day a holiday, weekdays and Sunday alike; how they messed around in the woods at night like brigands, consorting with fast women of the lowest kind. He heard it told how many of his acquaintances kept up a respectable front all on one side and threw away their honor on the other, indulging their lust with the maids, the first at the ready, and afterward killing scandal and buying off responsibility with a bit of money. Louis still had a high-minded and deeply virtuous contempt for those low deceivers, just like when he was fresh out of school, and he had no truck with them. But now and then, the young man sensed that such shyness no longer fitted his years: he experienced the weight of his father's stern nature wanting to keep him a schoolchild. He felt uncomfortable because he stood like a shamefaced boy, a stranger in the midst of the unruly confusion and the full life of the maids and hands on the big farm—and then he cursed the gentility that held him in check, because he was Vermeulen's son. His youthful nature came into conflict with the one as well as the other; he hesitated between holding back and letting go—but when the blood surging through his body in a wave began to boil, he looked ahead and promised himself the days of pleasure, of great, unrestrained joy that were still owing to him and in which he would indulge some time, later. He deluded himself about those good times, his crowning, joyous desires: he was intent on giving his appetites free rein for once—when the group came back, he would go along with them, shouting and unashamed, to celebrate the great harvest festival.

He understood now that outside the business of farming and the everyday work—the sowing, the tilling, the growing; good weather and bad, fortune and misfortune; stables and land, father and mother, house and yard—there was something else, beyond all those things: his own youth, his love for life, the glow in his healthy, strong body—something welling up, a kind of power, a swath of violence, a longing to revel—and he saw that once burst free, neither his father nor he himself, nor anyone else, would be able to tame and contain it.

Bloom

I

It is the time of the solstice. Now summer triumphs over the world.

The sun has attained its full ascendance and from morning to evening describes the same splendid orbit through the uppermost heavens. There it sits enthroned on high, where no one or no thing can touch it. Light streams out from it everywhere in a blaze of gold, heat descending like burning rain. Sunshine lies spread in splendor over the wide waves of fields that drop down with a sweep from the heights to the lowlands and then rise up again to other heights—over the whole double slope of the valley of the Scheldt, the thousandfold greenery of the various summer fruits resounding in a beautiful, echoing song of shading colors. Each within its bounds, one contiguous to the other, the fields form the fleecy patchwork in which each plant spreads over its ground and the abundance of similar growth strikes its distinctive note in that great harmony of summer's resplendent, color-filled sea. Thus the green of the meadows is green as grass and more vivid than the green of the clover, brushed on top with purple from the blush of living flower heads. The green of the beetfields glistens richly over the glittering land. Lighter, tending toward gray-green with whorls of pale brown and blue, the wide cornfields stand swaying under the wind's caress. The potato leaves have a darker hue, like square patches of downy, woven fluff. And yet lighter again, bordering on yellow, are the wheatfields, while the oats, scorched white by the heat, great blocks of pure brightness, stand with their little bells swaying. But resplendent above all the green lie the flaxfields: pieces of gold cloth, intense as the sunshine itself, shining out against the plain. Like clear lakes—basins of water full to the brim—reflecting the luster of the sky, so smooth is the surface of the stalks, all of the same length, grown arrow straight and slender; the brush on their bent tops twists together, looking like wisps of wool, and there the sunlight settles, sinking as it were to the bottom of a sheet of water threaded with curling trails of live yellow gold. Skimming above those mirrors of light, the swallows glide and trace out florid cursives. In flight, they snap up a beetle here, a fly there, carrying it away with a dart through the blue sky, over the meadows and the cornfields; but they are back again before long to resume their sport above the level yellow-and-green flaxfields.

The sunshine falls like a blessing over the summer crops, and the heat in the noonday peace holds absolute sway over everything growing in that wide valley. Like oases in that sea of green, the trees rise high up in stands, and under the shady domes of mulberry and the cross-branches of broad tops, the large farmsteads stretch out—like slow monsters, dormant and moribund—where man and beast now stay together inside.

In the open country alone are the great and eternal things, under the blue of the sky where the heat bakes down. On the bare fields, beyond all human interference, beyond all jealousy and petty, apish commotion, summer realizes its majestic course, the sun reigning omnipotent over all that grows and turns to ripeness. Only the birds take delight in it—swallows, larks, finches, and sparrows, all the feathered folk that thrive and play in corn and clover, in trunks and trees—each finding its way through the clean blue space, above a lovely pleasure-garden of green that seems to have been made for no other purpose but for the birds to feast there, forever singing and whistling, each in its own language. The land lies abandoned to the splendor of its own riches, as if the crops had sprouted from the soil of themselves, without tilling or sowing, as if growth and blossoming were designed to be the vain adornments of summer.

But on the farms lying sluggish, where the sun spills over the roofs, the peace is a mere semblance. Between the busyness of house and barn and stable, life prospers and the hands stay happily at work. The farmers, however, sit like lordly knights ensconced in their castles, safe from the heat; from each farmstead, a living consciousness spreads over the adjacent lands that appear to be without owner in the broiling sun. Every landholder sits peering through the peepholes of his farmhouse, not because of the beautiful array of colors but to keep an eye on the growth and ripening, for each knows the progress and condition of his own crops. As on a dial where the hands inch forward imperceptibly, they follow the advance of summer on their fields and the tenaciousness of everything growing outside. In the spring, they had worked from morning till night and slaved all they could to gain credit for their work. Now they sit looking at it and let the sun amble along. Satisfaction with the summer's profusion is alive within their withdrawn minds, but meanwhile they spin their thoughts over the profit and yield the land will bring at harvest time. Fear, nagging doubt, unease burrow as well through their consciousness, and they are stirred by envy to do honor to their name and surpass the others.

The sun, however, like a generous benefactor, shines upon all the fields at once, and the view is splendid everywhere—but by their nature and short-sightedness, the farmers know only their own holdings. They think of the sun as their property, just as the crops it shines on. In their dogged greed, they would like sunshine and growth for their fields alone; out of avarice to begin with, but also for the pleasure of shoving it under their rival's nose—to make him see that in the management of tilling and sowing, in the whole business of farming, they held all the knowledge inside their own heads and that their methods of work were the best. Everybody played the big boss, the master farmer, the expert in soils and crops, the artist who obtains the most produce for the least cost. All year long, each had followed his own judgment and headstrong opinion, and now, with nothing more for them to do in word or deed, they could only begrudge the sun sending its blessing over their neighbor's fields. For the harvest was imminent, and then it would be plain to all eyes who was the most steadfast, the farmer who held to the proper course. With fear and anxiety, they followed the daily progress of the summer growing. According to the location and the nature and composition of the soil, some farmers already required moisture for their fields, while others in their smugness sat reveling in the fierce heat that sustained their crops, turning their increase into profit. But there was still the final result to wait for: their entire business, all their work, all their expenditures, stood outside, left to fate's merciful or unmerciful game of chance. They could do nothing more there to help with their hands. Everything had been going well up to now, and the season was already drawing toward the end; but . . . premature fears kept their uneasiness awake—they spied on the small clouds in the sky, tracking the speed of the wind that carried them along . . . for the crops lay open to disaster until the very last week. In the distance, they saw delicate yellow flecks standing out amid all the other crops, and they remembered the fragility of the flax stalks: a rush of wind, with the slightest gust, might suddenly lay them flat, and they would go to waste—how fine and straight they stood there now, yet nothing would remain of all their perfection.

But with all the anxieties that fill the farmer's mind, he has simultaneously at his disposal a kind of broad indifference—once he has done his best, he remains resigned to the rest, reconciling himself to whatever misfortune falls on him from the heavens; for in his lifelong exercise of work in the open air, in his struggle with the great elements, he has learned to cultivate patience, and he praises no day before evening comes. He feels himself in opposition to nature, like a sailor on the sea: he has grown accustomed to danger; a disaster, so long as it is general, does not begin to ruffle the surface of his feelings. He attaches much more weight to matters that turn out wrong through his own mishandling, where the damage hits his crop alone and his reputation as a farmer suffers. All farmers are equal in the eyes of the Lord, and a hailstorm strikes the crops of everyone in the area. But under their own dispensation, they stand over against each other like so many kings, each ruling his country in his own way: the farmer has a farmer for his enemy and rival.

Seen from afar, the sunshine gleams over the plain in a general appearance of peace. The farmsteads with their many roofs lie isolated, the people living there to last like the trees that overshadow the yards and preserve for the ages the same tranquil aspect, through time's quiet progress. But on closer inspection, the houses sit there like dark monsters, each in its own peculiar style, obtuse, with long low walls, high pointed gables, and broad flat-thatched roofs. They lie scattered across the whole region, far from each other, separated by expanses of open air and level fields. Over there, on the other side of the Scheldt, and over the whole slope of the hill behind which the known world ends, they are nameless things, existing merely as objects in the landscape; but all over the left bank, they constitute so many entities, each in its distinct form and appearance, unchanged for centuries, and in use and occupied by the same families, passing from old to young from generation to generation. Down here, by the bend in the river, is Veroken's orchard with his fields all around; a little higher up, Legijn's farm, the oldest in the area, then Sobrie's, Verfleter's, Verschaeve's; and at the dip of the horizon, Vermeulen's farm, next to Stubbe's and Cannaerts's and Verstraete's. . . . So many farms, so many independent rulers across the countryside, so many stubborn heads, self-sufficient and willful, heedless of everyone and everything, governing their lands and letting the whole world feel that they are the masters and the power is theirs. The farmsteads rise like fortresses in their age-old architecture. House, stable, and barn form the four-sided whole that encloses the yard—all the buildings with their backs outward and their fronts inward. The narrow openings that look out suggest

embrasures more than windows. The low blind walls
and the heavy thatched roofs are overgrown with
moss, turning green, reddish, and gray with age; the
brickwork has had its share of so much rain and
storm for so long, while sitting under the open sky,
that the exterior in color and shape has come to
resemble the things grown all around it—as if the
whole structure had risen up out of the earth along
with the rough wrinkled shanks of the centuries-old
linden trees that stand on either side of the gate, and
at the very same time. A broad rampart surrounds
the buildings, while the large, solid gate, the only
entryway behind the bridge of stone, protects the
whole affair. Ranged around it are the cottages and
huts of tenants and bonded laborers, where teems
the whole thriving populace that lives on the farm
and finds subsistence there.

The prospect is quite sunny now, and a visible
calm reigns all over; everyone knows his property
has been staked and secured; enmity and disgust
exist in dormant forms only; where neighbors meet,
they greet each other with short but genial shouts
and chat awhile about the crops—but each remains
on his guard, ready to fall into controversy or
feuding for the slightest reason. Relations are cut off
at once, everyone sticking to his own side, and a
unfortunate accident can bring about calamities that
pass hatred and quarreling from generation to
generation. It is to good purpose then that those
large chunks of heavy masonry remain sturdy, with
their backs turned outward to repel attack and to

serve as a fast fortification. Even in a time of complete peace, the farmers keep to the homestead all week long, with no communication beyond the strictly necessary, determined above all to lose no time in the work; there is little running back and forth among neighbors. At a chance meeting in the fields between passers-by, a few words are exchanged about soil and sand, with gripes and complaints about dampness or drought. Not trusting one another, they hold their real opinions back, except where common interests are concerned. And each on his ground feels himself a self-sufficient, independent man. Proud in their stubbornness, they affect the dignity of kings, looking down on all with disdain, holding in contempt everything not their own. Beyond the private holding, there exists nothing. For the farmer, his homestead is the center of the world; from it, his will and his authority reach out across the surrounding fields, as far as the line where another living will, another authority begins to clash with his own.

The splendid summer now moved above their heads, and the farmers went on through it as if they themselves were its overlords and the cause of the sunshine. They acted cunning, immovable, hardened against all, indifferent to whatever was in store for them. Like giants bred in the wide open spaces, confident of the mighty elements, they acted as if it were in their hands to alter the course of things eternal and the appearance of the great life around them, according to their own will and pleasure.

Such an expression sat upon the closed, grim visage of farmer Vermeulen, and something also of that power was in his stride and bearing as he walked across the yard and took control. He was the first one up in the morning, every day, getting everything going and staying with it everywhere all day long to carry out his intentions. Of his crops in the fields, he understood only the value of their yield, feeling pleasure in their beauty insofar as it flattered his strong farmer's pride. Just as the weaver sitting at his loom values the lines and the curving flowers that form their pattern from the tangle of colored threads of warp and woof, so Vermeulen took delight in objects only for their worth: everything had interest merely to the extent that he could squeeze a profit from it and make use of it. Around him lived a flourishing world of young men and women in the full bloom of their youth, while he never suspected that every one of those heads harbored its own mind and an urge keener for fun and games than for work. He saw in them only hands and arms to be used, like other tools, to keep the farm going. Vermeulen had no notion of the inner thoughts, the longings, the desires that brooded in the simple hearts of the farmhands and maids: he did not understand that outside of their work they were subject to temptations of lust and loving; or how with their foolish goings-on, their romping, gabbing, shouting, and singing, they madly celebrated the luxuriance of summer, just like the birds in the fields,

for whom each day brings new delights—thought-
less, carefree, without aim or worry, envy or greed for
more and more and better and better, they let
everything come as it may, nothing bothering them
and no end in sight of their free and easy life. His
own son the farmer knew only as an underling with
no will of his own who was charged with a different
task every day, and who furthermore was assumed
not to have an independent thought in his head.
Louis was the foreman, the superintendent who had
to account for the workfolk and answer for the day's
labor in the evening. Vermeulen saw all the more
reason to make him work hard in the fact that he
was the son on the farm and a young man whose
love of life was just awakening. Of all who were
under him or in his hire, the farmer demanded no
more than work, the exacting toil of every hour of
the day. He himself regarded work as an urge, every
man's necessity—severe, pitiless, driving, with no
looking up, blind, life's only purpose—the way to get
on top, take control, and then to force yourself upon
what you have won, without compassion or
forgiveness. You had to fight to get there, like he had
to do himself, and everyone else had to do who is not
too lazy—it was the way of the world. Snarling these
things out from between his teeth, the skin of his face
was like bark on a tree: deep grooves held his ideas
fast in impenetrable severity, and nowhere on his
stubble-haired face could be detected in a single line
or tic a trace of anxiety or unsteadiness. What preoccupied him he kept hidden, and no human eye

could fathom it.

He walked across the yard, the sun burning as in an oven, and bore the heat without flinching. His piercing eyes looked through the harsh light that clashed with the white walls of the main house, to see if everything was in order, if all the stable doors stood open. Shaking off his clogs on the front door stoop, he walked barefoot on the clammy blue tiles, dampness tracing his footprints where he had stepped. The kitchen was quiet, filled with shady freshness pleasant to feel; his wife and one of the maids were busy with the food for the workfolk, as they had been day in and day out for years, without pause for rest. When Vermeulen walked into the room-for-show, the coolness blew against him from the raised windows where the tulle curtains fluttered in the open, shadowy air. The shutters were drawn in front of the other window, and a ray of sun pierced a crack in the middle like a blazing arrow, straight through the half-light, falling across the corner of the display bed, of solid oak, and the flowery damask of the wallhangings above it, all the way to the beams of the ceiling. The air swirled with tiny motes of color, as fine as pollen, in the shaft that like a flaming swordblade thrust through the room; and all the glossy appointments in the shining corners—the ornaments on the bedposts, the boxwood crucifix with its branch of greenery, and the silver bells among the wreath of flowers on the little altar of Our Lady on the mantelpiece—reflected the ray of sun with glowing sparkles of light. The summer's persistent heat had dried out the dampness and the musty air a bit in that seldom-opened room, but the smell of mildew permeating the bedclothes remained as something peculiar to it, associated with the solemnity of the atmosphere and the respectability that sweated from the walls. The placement of the furniture gave the impression of fixed immovability. The room-for-show was the soul, the sanctuary of the homestead. In the walnut wardrobe hung the cloth and silk garments of the farmer and his wife—apparel for the great occasions in life. The oak chest held safe important documents and papers—in it rested the authority and prestige, the strength and wealth, the very life of the farm. The bed was strictly a showpiece, a throne of woolen mattressing and feather pillows piled high, where no one would ever sleep. The writing desk contained the account books and heavy registers that, kept up from father to son with dates and figures, represented the chronicle and records of everything the Vermeulens had expended and earned and accomplished for centuries on the eighty hectares of land at their disposal, together with what had been raised in the meadows and stables and sold. In the high chimney corner stood the formal walking stick, the farmer's scepter Vermeulen's father used to take along as a royal staff when strolling through his fields: the white-metal trowel with its tip shining like silver and polished ashwood shaft studded with copper nailheads.

Summer's silence reigned in the room, and from

where he sat on the chair at the desk, leaning his elbow on the big copybook, Vermeulen looked through the open window, across the broad expanse of field and sky. He sat staring, and over that broad expanse of field and sky hung the great news that filled the whole district and seemed to disturb the summer's quiet course—the news that had hit people all at once, like sudden, miraculous tidings, so improbable that no one wanted to believe it until they actually heard it said, the way Vermeulen himself had learned it, right from Legijn's mouth, to wit: Legijn was giving up his house and farm and moving into a mansion in the village, going to live off his money! Legijn's fine large farm, where the old bachelor and his sister had spent all their lives, would be sold or leased: it was up for grabs, open to anyone who wanted to pounce on it. When he had learned of it, Vermeulen was seized with indignation and had called Legijn an idiot to his face. What a disgrace to leave such a farm and go wait for death in the village! "You'd have to be a horse's ass!"

But as Legijn remained determined and Vermeulen had to admit anyhow that the matter was unimportant and of no consequence to him, he had let it drop with a disdainful shrug, though grumbling to himself and later telling his wife:

"You'll see, we'll get us a newfangled farmer there, somebody who'll want to set up everything in the latest style to teach us a lesson! . . . And Legijn, I give him one more year to live! A farmer living off his money, he's got to die! Buying his meat, his butter, his eggs? He'll drop dead from hunger, the miser. And what's he going to do all day, the sap?"

So far, Vermeulen had only felt ridicule and contempt for Legijn's decision, something he brought up everywhere, incessantly, with other farmers and everyone else quite simply because seen from his standpoint, it seemed a piece of foolishness, a venial sin, but nothing more; until the first inkling, like a faint flash, stirred Vermeulen's mind, and he gravely tapped his finger against his forehead and raised his eyebrows. . . . Suddenly, it hammered through his veins, his throat tightened, blood rushed to his head, a shudder ran through his entire body. Yet . . . he restrained the surging turmoil—he wanted to calm himself first off. "I've got to think it over," he decided, "and think it over long, but . . . there *is* something to it . . ."

The rest he did not dare put into words, carrying it tucked away, a scheme come to him evilly and out of malice. He brooded over it, pondering it for so long that he became used to the idea and the plan took on a more rational guise in his imagination.

Once again, his tough old head rested on his closed fist, and under his elbow he felt the heavy account book; the fields lay open before his eyes, the crops stood luxuriant and vigorous in the sunshine, and that idea, that scheme played above it all like a mirage. . . . It appeared before him as a revelation from heaven: a means thrown at his feet to preserve his domain undivided—an ideal opportunity to ward off his rival for authority . . . and all at once and forever be free from fear and uneasiness. When would such a chance ever offer itself again? Wasn't it now lying all ready in his hands? Would it stir up notice somewhere, would anyone guess why he was doing it? Who better to do it than he? Buy a farm, a fine, excellent spread for his son, be on the lookout for a farmer's daughter to set up there with him. . . . In his thoughts, Vermeulen ran through the entire countryside to discover somewhere a fit wife for Louis. But that was of later concern—if only he could first get rid of him now, get him out from under his feet—control would remain with the "old man," *that* was Vermeulen's remedy, coming to him in a flash, like lightning from the sky—the solution that relieved him at once of his gloom and anxiety.

"I won't get my blood up about those two rotten, smartypants daughters of mine," Vermeulen thought. "They won't be staying here long!" But that he had found such an opportunity to cut Louis out of the race, the one destined to eat him alive—now that was something which took all the weight off his life. He nourished his decision, turning it over to savor its goodness; he looked again and again in his books, estimating the cost of such a takeover and then figuring out where he could cut back so as to clinch the deal. In all the years of his life that he had been a farmer, he had never felt pleasure in his wealth the way he did now. His excess money had been lying there a dead lump, an ever-increasing weight that became more difficult to deal with as it swelled and grew; but now that insatiable chest, always gobbling everything up and never giving anything back—that stupid contraption—had become a living force with which you could flatten mountains if they stood in your way, with which you could buy power. Vermeulen's intention was still a secret, alive only in his head, in the cast of thought—he could nip the thing in the bud, and no one would ever suspect what had gone on in his mind. But squelching or rejecting it was out of the question. There was only one uneasy thought still brewing: how would he break it to Barbele? and one fearful expectation: how would she take it? For he knew full well that it was not right and fell outside the regular course of things—an extravagance that would startle his wife. Shouldn't Louis succeed him here on the farm? But Vermeulen very quickly refuted that argument: what succession here? Weren't they both full of life and health? And wasn't Louis old enough, after all, to get married and run a farm? Nevertheless, Vermeulen waited with his announcement in apprehension, like a shy boy who has to ask for his girl's hand, or who goes to take some new important step and does not have the nerve. He kept deliberating within himself, counting his figures over again, making estimates, simply to gain time. And after that, he decided to wait further, in the vague hope that Barbele might perhaps come up with the proposal herself . . .

II

All the while Louis, the farmer's young son, stayed
with the hands on the sun-glittering field working
among the beets. Lately, he had become even further
estranged from his father and accordingly more and
more taken with himself. Intoxication from the heat,
the brilliance of the sun, fueled continuous joy in his
mind. When he sauntered through the fields, he
could see luxuriant growth wherever he had sown
that spring, and wherever he went, he acknowledged
himself as the great author of the perfect season! He
moved with a tremendous swagger, an intrepid
knight with endless room ahead of him, and every
day brought him fresh beauty and pleasure. Any
thought of seriousness or discipline irritated him; he
scorned it as not suiting the life full of sunshine that
lay open before him in a revelation of happiness.
The massive shape and obstinate face of the older
farmer dismayed the younger one and made him
hide the exultation of his heart when he was near,
out of a natural fear of exposing his overflowing
happiness to his father's stern glance. In the house

and in the yard, where his parents were near or around, Louis remained more than ever the decent farmer's son; but as soon as he knew he was alone with the workfolk, he again let loose his craving after youthful pleasure, giving vent to foolishness in utter forgetfulness of his position. He wanted fun, the wide enjoyment of a humming life, uncalculated laughter and shouting without afterthought, because he felt young among the young, in the midst of the growing, the noise, the commotion outdoors—because the sun heated his senses and brought them to a boil; because the flood of pleasures lifted him upward into sunny space! Everything had become precious to him; the whole countryside around was open, as it were, for his own—for everyone's—delight.

He had never, in fact, felt the way he did now how strongly he was tied to his entire surroundings: fields, roads, and byways, the trees along the paths, the walls and roofs of the yard, with its high wall and gate and bridge and lane—it was all so necessary to him; he would have nothing altered or taken away; he lived in it, and it lived with him—his eyes could not get enough of it. The work and the bustle were dear to him, and he exerted himself anxiously, hurriedly, without considering that his efforts had to yield profits or advantages, laboring purely from compulsion and in the awareness that he was drifting along with the great commotion, with all that diligent activity, in which everyone on his part understood his own role and pushed toward the same goal. He went to bed late at night, tamed and exhausted, and slept right through the brief span until the sun again began to rise, once more to start the new day cheerfully, with eagerness, and the promise of fresh and untried happiness.

Then too, the variety in the work and daily tasks was so pleasant, and it was so good to be outside, looking after the luxuriant summer crops in the field. It looked like a real pleasure garden! A uniform magnificence spread across the entire swell of the ploughlands: the thick foliage of the potato plants, the wheat, rye, clover, and oats, the beets—all equally beautiful in their growth! But the flaxfield lay especially close to his heart.

Given the chance, Louis would walk up by the high field, along the sandpath as far as the grove. That whole area held a peculiar attraction for him, without his suspecting there might be a different motive that drew him to it. It was not for the crop, really—that was not going to amount to much this year: the stalks were uneven, with leafless patches and blighted streaks that ran in snaking reddish lines throughout the yellow-and-green surface. All the magical beauty before him lay in his remembrance of that glorious month of May—deep inside, he carried the spirit and the energy of the young weeders with a constant feeling of inexpressible tenderness and happiness. The stretch of yellow-and-green now glittering in the sun, the delicate stalks unruffled by wind, held a prize in store: the promise of the great flax festival!—the harvest he looked forward to as he had never looked forward to anything before.

Schellebelle! Didn't that beautiful girl fill all his senses? Did he do anything, think anything that did not involve or concern her? Didn't his eyes seek her everywhere, and was he ever at peace when he did not see her? He looked for her, driven by compulsion. The ground, the crop in which the girl was working became important to him, as though she carried an essential valuable with her, and he wandered away from the other fields, following along paths where he might find her. The young lad had forgot his nice easy manner. A sharp agitation drove his heart, but he did not even realize what he had lost, for he considered the disquiet itself as his great happiness. His former peace of mind seemed a stretch of gray boredom to him now—days he had squandered lackadaisically, like an old man, with no other pleasure than sowing and tilling, and only trying to imitate his father's affected respectability. At the time, he was determined above all to hold himself stiff and intense, expecting to do credit to his position and gain authority over the hired folk. But he had not yet known then of his own glorious youth, which would demand its rights—the marvelous force that lay slumbering within him, though like plants about to bud, still enclosed in their shells, ready to burst open in a profusion of blossoms. What life's blossoming ought to mean to him, in what form that splendid happiness would show itself—he did not know, and did not ask. He

imagined it, however, as a surprise that was sure to
brighten his whole existence, something like the
magnificent long view across a wide plateau which
suddenly spreads open before your eyes when you
have topped the rise of a hill—a world where he
would have his full due, coming into its possession
again and again, doing everything he pleased,
accomplishing what he wanted—without super-
vision, going his own way undaunted. . . . For Louis,
this was what was meant by the fullness of all
human happiness, *this* was what the future held in
store for him. Right now, he merely looked on
whatever he was doing, enjoying the happiness of
others. The company of the workers on the farm
satisfied all his wants for the time being—he felt an
affection going out from them and gave out his own
in return. The honor and authority he would have to
secure to become boss of the farm and its people was
something he did not want to think about—that lay
in the farthest distance, beyond the horizon and
outside the sunniness of the beautiful summer in
which his heady youth breathed its delight.

Space all around was immeasurable, pleasure
waited for the seizing, and he was the proud knight
who would capture it. His youth and the summer
seemed one and the same to him—fused with one
another.

Neither his father nor his mother saw any change
in their boy, since Louis forced himself to remain the
same good farmer's son in his parents' eyes. But
inwardly, he was forever torn between holding back

and letting go. His sense of shame and deep-rooted honesty, his feeling of awe, and his concern for his appearance and bearing—these held him back. On the other hand, there was "youth": the irresistible urge for pleasure and amusement, the longing for emancipation and independence, breaking loose from everything that hindered his freewheeling or put bounds upon it. He felt himself man enough to go his own way. His gaze and his passion now reached out in that direction, he sniffed desire in the fragrance of flowers—it rose in him like a whirlpool; he felt himself drawn into it, willy-nilly, of necessity.

That new feeling, moreover, had given him a fresh insight into things, placing him on the sidelines of life and making him realize how ridiculous were all man's toils and endeavors—that senseless attempt, out of sheer vanity and ambition, to make a distinguished appearance and to strengthen that appearance ever and always. What did all the prestige matter to him if it set you outside the company of your fellow men and prevented you from enjoying life's pleasures! What did he care about his father's pride and self-sufficiency, which had cost a lifetime of work and strain and made him as feared as a werewolf! He would sooner go without deference and authority if fun and games had to stop wherever he showed his face. What was gratifying to him in the dogged pounding of one farmer against another, going at each other out of pure rage? When he looked out from here on high, he saw them all bent down to the ground, grubbing in the earth, and the pettiness of their useless, physical chase after some dead thing alive only in their sick minds. What joy did spring or summer bring them, if they knew nothing about the air, the land, the sun except the various benefits to their crops, and about those crops nothing but the value of the yield in hard cash? They worked, those clowns, with creaky loins, doubled, simply to pile up ever more money in the oak chest, a dead value, a store they themselves would never live to enjoy. But didn't those tightwads see that the whole world lay open beyond the limits of their property, and that it belonged to everybody? Didn't they feel the worth of the free wind around their heads? Were they forbidden the enjoyment of taking in all that space at a glance—of drinking in the splendor of the sun with their eyes—of tasting the fresh air on their lips, livening the luxuriance of the summer days with gladness? . . . Wasn't the glory of a summer's morning, the quiet peace at evenfall, worth more than the possession of money and property? And didn't the ringing laughter of a girl in the field sound a thousand times sweeter than all the jingling of silver and gold? . . .

And so Louis filled himself to excess with reasons for tamping far down his desire for a farmer's high standing. But the main reason for that change of heart he purposely kept covered, not willing or daring to admit it, for within him so far honor and decency still held sway. He was well enough aware of the reason but put it aside, since it was rather

awkward for his argument and could not be allowed
to count as his pretext, the cause of his penchant for
pleasures and delights. Stronger than the sun that lit
up his whole inner being was his confused
yearning—his secret need, his anxious longing, his
admiration—but also his fear of . . . loving
something: the inclination to make his boisterous,
boyish nature submissive, tender, to give himself to
something plump and soft, something to stroke and
caress with cautious hands, but above all to make
happy. Why hide it any longer? A pair of girl's eyes
held him under their spell, with all the mysterious
allure of femininity haunting his mind and driving
him to a hot fever.

It had entered him while on the flaxfield, starting
with the wonderful days of the spring growing—he
knew it only too well. The young girls with their
loose, carefree blitheness had shaken aware his love
of life. He followed their brisk, springy step, and in
his memory he still saw their slender bodies ever
dancing along the lane in a group. He knew them all
individually, the blushing creatures with their bold,
shining eyes. Their singing had set the whole farm,
the whole neighborhood into commotion, and the
light ringing of their voices and their playful
swaying . . . were like the sunshine itself.

But Schellebelle—strange girl—was the flower that
bloomed in that sunshine, carrying with her
wherever she went brilliance and joy. Louis' eyes had
been dazzled by her—long before this, he had
stopped noticing the shabby, worn-out jacket

stretched at the seams, or the threadbare skirt she had outgrown taut across the roundness of her hips and reaching barely to her knees. When she walked ahead of him on the way to the field, he could see even better the supple movements of her straight, slender shape, the undulation of her alert hips, and the curving lines of her young, attractive body. And when he had her right in front of him, she seemed a true summer flower: a touch of sunshine on her blondish-red mass of hair, a touch of morning blue in her clear eyes, and a burst of the white delicacy of summer clouds on the carnation of her neck, the skin of her face. As soon as their eyes met, a smile appeared on their lips. When he shouted out a bantering word, her mouth broke open in a loud burst of laughter and he had the treat of seeing her perfect white teeth gleaming and the two dimples on her soft cheeks. He spoke nothing to her except silliness—of course he teased her now and then, the way you tease a girl you like, but she did not yet seem to suspect because of it that she was all his joy from morning to night, filling all his thoughts until there was no more room for anything else. She did not know it—was not allowed to know it, for it was only a game and he would not want it to hurt her for anything in the world! The feeling he did not dare call love (such happiness!) had come at the same time as the summer, and perhaps would go out with the summer as well. He looked on it as a passing fancy, a superficial inclination. Nevertheless, he was filled with deep respect, and the rich farmer's son considered the penniless girl a treasure destined for another, something like a fragile plant still too young for him to touch.

And so, he decided to be careful and take in his pleasure silently, with his eyes alone, for he was especially afraid of injuring the virginal girl or causing her sorrow. After that first and only time when the temptation had been too strong for him, he had not touched her again—having made the decision to put such foolishness out of his head, and compensating himself with anticipation of the great flax harvest festival, there to join in the wild merriment of the group for the last time. But it was turning out entirely different than he had planned. What had then appeared to him as a mere trifle had brought about a complete revolution in his mind: that poor girl had made his spirit restless. He still, as ever, looked forward to the harvest celebration as the main event of that beautiful summer; he longed for it, yearning to be in the whirl of the loud feast, to make the most of the occasion and really enjoy it. But in the meantime, his senses were arrested by Schellebelle, and he followed her with his thoughts where he could not reach her with his eyes. Yet even as he looked for her he avoided meeting her, fearing for himself and for the girl most of all. He knew it must not be allowed to turn into love—and that it was love already; for that reason, he had to keep away from any word and gesture that could create bad suspicions or compromise him. Though up to now there had been nothing, an inconvenient accident could spoil it all; for he knew he had only to stretch out his hand and the girl would jump smack around his neck in her artless exuberance—and be lost before all the world. That it could end in a scandal frightened him off the most, and not for anything on earth did he want to face his parents in shame. No, just a bit of quiet friendship and the pleasure of his eyes—he did not ask or long for more, and after the summer, it would all pass of itself.

 Schellebelle too seemed content with what little there was—the knowing glances, the smile of the farmer's lively son were favors that brought her to the very peak of happiness. She stood like an innocent child who does not know where it has come from or where it will go, overwhelmed by the plentifulness, moved by the extreme good fortune she could not understand and that intoxicated her. She still supposed her encounter with Louis in the stable had happened in a dream. Now she only wished the dream would last. She watched Louis moving around early in the morning while she was busy in the shed; when she was working in the field, she was restless until Louis came walking up the path. Then she felt it, like a caress on her hands, and from under the broad brim of her straw hat, she knew his eyes were on her—all of her—those eyes that were as good for her as the sunshine itself.

 At noon, Louis ate at the small table in the kitchen beside the farmer and his wife, but with his face turned to where she was sitting among the workfolk at the long table. He came by and drank coffee with them every so often in the afternoon, and then invariably he would sit—as if by chance—directly opposite Schellebelle, and while everything about him remained calm and indifferent, his foot would search for hers where he could find it under the table, and he would linger, too, until the girl had to jump up because the others were already leaving. Schellebelle let him. Her heart was so pure, she did not see mischief or danger anywhere, and the silent, secret love-game became a sweet habit for her. But if it happened that the girls were chattering among themselves after work or during the noon break and the farmer's son came uninvited to join in the banter, then Schellebelle would dare to go at Louis, bolder than the others, and in their mutual excitement, they betrayed the familiar goings-on between them. There could be no harm so long as the farmer was not around, and Louis gladly allowed himself to be pestered, drenched with water, or otherwise be made to play the fool. And so it came about that Marietje Verlinde and Fientje Vandoorn would tease Schellebelle later on, saying she would surely be the lady of the house here and marry the rich farmer's son! Then she would shout with laughter, as if wanting to scatter around her in ringing peals the fullness and strength of her happiness.

But what the girls said all joking, in fun and foolishness, was rumored quietly and more seriously without Louis or Schellebelle even suspecting it. It went so far that Sofie, the oldest of the women, heard whispers about it, then later noticed it with her own eyes: yes, something was going on between those two. The grave, fortyish housekeeper thought it her duty to see to it the young master avoided disaster; the exuberant laughter of that fetching young thing had annoyed her for a long time now. And so she took the pushy flirt aside into a corner to spell it out for her, carefully but firmly.

"Child," she said, "you've got to hold back a little more. You've got no experience, and you're much too young to twist Louis around like that. . . . I know for sure you don't mean harm, otherwise you'd hide things a little better—right now you're carrying on in front of everyone, and people are beginning to talk! Believe me, girl, no good will ever come of it, none, and if anything happens, you're the one who'll have to put out the flame. You've got to act a little more modestly or people will laugh at you and say you're spreading your net to catch the farmer's son—really! You're just a kid, and Louis doesn't think of stablemaids, does he? And if Vermeulen happens to hear about it, you'll be out in the street in no time!"

Schellebelle stood like a cheat caught redhanded—she blushed all the way down her neck, her throat drawn tight so she could not get out a word. Her whole body trembled. It had come so unexpectedly, dropping on her heart like a stone, and what she did now she had never done before: tears of regret fell like pearls from her eyes, rolling down her cheeks in fat drops.

"I can't help it! It's not my fault!" she stammered

at last, sobbing.

Sofie, who had not meant it to be so harsh, wanted to soften things now:

"Do what I say: Louis is a tease, let him alone. He'll turn your head and only laugh at you later."

It hit the girl harder than a thundersquall. She was filled with regret and annoyance, despair and shame, suddenly facing reality in all soberness. Her resolutions were cruel: she would never laugh again, never look at or talk to anyone.

The first time she encountered him and averted her face, Louis came over and asked what was eating her and why she was so angry. Immediately she began to blush, then burst into a flood of tears. On his insistence, she gave him a full account of what had happened. He roared with laughter.

"Well!" he shouted, "that old bitch! Don't worry yourself about it! She's jealous because I don't play up to her. Nobody's going to hurt you one bit," he said, suddenly serious. And immediately after, again in a familiar tone:

"You're looking forward to the harvest?"

"Oh!" she cried out, her eagerness radiating out to him. "And you, Louis?"

"Me too."

Their plain understanding restored her happiness and brought peace to her mind. They knew that, no matter what, their pleasure aimed at the same mark. The flax festival glowed in their imagination, their anticipation of it rising as if that day would bring them something more than just noisy, exuberant fun and singing and dancing. For they knew from each other that their tender dream of happiness in love had flowered on the same ground, and they expected in return from the feast on the flaxfield something similar to what they had already enjoyed in that wonderful time of spring.

III

Steadily and undisturbed, the sun carried out its grand summer's task across the land. The crops in the fields now reached their full growth. They stood luxuriant in rich verdure where the soil gave them moisture and nourishment; where they had to fight against dryness, they were beginning to suffer, their color fading, for it was long since the sky had let fall any rain or refreshing dew, and from on high came an insistent heat that increased with the days. As if by a miracle, the flaxfields had survived thunderstorms and violence from the heavens, and now the fragile stalks this far into summer stood firmly at their full height, unbowed, as fine as threads: it seemed a wonder a crop that had come up so slender was holding its own on such delicate stems. No wind had troubled it in all the time of its growth. The green bark was turning paler, almost yellow, ever improving the value. The swift swallows darted over and away, while the linnet had made good use of the beautiful peace and solitude to build its nest in the midst of the plushness, and now it sat there all day long, weaving the same little song, rocking at times on one of the threadlike stalks as if it were the lightest butterfly. Other birds had made their dwellings there too and lived undisturbed in a joyful congregation. Sunny mornings and warm afternoons, they busily did what they had to do, each after its rank and status; for the rest, they sat there, chirping and chattering or frolicking, as though they had all the time in the world and summer would never end. Not one among the feathered multitude seemed to have a care or notice how something was beginning to swell on the bud end of each bent and fuzzy stalk of flax—how a tiny blue eye blinked open unobtrusively here and there; and gradually more; and finally so many that a haze of blueness dappled the whole surface, like powder blown over the fluffy gold threads. One day later, the blue had already expanded and lay spread wide in a delicate coating. Before long, you could see the flaxflowers, beads blue as eyes, so many miniature bright bells, countless small blossoms hanging one from each stalk. Bloom lay over the flax. The fields had now become so blue, it was as if they reflected the sky with their whole expanse.

As far as the people were concerned, the crop now was as good as in. Now, too, would the peace and the pleasant silence be over that had held the land in a windless calm. Movement, commotion began at once: strangers appeared everywhere to despoil the land—flax appraisers, hacklers, merchants, scouts—tough fellows all, with heavy shoes, wearing blue smocks and silk caps and carrying curved walking sticks or cut branches in their hands. They entered the district from the west, always in pairs, side by side, following all the paths along the fields where flax was to be seen. And when they found one to their liking, they tore through it on rough feet, pulling up the stalks by the handful, inspecting them and measuring the length against the width of their fists, then yanking out a further handful from the middle of the field and weaving it into braids to take along the way. As soon as one pair was gone, others came and did the same, blazing trails straight through the smooth, lovely crop, paying no mind to the tracks of their predecessors.

Now, too, the farmers emerged from their houses, and wherever they met each other or ran into purchasing agents, the endless talk began of the unbelievably fine quality of the flax, and impossibly high prices were quoted. All the "experts" wanted to take part. You could see farmers and buyers haggling and shouting in the middle of the fields, and everywhere else—like comedians, making wide gestures, stepping back, leaving and returning, but shaking hands in the end and disappearing through the doorway of a tavern or the farmer's house, where the deal was clinched. In a few lots here and there, a may-branch appeared, a sign that the flax was sold and that the buyers and appraisers should stay away from now on.

On Sundays after High Mass, the farmers stayed in the taverns until well past midday, and again in the

afternoon until late in the evening, in hard
contention over the outcome, sale, and delivery of
the flax. That was the only thing of importance
throughout the whole region. In all their born days,
they had never known a year like it. Never had there
been so much flax and of such quality! And most
wonderful of all: each and every one of them was
getting an incredibly high price for it. The final
condition of all the flaxfields was now known: as the
crop stood, so it would be harvested. The bold
predictions were jokingly dredged up again and the
earlier "authoritative" opinions compared with the
present state of growth. Many a farmer who had so
loudly boasted in May had to sit silent now, keeping
to himself and swallowing his anger. The region was
busily discussed as a whole where they gathered in
clusters by the bowling green or at small tables in
the coolness in front of the taverns, every man with
his pipe and pint of beer. Best off were those who had
manured thoroughly or had sown in moist soil. You
just had to look at Legijn's flax and Veroken's . . .
and Vermeulen's. Legijn had been sparing with the
manure out of stinginess; Veroken had wanted to
demonstrate what he could do farming in the
newfangled way, spreading chemicals; and it would
have been better and wiser for Vermeulen to have
sown his flax lower—that was the farmers' general
conviction.

"But who'd have expected such a drought? . . ."

"If you could only know in advance."

"A little bit more rain and Veroken would've had

his flax for sure!" Bovin supposed. "I saw that field in its early growth . . ."

"And who'd have expected it of Verschaeve's lot? Just let the good weather hold for another couple of weeks and Vermeulen's flax will really push ahead too—it's still growing!"

"Verschaeve and Sobrie are the two winners! Now that's *flax!* You ever seen anything like it?"

"All of it the same grade, smooth as a sheet. Fine, rich stuff, golden yellow—and what tops! Ten hands high, I measured twice!"

They prodded each other to find out prices, curious above all to know what the sales amounted to.

"I heard tell that Sobrie sold at a hundred and fifty . . ." Stubbe observed.

Bovin commented: "I'd have to see it to believe it!"

However, it all remained guesswork; among those who sat there, not one came out with it and admitted what he had been paid. On the other hand, they would not have believed each other anyway; they knew enough about themselves to be aware that when prices were given, there were invariably lies and exaggerations. Anyone could easily learn whether or not a flax crop had been sold—the may-branch proved it. But no farmer would ask straight out "How much did you get?"—since, after all, he could not count on a reliable answer. So proud of their own produce, everyone insisted on inflating its worth. Another point touching upon their ambition came up as well, that of the nature and quality of the crop. With the harvest now fast approaching, it would have to be decided for each lot whether it was good enough for the river Lys or not. Which of these was it: what would they term "Lys retting" and what "blue retting"? What would be soaked in the river and what in the field? The farmers got around the words and posed the questions without calling the things by name. They understood each other with the winking of an eye: "How's your harvest? How're you delivering? Is it going to the Lys? You having it retted here? Is it or isn't it blue flax?"

Those "words" were flying now around the whole district. Were a farmer allowed to decide the matter for himself, all of his flax would of course be brought to the Lys, if only to maintain his honor against the others. But getting up and going was of no use here: the buyers did the choosing. A farmer usually held on to the ordinary flax until he had retted and hackled it himself in a pit on his land and blanched it in his fields. They call it "blue" or "field retting." It was the good quality flax, of sound stock, that the agents from the banks of the Lys came to buy up with hard coin. Dried on the field, the flax was then stored in his barn until the farmer was allowed to deliver it to the river three months later or more. Anyone who could not get his flax sold in this way was looked upon as a flop, and counted among the small cow farmers who dump their little piles of rubbish in a puddle somewhere, spreading dry rot over the whole area, and work at it for months, laying it out and turning it over until the blackness is blanched out of it somewhat. A farmer's glory consisted partly in the high profit from the price, but above all in exhibiting his harvested crop on his field, first in hedgerows, then tied up and stacked in sheaves of golden yellow; having stored it crude in the barn, to load it in high cartloads later, when delivery fell due, and set out for the Lys, five or six men together, with all the horses they had, the whole row of wagons one behind the other in a long caravan. That was why they delighted now in babbling, bragging, and misrepresenting each others' crops as much as possible.

"There's a lot of good flax," Verstraete claimed, "but a lot of junk toadflax, too. I saw some today, all the stalks ruffled."

Verfleter commented: "The ones with bad stunted flax, they'll boast all the same."

"I walked by a lot today," Bruintje said, "that was completely shot, rust on the stalks like freckles of iron."

Bovin shouted: "Cannaert's flaxfield's overgrown with mold and less than four hands long, but to listen to the man talk, he'll be getting a hundred francs for his Lys flax!"

They laughed among themselves but knew very well that this year, except for one or two lots here and there which had failed and some small pickings, there would not be much field retting and stunted flax in the district: the agents were moving too frantically, by and large, for all the Lys flax that was for sale. And so the farmers stood themselves to a good pint that evening, stretching their legs to show they were sitting at their ease and had plenty of time.

"Sales'll be just about over by next week," Duitschave said, "and before harvest comes, there's not much us farmers can do—give me another pint."

They stayed put or walked on to the Eagle, the Village Hall, the Flaxflower, to while away their Sunday, unconcerned with the valuable crop, nearly mature, that stood under the open sky, carelessly exposed to ruin and destruction. Their heavy, fat, hardy laughter rang through the evening, their clean-shaven, brownish-red faces shining with pleasure and good cheer.

The countryside felt the pressure of business for a few more days—the flax was already past bloom, the cheerful blue gone like a dream, but agents and buyers were still combing the area. Six or eight of them came to Vermeulen's farm every day to haggle about the flax on his field, but again and again the farmer invariably told them, brusque and curt, that he had no crop for sale. Scarcely had two left when a couple of others would arrive, constantly having to go look for Vermeulen or pulling on the bell to make him come to the house. They brought along the braid of flax from the high field as a sample, and even though it had developed poorly, they nevertheless offered him a fair sum, since the crop was by nature a good and noble one. His wife was very eager to accept an advantageous offer but did not interfere with any business matters. Vermeulen, however, would not hear of it. He remained obstinate.

"I'm going to keep it in the barn for a year or two, my friends," he would answer, stiffly. He preferred to delay, since there was not much for him to be proud of. He could get rid of it later on the sly, and no one would be around to crow about it. Besides, his mind was entirely on other things: ever on the go, worrying, doubting, struggling to arrive at an agreement within himself about that important transaction, Legijn's farm. When it came to a serious matter, he would turn it over continually in his mind, exploring the advantages and disadvantages. But once having made a decision, it had to be carried out immediately, without hesitation or delay.

Now especially, he wanted first to reflect deeply and carefully, so as not to feel any regret about his actions after his yes or no had been given. He walked around day and night with the thing on his mind, unable to make a final decision. Vermeulen had all but settled the matter with himself, not hesitating long between choosing to advance the money or lose his supreme authority: his son had to go! He would have no one rising while he was sinking, no young farmer against old—*that* he would never allow. He was already firmly resolved to negotiate the sale and fit out the farm. He had sounded out Legijn and learned that the house and fields would be sold at auction, both the assessment and acquisition of the cattle and fields on terms agreed to by the purchaser. In a few days, the notices would be posted. So far, Vermeulen had it all in hand; no serious competitor

was about to turn up there—to jump on such a
chance, you had to be waiting on the spot, money
ready.

But then, there still remained the question of that
"wife" for Louis! Vermeulen ran into that one like a
wall. Looking around and thinking were getting him
nowhere. He needed a woman's assistance—Barbele's
intercession. Yet now that he had gone so far,
confronting the deed and having to act—now that
the opportunity to carry out his will was within his
grasp—he hesitated to break his proposal to Barbele,
manfully and straight out. Not that he was afraid of
her, or that her objections and resistance could alter
or check his determination—but still, he did respect
it. Through their long years of living together, his
wife had become something like the better part of
himself, his own conscience, as it were; it was she
who held up the truth to him when, against all
rhyme and reason, he wanted to carry out what had
been decided impulsively or in hot temper, without
his having taken the consequences into account.
Barbele never interfered in the ordinary course of the
day-to-day running of the farm, but concerning
everything beyond that, she would pass judgment
and get in her word, bringing up the pros and cons
in a calm mood, and always with proper
moderation—and her opinions were correct about
many matters. When it seemed necessary, she could
cut Vermeulen down to size, rake him over the coals,
lay him out flat, make him see how wrong he was
when he dared come up with any nonsense. With

this result: he still did what he intended just to show who was boss—the master—but carrying shame inside and the conviction that Barbele had been right and he had done something brutish.

"How'll she take it?" *That* was what made him uneasy. He anticipated an exchange of harsh words and that he would have a hard time of it. Which was the very least of it, however. He was afraid she would see through him as usual and guess at once the real intention behind his plan. For Vermeulen knew deep in his own heart that the whole affair ran counter to the plain course of things—he felt there was something wrong with it and Barbele, with her sound judgment and simple humanity, would demolish with a few words the entire edifice he had constructed in his head, piece by piece, including all the arguments he could bring forward as proof. He walked around the yard with his face in fury. He hung around the kitchen looking for a pretext to start talking but could not get out the first word—he was apprehensive about making the matter known in the house. Undecided, angry with himself, he again withdrew into the best room to be alone, ostensibly to go over the accounts once more.

Vermeulen spied on the yard through the curtains, behind windows where no one knew he was sitting, and from there he watched everything the workfolk were doing right up to the open doorways of the sheds and stable. It had become his favorite pastime lately. With those worries on his mind and his dogged sense of discontent, he could now less than

ever tolerate noise and jabbering: the fun and
laughter grated against him. He saw the boys and
girls looking for each other, enjoying their sport
more than their work. He had already observed a
number of times how Louis, that young show-off,
took delight in this foolishness, how familiarly he
behaved in the company of the maids. In other
circumstances, he would have seen no harm in it,
but now that he had been woolgathering, he was
eager for what he had wished to avoid by all means
in the past: a clash with his son—he was looking for
a reason to get angry, to blurt out in a fit of rage
what lay in his heart.

He could see Louis always latching on to that same
red-headed scatterbrain of a maid. He had already
observed in the kitchen how their eyes locked: as if
they would swallow each other with desire. During
the noon break he had followed the pair to catch
them in the act and jump between them screaming,
to terrify them with a curse. He saw himself carried
away in rage, beating the slut and barring the farm
to Louis in disgrace. . . . He wanted such a discovery,
longing for it, but until now it was just as he had
seen, nothing more than kittenish cavorting in
public: drenching each other with water, some
pulling and teasing. Vermeulen kept a lookout. He
sat like a tomcat in the shadows, ready to leap.

Meanwhile, fun and games went on all day long
in the farmyard, the young people at it full tilt every
noon, things becoming pretty wild at times, with
plenty of noise. Louis, who had now made of the

girls his hobby and cheerily wanted to take part in the tussle; and Schellebelle, who was as crazy as a horse at a fair—neither knew they were being spied on, neither was aware of danger or that their happiness could be so near to an end. Louis especially deferred to no one. Ever since the housekeeper had poked her nose into his affairs, he did what he was doing on purpose, simply to get a rise out of the old bitch. Inwardly, he reproached himself sharply for taking up with people of a lower standing; he knew it was not right of him and that, sooner or later, the girl would suffer for it. He did not want, however, to acknowledge or reflect on those conflicting feelings—he carried on because the urge was too strong for him, he could not help it, but also out of a sense of rebellion, to show he had the nerve. "What's the world coming to if I, a young guy of twenty, can't look for any fun! And I'd sure like to know who's going to keep me from it!"

He was as yet unaware of a deeper desire in his heart or that he was crazy in love with the girl and could not do without her any longer—that he had to watch her to satisfy his very eyes. He still took it for a passing fancy that had come over him in a wide wave of tenderness, an urge to love and embrace everything, harmonious with the summer's heat—a by-product of the beautiful season, of the whole environment he lived in, whose priceless riches had only now been revealed to him. Otherwise, his purity of conscience put him at rest: whatever he did was done in the open, in broad daylight, for all to see.

When sensual desires began to burn in him, his deep, innate sense of honor would surface, serving as an immediate brake that reined in his passions and made him alive to the danger. No matter how he hankered for it, it would never occur to him, with conscious intention and premeditation, to look for an opportunity to meet some girl privately or abuse his superior position. When the chance was right, he seized it, whispering a little word in Schellebelle's ear and teasing her a bit. Then he would look long and deep into her eyes, where all that playful mischievousness, that roguishness of her artless soul, was disclosed as in a clear mirror, feeling more than ever the temptation in her dimpled cheeks, in the flush of her neck, and in all the liveliness of her supple shape and trim body. Louis knew when Schellebelle was stirring the cheese vats and butter tubs in the dairy; he knew she sat milking the cows in the shed every morning, noon, and evening, and afterward made the rounds to water the hogs and calves—he was able to keep track of all the chores of each hour of the day and guess where the girl could be found, but he was content to watch her from afar.

Today, however, Louis had come back from the field a little before noon. Having taken the horses to their stalls and knowing there was nothing left to do, he stood waiting for the lunch bell in the stable doorway and saw Schellebelle coming out of the dairy with two buckets full of milk. He knew she had to go to the orchard to tend to the calves. In a flash, desire flamed in Louis: he would, for once, thoroughly satisfy both his eyes and heart with the delicious girl. He pictured the exciting prospect in his mind's eye, framed by the charm of the mysterious spot, where the thick foliage of the elderbush vaulted a dome of shadow above the small fence gate. This was the forgotten clearing tucked between the high hedge of fennelwood and the stable walls. It remained in a half-light, no one ever passed by, and garden grass with nettles and madder grew wild there, rank and full. The nook had a peculiar enchantment, lying hidden and isolated a few steps away from the yard, cool and quiet as a bower.

Louis looked intentionally in another direction, but no sooner than Schellebelle disappeared around the corner, he slipped out of the backdoor of the cowshed to that shaded little corner to wait for his "sunflower." She was singing a nonsense song, just to ring out her abundant delight in an echo of lovely sounds:

Le-lia-a-lia!
Alona-sa-sa!

He heard her coming and held still. Passion throbbed in his veins. . . . She looked up, and immediately her whole face lit up in happy surprise:

"Ah! This is the place to be, where it's cool!" she shouted, half in laughter.

Louis stood leaning against the small gate the girl had to walk through, protected by the arching leaves of the elderbush. He saw she was defenseless—with a full bucket in each hand, it was easy to tease her now.

"No one passes here unless they pay the toll!" he said grinning.

She pouted and looked at him with a lingering glance of enticement. Louis did not give way, blocking her passage with arms outstretched. Then she laid into him with anger: impatient to walk on, her eyes blazing like stars, she tried to convince him:

"Silly boy, let me through. The noon bell's about to ring, and nothing's ready yet!"

She stepped forward to force him, bold and deliberate, with her chest thrust out. But he threw his arms around her neck at once and held her caught in his trap.

"Oh you crazy bee with your angry looks! Can you still say now that I think myself so big I won't grab poor you!"

Schellebelle did what she could so as not to spill any milk, squirming to get out of his grip. But not daring to shout or make a racket, she had to allow Louis' heavy hands to touch and paw over her, willy-nilly.

Suddenly, the girl let out a terrible scream. She dropped both buckets, scratched desperately to break free, and fled with a single jump behind the elderbushes.

When Louis turned around, surprised, he was standing dead level with his father. The boy apprehended immediate disaster.

"What do you want with that filthy slut?"

Vermeulen shouted, looking at his son with the eyes of a maddened bull. "You let the womenfolk hang on you like that? I'll kick you off the farm if I see it again."

At that, Vermeulen turned and walked away, as if he had caught his son there with the girl purely by chance.

Louis stood there stunned, emotion convulsing his whole body. He had not answered back a word, the shock had been so great. His father's bristly face had never seemed to him so ugly and deformed, but he had looked him straight in the eye all the same, until the farmer's heavy frame had vanished through the doorway of the cowshed. In that first startled moment, when he stood in his father's presence with his hands still on the girl, Louis felt humiliated and ashamed, like a bewildered schoolboy who has misbehaved and can find no excuse for his foolish conduct. In his father's look he had seen the reproach of his own proud heart. It blazed inside him as the severest of punishments: he who was so set on appearing respectable and proper now saw his good name lost and was thought of by his father as a skirt-chaser who hung out with trash. But at that one word of abuse—when he heard her branded a "slut"—he had overcome his shock: he had caught hold of himself with the awareness that his honor, and hers, were beyond reproach—and his confusion turned to rage. The insult got his blood up as though the word had been directed at himself. He cursed his own timidity, since he had stood there like an idiot, unable to find a thing to say to defend his case. He was exasperated with himself for having undergone it so passively—too late to make up for it now. It was not fear but a sudden start that had made him lose his tongue. What was so "filthy" about it? He knew his affection was as pure as sunshine—he had never touched the pleasure of his soul, except with his eyes! Then, all at once, perplexity gave rise again to hatred and bitterness toward that gruff character who served everywhere as a wall between himself and his youthful happiness. He felt offended by the blind authority oppressing him. In the heat of excitement, not knowing how to vent his rage, Louis shook his clenched fist at the doorway of the stable into which Vermeulen had vanished.

"I'll just wipe my boots on your threats, you old pig bastard!"

This was how his pent-up mood expressed itself, but it was a declaration of rebellion as well, with the grinning satisfaction of someone who knows he is stronger and sure of victory. Grinding his teeth, Louis let his explosive feelings out in the open, and his revenge was contained in the cry: "I'm young, you're old! We'll soon see how long it'll last!"

His future lay open before him, making his hands itch to claim his place in life with main force. He would walk right over anyone who dared trespass upon his true nature! It was certainly time his meek submissiveness came to an end—time to let the old man feel that there had arisen a will alongside his own.

"'That dirty slut'! I'll go with her just to rile you!"

Little by little, however, calmness set in and quieted the boy's heart—he looked ahead to the inevitable feud, and before long a great sense of sadness came over him—as if something beautiful had been shattered and obliterated which could never be restored: the pure, peaceful summer's dream had been violated—just now, when the best part was about to happen.

The shock had awakened Louis suddenly to reality: the carefree joy, the boyish delights were over. The girl would not dare look at him again—would she, perhaps, be sent away? And now, all unexpectedly and unprepared, Louis stood at the crossroad—he had to go in one direction or the other, choose between two things: be subservient and give in, or else rebel and obstinately carry out his own will and desire. But such a outcome alarmed him: what would become of his position as a proper farmer's son? It was clear now how dangerous misplaced affections can be and where they would land him. He had staked all his happiness, all his wants, on that lowly girl—a girl like a flower, but nothing more than a flower, and as fleeting. His sunny dream had suddenly vanished in a blaze—the whole show seemed ridiculous to his mind. The wondrous magic had lost its splendid glitter; like a green kid, he had given in to a false game of enticement, allowing himself to be seduced by some ogling eyes and laughing lips.

No, he had done it himself, the guilt was all his.

Why hadn't he left that girl to her work? Why did he go and disturb her pure peace of mind with his silly showing off? Pity, compassion filled his heart. He saw through his own cruelty, since he would have to undo what he had done, and cursed his senses for leading him along for so long, and because he could not play with his affections the way other fellows do, throwing their love away when they liked. No matter how he measured it, the shame was his alone, and he did not know how to better the situation . . . . His heart pounded with emotion. He ran up and down in excitement, with fists clenched, not knowing on whom to vent his anger. At length, he sat down right where he was to mull over his plight. He dared not, would not show his face to anyone before he had sorted himself out. Looking around where he sat in that quiet corner behind the stable, at the small wooden gate, at the elderbush, all the usual things seemed strange to him now . . . . Louis stared at the buckets she had let fall and at the milk streaming over the dark ground. . . . An excess of pity came over him. He saw himself and the poor girl as two innocents wronged, driven apart by cruel fate. "Why did I meet her? Why throw a glance at her? She was so happy by herself, so full of life and buoyant as a bird in the sky." But can a man, in fact, control his affections? How could he not have fallen for her loveliness? He reflected on how the fondness had grown in him by degrees and firmly taken root, how his love turned out to be something tangible, of substance, without which he could no longer go on living. He remembered how the girl had stood there before his father—the fear in her eyes was that of someone drowning and pleading for help. . . . Suddenly, he was seized by the urge to prove his compassion to her, to pour out his feelings of tenderness. He would not deny her—it was his fault, and he had to make it up to her. "What do I have to be ashamed of?" Louis thought. "I'll spill it all out, tell her straight off that I love her. What'll come of it, we'll see later."

Meantime, the bell rang for noon. The meal passed, and nothing at all of what Louis had feared so badly happened: not a word, not a look. Everything remained as usual in the kitchen, and the noon break also passed, as quietly as on other days.

And Louis was astonished at his first unexpected impression when he met Schellebelle again—the girl seemed strange to him and unfamiliar, so much so that he had to ask himself: "What business do I have with that redheaded thing?" He said nothing to her, not a word of his intended declaration, looking at her with cool indifference. And to explain and excuse his odd behavior, he placated himself with the notion that he would talk later, that he wanted to wait a little bit. But already he was glad he had not spoken.

IV

Vermeulen now thought he had a valid enough reason at hand to broach his decision without fear; his hesitation suddenly fell by the wayside. He tried to get Barbele alone in the kitchen that afternoon, and as soon as the housekeeper was gone he started in right off:

"I'm interested in buying Legijn's farm."

His wife understood perfectly what he had said, word for word, and yet she stood there with her mouth open, looking at the farmer with uneasiness in her eyes, as if she were afraid something was wrong with him.

"What?" she asked loudly, for the second time.

"That I mean to buy Legijn's farm—for Louis!" he shouted impatiently, as if at someone hard of hearing.

"But farmer!" Barbele cried, now entirely alarmed, "you're not really going to do that?"

"Why not? Do we always have to miss such opportunities?"

"Opportunity? What opportunity? For Louis? Does

he need to be set up . . . when he *is* set up?"

"Where is he set up?" Vermeulen put in with mock amazement.

"Well, here on the farm! He's our only son. Neither of the girls'll take up with a farmer . . ."

"Here?" Vermeulen cut off. "*Here? I'm* set up here! Louis? . . . Or do you mean we're going to do like Legijn: bury ourselves alive in a house and live off our money?"

"But what's the matter?" the woman asked anxiously. "How come you're on to this? What's happening to Louis? Does he want to leave? I don't know anything about it."

"Don't . . . know . . . anything!" the farmer mimicked her.

"Well, aren't we all right together like this? We're getting old, and when we can't get around anymore, then who will? . . ."

"Here? We? Old?" Vermeulen shouted. "Are you old? Am I old? Who says I'm old? Louis, he's at that age now where you can really see he's wild about women, right?"

"Women?" Barbele shrieked.

"He's got to get married. You get him a woman, and I'll get him a farm—and so then," Vermeulen concluded, "we'll have done our duty."   "Am I going crazy?" Barbele cried. "What's this I hear? Is he messing around? With who?"

"Are you blind, woman? It's high time he changed . . . otherwise he'll get hung up on some slut of a girl and you'll have a scandal on the farm. I saw him doing it out there just before, making a play for a girl, a stupid maid!"

The farmer's wife wanted to speak, but the words stuck in her throat, her eyes showed amazement. "Lord God, help me," she sighed. At that moment, the housekeeper walked in, and the ugliness was caught up in the silence that suddenly reigned in the kitchen. Vermeulen went off to the field.

Barbele did not know what to make of it. She was in shock, trembling in nervous agitation, unable anywhere to stay in the same spot. Restlessness drove her outside. She was afraid that something worse had happened, that Louis was carrying on some sinful affair, that shame would come upon the house or . . . that perhaps Vermeulen was exaggerating? . . . Had they had a fight? Was that why the farmer wanted Louis out of the way? It had been her fear for a long while; she had been expecting the showdown as something inevitable. Vermeulen was erratic, at times filled with odd ideas and hard set on his authority; Louis had reached the age when he too, now, had ideas and opinions of his own—and it gets difficult to give in all the time. Would she still be able to remedy it, put things right between the two of them? She wanted to know the answer, but Louis was out in the field. The uncertainty tortured her. What could the farmer have seen? What was going on with the maid? And which one? All afternoon long, she racked her brains on false suppositions. She did not dare mention anything to Sofie. She had to wait. With a maid, Vermeulen had said. Schellebelle was

still only a child, playful and always chattering . . .
but there could be no harm in it. With some other
one? Louis must have done it as a game. The
farmer's wife did not believe he would throw away
his honor and his future. She knew Louis was too
sensible for that. But she wanted to ask him. She
kept a watch long before dinner time, and as soon as
she heard the horses' bells, she was already on her
way from the doorstep to the stable. She followed
Louis at a distance wherever he went, to the feedhut,
to the barn, and then she headed toward the pigsty,
furtively, and there motioned to him in silence.

"Come for a walk, Louis. I have to ask you something." She went through the cowshed straight to the
same secluded spot by the small fence gate leading
to the orchard, sure that no one would hear them
there.

"What's this I understand, my boy?" she asked.
"You'd like to get away from here?"

"Get away, Mother? Where? Who says so?"

"Didn't I hear that Father has to look for a farm
for you? That you want to get married?"

"Look for a farm? Get married?" He laughed out
loud. "And who to? I don't know anything about it!"

"Is there something going on between you and
Father? He looks so discontented."

"Father's always discontented."

The woman wanted to ask something but did not
know how to begin. She stood there, shamefaced and
shy, blushing as though she harbored an improper
suspicion.

"What is it? Tell me, is something the matter, Louis?" she stammered. "You've been moody all day, walking around without talking."

The grown boy began at once to open his heart, but his voice caught:

"Because Father can't stand anything," he sobbed. "Because he reads trouble into everything!"

The woman's expression brightened, her lurking suspicion was softened: she knew she had nothing to fear for her boy. Those few words had set her at ease. She dared now to speak further:

"And what's he taken the wrong way, child?"

"Because I was teasing Schellebelle here while she was tending the calves . . ."

"Pshaw! You have to be patient about that with your father, Louis. He's getting old and doesn't understand such fun. Is there really nothing else?" she asked softly. "No thoughts lately of getting married?"

Louis looked up, surprised.

"How so, Mother?"

"Well, son, Father heard some talk about marrying and wants to find you a farm right away."

"Ha, ha! Are they saying I'm getting married?" Louis laughed. "And who to? And where does Father want to set me up on a farm?"

"Then it must've been just gossip, son. Don't let it upset you. Besides, who'd do the farming here when we're old? What would we do without you?"

The boy looked at his mother's open face. As she stood there before him in her fleshiness, with her hands in the pockets of her blue apron, he realized how kindly was her intention to come out and speak with him simply. But at the same time, Louis knew that she, with her sound insight, grasped the entire state of affairs—she interceded everywhere with calm and goodness to bring about peace and harmony. Louis could be so much more confidential with his mother than with his father; she always gently put in the best light whatever Father grimly thrust away from himself.

"You'll have to use sense and have patience," she added as they walked through the cowshed. "Father doesn't mean any harm, he's just somewhat obstinate. And if he's insisting on his authority now, leave him that satisfaction. In a little while, it'll come to you anyway: he can't keep on being everywhere much longer."

She picked up a pitchfork from the ground, lingered to do a few things in the stable while Louis went out, and then returned to the house through the back door.

The next day, Vermeulen came in from the fields in the afternoon and marched into the best room. Silence hung throughout the whole house, and over the farm burned the heat of the summer day. The farmer's wife looked around, softly opened the door, and approached her husband on bare feet. Vermeulen was at the writing desk, and Barbele sat down on the edge of the table, intending in a good-natured way to talk things over.

"You're not still going ahead and buying that

farm?" she began.

"Mm-hum. I certainly am," Vermeulen said, without looking up.

"And why? And who for? . . . Louis isn't thinking of getting married or going away."

"What do you know about it?"

"He says so himself!"

"Then why's he hanging around with the women?"

"Women?" the farmer's wife mocked, crossing her arms over her breast, "because the boy is having some fun with that slip of a girl? But don't you see, he's past twenty! Does he have to be so stiff? Weren't you as playful when you were young? Or have you forgotten? You don't have to add another twist—if those are your 'reasons,' then you'd be better off saying you can't stand Louis, that you're looking for an excuse. You'd be better off saying point-blank you want him out of here! Pushing him onto a farm . . . and you knowing he's dead necessary here? If he was rebellious or headstrong or bad, but people know different and they'll cover you with shame . . ."

At that, Vermeulen turned suddenly toward his wife.

"People?" he asked, surprised. "They'll know right away that I *can* do it and that I *will* to do it. Where are the farmers who'd do the same for their sons?"

"So, you're doing it to show how rich we are? What kind of foolish talk is that? When Louis wants to get married, you don't have to look further for a farm: his is all ready, here."

"What!" Vermeulen shouted. "You don't think a single straw'll be moved here so long as I live, do you? That a stranger'll come in here? That I'll make room and let someone else go over my head?"

His wife remained calm.

"That's not the question," she said. "I repeat: Louis isn't thinking of getting married. But if he had to leave now, what in God's name would you do? We're without another man of our own kin! Besides, you won't stay so eager to look after everything."

"Me? I can do whatever I want! Where there are two bosses, one has to go—I'm master here, and I'll remain master."

"Who's saying anything against that? You're respected like a king . . ."

"A fine king!" the farmer scoffed. "I can see it coming: once children get any brains, they want to be boss, and the parents are shoved into a corner. But that won't work with me! They'll have to go before things get that far—I'm not giving up. They'll have to go!"

"They do *not* have to go!" the farmer's wife said firmly. "They have to stay. Listen, Vermeulen, I'm going to tell you something: it's the case in your house, in a lot of houses—when the children get a little older, the conflict starts, the fighting and wrangling—life becomes hell because everyone has their own idea and gets stubborn, and no one will give up. The house and the farm are too cramped for them, too small—everyone pulling on their own rope and the family goes to ruin: parents and children grow apart, they all want out instead of wanting in. You and your father and mother, your six brothers and two sisters, the whole lot of you have grown apart and gone off—every one of you finding your own way because you couldn't bear each other, because you couldn't breathe, couldn't move anymore in a house that had become too small. You pushed and shoved to get each other out, one against another—as if you were strangers wanting to devour each other—and nothing's left of all that fine family. We've only got one son, and you'd like to play the same game here? Now that he's barely home from school, that he's full grown and can help, you're already feeling cramped and want to shove him out? What has he done against you? He's honest, he's diligent, accommodating and willing and amiable, but you treat him like an underage child. You can't bear that he's young, his fun and laughter grate against you! You belittle him in front of the workfolk—you want to wear him down . . . shove him off onto his own farm! You know our two daughters don't have farming on their minds, and we won't live forever—so who profits from this place of ours if you chase Louis away? Does it have to fall into strange hands? And all that just so you can carry on in your rough way. All my life I've done what you wanted, tried to please you in everything, but if you're going ahead now in that pigheadedness of yours and wearing the life out of Louis, then I'm leaving with him and you can farm here alone!"

"Right, but only if you pack along your pretty little

daughters too. I can do without them as well!" the farmer jeered.

Two tears shone in his wife's eyes and ran down. Her voice changed:

"Vermeulen, you don't mean that. It's a shame to say such things. All parents take pleasure in their children, seeing them grow up and become adults . . . getting help from being happy with each other, trying to stay together. And you . . . you always go against the grain—you make yourself hated instead of loved. You estrange the children from you with your harsh ways. To me myself you've never spoken a good word . . . always acting like a brute with me, as if I was your servant. In all the years we've been married I've never heard you call me by my name. But you don't have to do these things for me: my father and my brothers at home never pampered me with kindness either—but the children, why do they deserve it? . . . And what better can they ask of their parents than some peace and affection in the house? Why can't we deal with each other sociably and politely? We're well off, we've got fine children—all our trouble is what we inflict on ourselves—what more could we want than for all of us to stay together?"

"Ha! A nice thing staying together, when the children you've raised tower over your head!"

"Well, *let* them. We've had our time: we're headed down, they're coming up—to each his turn. It's a consolation to see our place taken by our own family."

"Consolation! Our place taken? Give up while I'm alive? As long as I can stretch my legs, I won't let anybody take anything! I'm not dead yet . . . I'm still living! . . ."

"The longer you live the better, but put those silly ideas out of your head. There are parents whose position is entirely different, who've got reason to complain about their children growing up. But you least of all. You're lord and master on this farm, nobody puts so much as a straw in your path, all your orders are carried out, you do as you please in everything . . . what more do you want then? Better you said that you're too fortunate and considered that you're trampling your good luck to pieces under your feet! If you had a reason—like you pretend you do—and were forced to buy a farm, I'd pity you from the bottom of my heart. But this here is nothing else than a whim, something you take out of thin air to satisfy your own pigheadedness. . . . I think I have a word to say too in such important matters—well: I shall fight this nonsense with everything I have."

"Do what you can—it's a tug-of-war—we'll see!" Vermeulen cried, and he smashed down his doubled fist, shaking the writing desk.

With that, the quarrel came to a dead end. Though he had been exposed by Barbele, his proud heart prevented him from admitting to his wife that he was wrong. He then made as if hurt and insulted—he exploded, loosing his rage, shooting off at the mouth, and marched out of the room with his head held high.

Days of heavy silence usually followed such a quarrel, a stiff-necked silence the farmer found hard to bear; yet he could not get over his mood and bring himself to speak the first word of reconciliation. Barbele, on the other hand, tried to make it easy for him and acted as though she had long forgotten the fight. But inwardly she felt reassured—she understood her husband, she knew bad thoughts brewed in his mind at times without his being able to find his way clear, and she had to talk him out of them. His fit was over now, and Barbele was honestly convinced that she had persuaded him, that he was ashamed of his stupid idea and would never dare mention that farm again. Vermeulen, for his part, kept his real intention secret, deep behind his dark brow.

Smoke from the hearth twisted upward through the broad chimney and curled lazily in the thin, white-hot air. Even less than that small smoke cloud showed, however, of the thoughts and opinions of the inhabitants there, their deeper understanding of life. They all did their work, laughing and chatting, but concealing from one another what went on inside.

The farmer's bristly face was like a board gouged full of cuts and furrows—not a line of it would go away or change. His wife as well wore her usual expression, the friendly features of someone who has to bear no other burden than her own heavy flesh and no concern except the care of the household. Louis, for his part, sounded his happiness and joy in life, as if nowhere were there troubles or disturbances to be feared in the endless progression of beautiful summer days. Undaunted, he strode along through the tumult of life, the noisy bustle of boys and girls in the yard. There seemed no place, no opportunity for personal thoughts and reflections in that steady excitement, with new activity always presenting itself, one long day after another, from one early morning to late the next night, throughout the smooth turning of the steady summer. In all that great, overwhelming, perpetual motion of farming, each private tendency widened into the general flow of the common stream, in one and the same direction, toward one and the same end: the harvest—the yield of the crops in the field now swollen to ripeness. The main event, for which all the other work the rest of the year was mere preparation, was going to begin at last.

Beyond the walled enclosure of the farmstead, summer reigned in full splendor over the land, the crops standing in all their glorious abundance. And next to that endless luxuriance and beauty, all man's brooding and petty cares seemed to have been swept from the world.

Though the lovely bloom had vanished like a dream, the regal summer still hung in perfect peace over the expanse between the four horizons.

Harvest

I

While the crops still stood in the fields—the pure splendor and ornament of a beautiful world—the endless peace of the long summer days still spread over them, people were getting ready to launch the assault. The calm would soon be over and done with, now that the time for blossoming was past and the myriad colors of living flowers were fading and dying—a ray of sun might shine down on them in a golden luster, but the racing shadow of a passing cloud would again turn them drab and gray, all youth and joy gone in a breath. That expanse of loveliness was now to be touched and violated; everyone would lay hands on "what's mine," clutching at their own property.

First here and there, then from all around, the farmers were setting out for their fields, where they searched with open hands through the stalks of flax, inspecting the color as they walked on and rubbing an occasional stem open to test the toughness of the fibers. The time indeed had come, and the farmers were determined to make use of the remaining

sunny weather to work their flax and to haul it in.
They said:

"Who knows, a thunderstorm can come on quick
enough, and now while it's still standing,
undamaged . . ."

The commotion started, without consultation or
loud warnings. The workfolk set out, just as in the
weeding days of spring, and whoever did not have a
fixed daily routine joined the throng. Not only
women and girls, but all able bodies—young fellows,
boys, everyone following the flock and looking out
for where you had to go to get hired. It was like a
great trek, a migration, with all those people on the
road—the movement was altogether new and
strange to the countryside, which had become used
to a peaceful and unfrequented scene. The men
walked purposefully and seriously, vests over their
shoulders and clogs in their hands; the women went
barefoot, with straw hats on their heads; the girls
and boys laughed and cavorted all around, half
dressed, suntanned brown on their faces, necks, and
bare arms and legs. Even old, withered women,
doubled over and gnarled with toil, burned black by
the sun, tottered behind with broken little steps,
trying to keep up with the crowd. It was as if the
whole population, driven all at once by necessity,
was setting out to gain its food and sustenance.

Early one morning, harvest song echoed for the
first time, unexpected, powerful, shattering the
crystal silence of the pure morning air. It resembled
the battle cry for a general attack, that sudden noise

in the heavy stillness, along with the tumult of so many people moving through the countryside, gathering to signal a full-throated shout of victory. The harvesters began the day and the work with dancing and singing. After that, they got down to business furiously. Men and women together, standing with bodies bowed and arms hanging low, pulled the stalks out of the ground by the handful, roots and all, while a pack of hollering boys and girls ran back and forth, carrying the piles away. Something was released now, something awakened in the withdrawn mood of the workers. They were usually taciturn, with seriousness written on their faces, apprehension and submissiveness on their bent backs, as all day long they performed their hard labor until going home in silence through the dusk, weary and exhausted, with feet dragging—the harvest did not seem an especially heavy exertion. Indeed, there was an elated cheerfulness in the crowd, happiness stirring in the air; they took pleasure in the light lift of their steps, the open swing of their arms, and the exuberant wagging of every tongue. The great, long-repressed shout of joy echoed and re-echoed loudly from one flaxfield to the next: a shout containing the end of their longing, the removal of all fears over the uncertainty of yield and profit; a shout signaling triumph over the season, the victory of the beautiful golden crop on which so much toil had been expended all summer long and to which were attached such worry and care. The weight of all those days, the suspicions, the dread

from start to end all seemed past now: the precious
crop was won, and the farmers would now reward
their hard labor. Exultation rose like a flood across
the whole region; everyone felt it as pure joy, with no
side reflections of self-interest or gain—the welling
up of the broad flow of life. Whoever had helped or
joined in the work claimed the right to share in the
joy of the harvest. From the east side of the valley,
hoarse and strong, went the collective call of the
throng:

"Is the farmer's flaxfield ripe?"

And the long drawn-out whoop of the womenfolk
and boys, their high-pitched yell, came roaring back
in answer:

"Ye-e-es!!!"

The cry shifted west, just as strong as the echo
from the east:

"Are we harvesting the flaxfield?" And there too
came the subsequent cry in answer, equally wild and
full:

"Ye-e-es!!!"

From north, from south, from the four corners at
once, the shout of joy crisscrossed the whole land.
One and all, then, took part in the great commotion,
for people were now harvesting everywhere.

That same morning, Vermeulen's workfolk went
haying in the meadow, and from the lowland where
they stood, against the slope in front of them, they
viewed the open heights and, flat as the surface of a
table, Sobrie's flaxfield, lying bare between the green
of the other crops, like a large piece of smooth,

ocher-yellow cloth. And before Schellebelle and the other girls had even gotten to work with their pitchforks, they already heard from far away the beginning of the song. From the distance, it carried through the thin air in all its sweetness, the words distinct:

We're up there early at the dawn of day,
Off to our flaxfield, gone and away!
  Na-ve-va! Na-ve-va!

They saw the group in a round dance, holding hands, twisting and turning, slowly at first, then livelier with the rising pace of the beat, the song gradually unwinding:

And flax as growing up so soon,
Tops and bottoms ready to prune!
  Na-ve-va! Na-ve-va!

The farmer then showed up with his bottle of gin, and suddenly the voices changed, the harvesters bawling louder in triple time:

What is making our host so late?
Let's rub pepper in his hairy face!
But on him my mind is set,
And I alone his love will get!
  For look—there's oily-oil in it!
  But look—there's oily-oil!

They closed the circle around the farmer, turning at a swifter pace as the singers fell out one by one and went to the center for a drink. All the while, the spirited dancing song continued:

I raise the tumbler, drink it down,
I smack my lips and watch the ground!
    Na-ve-va! Na-ve-va!
And our farmer's such a cull
He pours the glasses just half full!
    For look—there's oily-oil in it!
    But look—there's oily-oil!

When everyone had had their turn and the bottles were emptied, farmer Sobrie left. Then came the friendly last refrain:

Thanks to our host, his heart's so sweet,
For all of us a happy treat!
    Na-ve-va! Na-ve-va!
It's harvest here, it's harvest there:
Harvest comes but once a year!

With that, the circle broke apart and everyone quickly got down to work. The flax was gathered by the handful, and by the handful carried away and set up in hedgerows, the task progressing like a game, light and easy.

The same lightness and ease, of play rather than work, prevailed on Vermeulen's meadows as well. The young women now stood all in a group, legs bared, in the cut grass where the mowers had been the day before. In the full delight of life, they moved their arms, swinging their forks—catching the greenery on the sharp glittering tines, scattering and raking the windrows apart, throwing the strands high up in the air and letting them rain down all around. The smell of balsam that rose up from the resinous grass made them drunk, so intoxicating them that they all stood there together laughing. The dance and resounding music of the harvest songs kindled their eagerness. And although all lay in silence again, far and wide, they felt a great joyfulness in the air and expected that their turn would soon come to shout and join in the celebration.

The silence lasted until around noon, but then the dancing and the singing resumed on all the flaxfields; and once more in the late afternoon and again in the evening—with each meal break, at regular intervals, the festiveness suddenly sprang awake again, the noise and shouting taken up everywhere. Far off, from the flaxfields lying out of sight behind a hogback rise, from all over, came the high cries and wild crowing calls, an endless echo without end, the perpetual "oily-oil in it!" It kept up for days. The happy lilting song seemed almost to belong in the air, rooted in the entire surroundings, the way it was resumed so steadily and firmly, returning with each mealtime all the days of the harvest.

From Vermeulen's farm, through the wide opening

of the gate and from the high fields all around, you could take in the whole region at a glance, and wherever the flaxfields drew their yellow four-sided planes among the other greenery, you could see the harvesters at work on every one of them. They looked like little manikins, each playing on their own bits of ground, busy with some nonsense.

Vermeulen's flax was still far from ripe, and his people would have quite a wait before they could join in the general excitement. Meanwhile, they quietly worked on, young men and maids together, in the hay and among the beets. But they enjoyed looking at the dancing and the fun before the meal breaks and every time Sobrie's harvesters got their gin and the singing rose. And they talked together about wanting to start in on the important business too.

Schellebelle was more deeply affected than the others, since she had never been allowed to participate before and was seeing it now for the first time close at hand. She was no longer in control of herself; her legs trembled under her body—if she just had wings, in short, she would have flown in her longing to where the fun was going on. She could watch every movement from here, the whole show, so distinctly the harvesters stood out in their motley clothing against the clear, translucent sky and the white-yellow field that had been reaped: young men and women in a single line, girls and boys running with handfuls to the men laying out the flax in even hedgerows. Everyone understood so perfectly where to go and what to do that it looked like a game they had learned—the way children play grown-up for fun. In all that live commotion, Schellebelle recognized among the other people Marietje Verlinde and Fientje Vandoorn; in the crowd, too, were the two boys she knew went out with her friends. Her own heart beat in fits and starts at the thought, the fancy of what seemed to her supreme happiness, for she had noticed before long how each of the two couples held hands in the circle with every round dance. She spied, furthermore, on their doings while at work and could certainly guess the rest: how there was a good chance to whisper and pet among all that singing and noise and merriment, so that now the game must be doubly pleasant with love involved.

The flaxfield, that luminous yellow plot, was a promised land in Schellebelle's naïve imagination, a stretch of warmth to which she was drawn by all the fierceness of her desire. What others took part in so casually, without looking upon it as the peak of happiness, seemed unreachably far-off to her, forever denied, because her longing was too high-strung and she expected too much of it. Every day she heard about a new gathering, a new attack on another flaxfield that had lain untouched until now. The boys and girls talked of nothing else on the field where she herself was working; they could feel the itch and the pressure, the waiting, the uncertainty testing their patience.

"The weather could turn bad, and then the fun's

pretty much all over," someone said, to tease Schellebelle.

But the others reassured her, claiming the farmer would start tomorrow or the day after. They told her about how the maybranch had to be taken up and what happens at the farm on the last evening, after the harvest pudding . . .

Her whole body quivered with delight. She felt the pressing desire to dance and sing, now that it seemed the same for everyone elsewhere—now that it rode the four winds through the air, a wave of irresistible joy, and people were celebrating all over the place. She did not know what would become of her or what would happen to her during the days she pined for—she wanted only to let herself drift with the general current, for in the neighborhood there had never been such a whirl of excitement around her. She could see no end of it and had to force herself to stay calm on her feet and rein in her delight.

Louis stood in front of her, on the edge of the beetfield. He too found pleasure watching the tumultuous crowd of harvesters having fun. The farmer's son spoke little to his hired folk, but whenever he came near their work, his eyes stayed glued to the distance, around to where the harvesters were laboring. And when the maids teased him and asked, "Farmer, when'll it be our turn? When do we start?"—he replied, smiling:

"If I was the farmer here, we'd harvest tomorrow! But I'm not the farmer—so ask my father."

The maids laughed at him and made out that he,

and he alone, was really the boss.

"Who did the sowing?" they asked.

He let them babble on, and walking away he said casually to Schellebelle, but with a knowing look in his eyes:

"You're looking forward to the harvest, too?"

The girl lifted her arms, her ten fingers spread open like stars. Longing shone in her eyes, her keen desire flaring, and showing all her teeth she laughed in Louis' face like a child excited by a wonderful promise.

He was not allowed to show it, he had to maintain his dignity in front of the workfolk, yet inwardly he yearned as much for the harvest as Schellebelle herself.

After the encounter with his father, Louis had made a resolve not to engage in any more foolishness, to behave properly. . . . But just as the celebrating started up in the fields, he felt the desire awakening to join and have his share in it. The singing of the harvest songs along with the maids' giggling went through his head constantly: everywhere he looked, there was fun going on, and he itched to mix with the excitement, roughhousing with the young people, for once letting himself go. . . . The impression of sensuality wrapped in a filmy veil of tenderness, which had been revealed to him on the flaxfield in May as an undiscovered salvation, still hung ever on his mind. It had come unexpectedly then, overpowering him; he could neither get quit of it nor drive it away and only truly realized its preciousness when the happiness had passed; and ever since, it had stayed with him as a wistful sorrow, a longing for something that can never be again. But now he would catch hold of it again on that very flaxfield at harvest time—now he was waiting for it, aware and ready to enjoy it to the full, letting nothing of that wonderful magic be lost. In his mind's eye, Louis increasingly indulged his anticipation of that immense joy. Eagerness for pleasure stirred up his longing more and more, and he regarded what was waiting for him as the crowning splendor of the first royal summer he had really lived in the full sense—enjoying the sun, the bustle in the fields, the growth of the crops, the company of the workfolk, and everything that thrived outside under the open sky. He would not see how exaggerated his expectation was; knowingly and willingly, he embellished it in his imagination, egging his desire on; he looked upon it as the event that would free his life from all bonds and bring with it his future happiness. He took great pleasure in going over the details of that imminent success: the deliciousness of bathing up to the knees in flax, helping to harvest with the crowd—grabbing by the handful, fooling around, joking, laughing, romping and cavorting without suspicion and without being watched over, like an ordinary young fellow with his equals—to hear the sound of the loud prattle and laughter and teasing of the lusty young women, the girls with their shining eyes and their bodies itching with life and mischief.

Each time he left the beetfield or came up from the
meadow, Louis wandered back past the high field
just to look at the flax. It was his favorite walk, and
all his interest lay there. That square plot of bright
green with the luster of yellow-gold upon it, light
playing among the straight-grown stalks, excited his
admiration from afar. Yet he stood at the spot like
someone looking to find there what he had lost: the
happiness of the beautiful days in May! It seemed in
fact an eternity ago: then the stalks were barely a fist
high, and the spring dew lay glistening upon them.
The memory—something from another world—affected him like the pleasure of a good refreshing
drink in the fierce heat of summer. How pure and
peaceful, how enchanting had the air been then,
hanging above the field! How pure too his own heart
in those days. . . . It seemed impossible to him that
that spring should belong with this very same
summer—nowhere was the bond still noticeable; all
that he had experienced then appeared to him as if
in a dream—everything so soft and hazy in color, in
the glow of a magic lantern. . . . And what, in fact,
had he carried over from it? An uneasiness of mind,
an agitation that made him happy. Seen from here,
his former way of life appeared drab and colorless to
him, in unbroken sadness. How his heart beat more
fiercely now, how much more boldly he scanned the
things around him—he felt like a ruler for whose
sake all things exist, with a rich future in prospect.
That spring had made him conscious of the place of
his own life in the passage of time. He was aware of

his blossoming, on his path to deliverance and a
certain position in life. He perceived it as a transitory
happiness, whereupon beauty would vanish, along
with pleasure and joy, and he soon realized the
preciousness of each day when evening came,
regretting he had not enjoyed it more. He wanted to
live every day through without missing a single
pleasure. He felt his desire as strength, tangible in his
hands—a living thing he could use to fulfill all his
deepest wishes. He had to fight his innate
seriousness, and with it his exaggerated decorum,
and push them under—that stiff attitude was
unbecoming in youth, the deathblow to every
pleasure.

"Later, when I'm the farmer, I'll be my own boss
and suit myself," he thought. "And now too."

The doubter was dead in him; he wanted to smash
his way through, boldly, without looking
back—things had gone on much too long. Life was
rushing right past him without his taking part, and
he was standing in the middle of it. Now for the first
time was it awake inside him: the sun had laid it
bare, and he stood, saw himself standing, in full
bloom. He was the sower and would become the
reaper all through the beautiful progression of the
seasons. He did not regret the time he had let slip by,
unused and unenjoyed—he saw all his happiness in
the future. He felt uncomfortable only because he
had no way of knowing what to do with his
exuberance: here he was, a big, full-grown fellow
without experience; a first-born son, shy and

timid—ashamed to give himself up to sensual pleasure. The boys and girls he had under him did not know that difficulty—following their natural urge, they grabbed what fun they could get. In his wistful yearning and desire, Louis nevertheless still carried second thoughts with him, a holding back, a hesitation to let go, a fear of excess—the weight of his father's respectability. His entire social environment and past conduct stood in the way, hampering such easy looseness. But it would come: outside, the whole wide space was filled with it. It all still seemed so new; to be sure, this was the first summer when he had been overwhelmed by the desire to join in, when his eyes had seen what there was to seize and hold. He would sweep it up in his hardened arms: the foolish nonsense, the wild, unrestrained fun the boys and girls indulged in freely, without an afterthought. He wanted to love whatever pleased him, and he had love for everything!

As he strolled along, no sign of inner struggle or hesitation could be detected in his quick step or the tilt of his head; his sweeping hand trailed through the fine stalks of flax. The bolls struck like hard little bells and slid, rustling, between his open fingers. But while walking, the farmer woke again in the young man's heart, and all at once he began to regret that the crop was so ordinary this year:

"The flax should've turned out better," he thought. And immediately, all the daydreaming about the revelation of his happiness, his longing to see it accomplished with the harvest, was gone and forgotten; he was thinking, with disgust, of his father's obstinacy. There was something wrong with the crop, and the whole lot, as it stood swaying, annoyed him, because it had gone bad through his father's fault, against all better advice. He no longer felt himself now the great performer as in the spring, when he had walked across the field, step by step, elated, sowing. . . . The expectations of that moment had not worked out, and all his preconceived plans and calculations had miscarried. The farmer in him required results as direct proof of what he had done, with his every action, with every expression of his will; he tried with all his might to create beauty and abundance everywhere, wanting to be the guardian of the land—to make the growth and increase fit his strong opinions. The fields that were his responsibility, his to cultivate, he viewed as a space in which to effect his taste for beauty. That was why he took no delight in the flax now. He did not feel it was his, lying there like an unwanted excrescence come into being against his will. He felt ashamed to have sown it.

"Wait until I'm the farmer myself!" he grumbled under his breath. These words shot blazing to his heart, and for the first time now Louis wanted to run the farm in his father's stead. Contempt for his father all at once stood clear and fixed in his mind. He expected the great change to take place before long, counting on it as a certainty not to be doubted. As day follows night, so one life follows another. He would fight for control year after year until the old man had to quit, leaving him the legacy of his authority. Louis considered that heirloom the finest thing waiting for him in life. The farm with all that pertained to it of land and people and animals—the whole works lay there like a kingdom that would one day come under his rule. Enjoying the comings and goings, with full opportunity to carry things out in accordance with his own views and after careful consideration, he would continually convert his ideas into actions. He wanted to start on it while still a prince.

Suddenly the joyous shout echoed again through the air, the long-drawn-out song with the endlessly repeated

oily-oil in it!

It sounded like a burst of laughter: the echo of exuberant fun, the joyfulness of people unselfconsciously celebrating a farmer's gains, or rather, the pure gladness of summer, with the frolicsome, senseless daring of their bold love of life.

Louis, the prince, watched his kingdom and his rule sailing off into the clear blue sky, and from beyond all conscious thought, his own pleasure in his twenty years surfaced again.

"Later, later," he thought. "Let's have some fun first. I'm in my youth now, my prime! You can hear desire rising up everywhere and bursting out in wild song! Heady excitement running through the whole countryside!" Dancing could be seen in the fields on three, four sides at once, accompanied by full-throated singing:

> It's harvest here, it's harvest there
> Harvest comes but once a year!
>   Gloria-excelsia-pari-mondi
>   Van-domi-ni-co-dema
>   Van-sim-sa-la-pari!
>   Na-ve-va! It's comparea!

It sounded from a farther direction too, in a different tone and with another melody, but just as lusty and provocative:

> And mightn't I have a little glass!
> Would I for that a drunkard be?
> Would I for that, would I for that
> Would I for that a drunkard be?
> Mietje, fill up full the bowls,
> No more flies are swimming in them.
> Have we no money, we'll sell our clothes,
> No more fleas are living in them.
> I merrily take the jug by the ear,
> Merrily take the flask by the butt.
> Merrily, merrily, merrily, merrily,
> I merrily like to souse my gut.

When Louis was even in the farmyard, Sobrie's harvesters could still be clearly heard late into the night, singing their closing song for the final hour:

And our farmer's just a glutton,
He's made us get tipsy, made us get drunken.
   Na-ve-va! Na-ve-va!

And after the swaying sigh of the refrain, you could guess the mad, foolish dance by its tripping melody:

And on him my mind is set!
And I alone his love will get!
   For look—there's oily-oil in it!

The insatiable excitement expressed itself in wild shrieks, and although their voices went hoarse with shouting, the harvesters had to tell it to the whole world: the farmer's flax was gathered, and they were drinking and celebrating to overflowing!

So boisterous and lively were the goings-on out there, Louis had never found it so fearful at home, so oppressive, lonely, and hushed in the yard and everywhere on the farm. The singing and the noise penetrated inside, but no one paid any attention. The workfolk kept silent, and you could not tell from their quiet behavior that they wanted to have their turn, too, in the general events. More than once in the stillness, the maids, impatient with all that dillydallying, asked Louis:

"When's it to be?"

But the young farmer would answer joking, to tease them:

"We harvest when all the others are through, then we get all the fun to ourselves." And after that, he would whisper roguishly in a girl's ear:

"But this time, no women are allowed on the field: the girls have to stay home—the farmer doesn't want their silliness."

They looked at him, scheming, with mischief in their eyes.

"Hm!" one of them would say. "And you don't want them either, of course!"

Another time, he would think up something else: to make them feel low, he said the farmer had sold his flax as it stood on the field and that the buyer had to harvest it. But not a one of them believed a word of it.

II

The days passed, and still no maybranch was placed amid Vermeulen's flax.

Buyers and agents came and offered money, but the farmer, always used to having the best crop and the highest price, had to make them clear off again and again. He remained obstinate. . . . Even at the last moment, he still would not admit being wrong and kept blindly claiming his flax was worth more than any other. He did so to save face with Barbele and Louis, acting as if he were right and had done well to locate the flaxfield on the heights. But for all that bluff, no deal was made.

"I'd still be more reasonable," his wife insisted. "You even know yourself you're asking too much."

But the farmer flared up, repeating the changeless apothegm he habitually used to brush off any line of reasoning: "What do you know about it? I'm the farmer, I sell the crops. You mind the butter and milk."

Louis stood by, leaning his shoulder against the chimney piece and grinning foolishly, like a big clod who couldn't care less if the flax is sold or not. He watched his father's senseless behavior and kept quiet. "Sold or not," he thought, "it'll have to be harvested anyhow, and that's the main thing." He felt, in fact, inclined to give in to his father's stubbornness.

"We can keep it in the loft for a year," he mused, "take it to the Lys ourselves, and swingle it at home in the winter." And with his next word he asked, carelessly and without design, simply because there was an opportunity:

"When can we start, Father?"

"It can stand some more sun for sure," Vermeulen claimed. "If it only could get a good rain, it'd still grow another span . . ."

"If the rain just doesn't spoil it, Father."

The farmer replied with a surly growl. A jerk of his shoulders, and that was the end of it. Louis found it intolerable that his mouth clapped shut again, like an oven door, and that you had to put up with it until the mouth came open again of its own accord. Elsewhere, the harvesters were working without delay; they had been gathering and setting up hedgerows so long and so diligently that whole lots lay shorn and bare, ready for the harvest home celebration. In some places, it was already long past. The poor flax had been hackled in the fields and sat in the retting pits, or having already been hauled out, lay drying on the meadows. The stench of the retting hung in the air, like a plague infecting the whole region.

Schellebelle had carefully followed it all, asking

questions, forever anxious to see the flax festival on Sobrie's field begin.

Something extraordinary was at hand—you could notice it early in the morning. The harvesters sang louder, they danced harder, while Sobrie brought along a double ration of gin.

"We'll see something happen today," Kate Verwee guessed.

"It'll be all the oldtimers and boozehounds," said Zenia.

"And there'll be some real dancing. Wantje's with them, and then they always go by the rules, like in the old days."

"She's still light on her feet," Poortere maintained, "though she's past eighty."

"She could even outdance a girl of twenty," Triene Loket claimed. "Young folks nowadays don't know the steps for the festival anymore, they just jump around like crazy."

"In my day," Tale Kok told the others, "it was a joy to watch the harvest. It doesn't stand for much now, not since your young jumpers learn dancing in taverns."

They chattered on about the old customs of the flax festival—the games, the harvest celebration, the sense of fulfillment—while rooting up the weeds from among the beets with their hoes. Schellebelle listened in silence but now and then stole a look at the field, longing to see the fun there get underway.

The harvesters were falling to work with unusual haste and agitation. At no time had the sun burned so fiercely, but not one of them grew giddy or suffered from the heat. Today, they had to gather in the may! Their shirts hung loose and open on their bodies; standing barefoot, they stooped over their work. The right hand gripped a braid of flax from below against the foot and with a quick jerk ripped the roots from the soil, hard and dry as a threshing floor. With a sweep, the braid was whisked under the left arm, where it was held tight until the small barbs were pulled out and the stalks shaken smooth. From there, the flax went to the girls who carried the handfuls, or "pawfuls," away back to the hedgemakers. The work moved deftly and fast, the girls reaching and gathering, giving and running, from the harvesters who stood in a single row to the hedgemakers, constantly back and forth. The harvesters continued until noon without looking up, and they hurriedly resumed right after eating, working all through the break. The air was windless and still over the region, the intensity of sunlight dazzling to the eyes. The heat further increased in the afternoon; it became close and stifling and difficult to work, the burning sun beating down so hard that every living creature looked for cover.

"There's a change coming," a hand on Vermeulen's field forecast. Everyone agreed it was impossible to stay out in the hot weather.

"He won't come, he's afraid of the heat," Schellebelle was thinking as she looked once more at the wagon road behind her to watch Louis appearing. They had let him know Sobrie's would be holding its harvest festival, and he had promised to come, but he was staying away.

It was after vespers that the excitement on Sobrie's flaxfield began.

"They're going after the may!" one of the maids yelled.

A couple of girls were seen leaving their work be, tearing away from the field in a flash. They returned a little later with something they kept covered with their aprons and went and tucked away in a small ditch at the edge of the field. Schellebelle recognized Marietje Verlinde and Fientje Vandoorn.

"It's the flowers for the may," Zenia claimed.

Two other girls came to help too. But when still more wanted to join in, they were unceremoniously sent away—nobody was allowed to see what was being hatched in the ditch. Finally, they brought it to the light of day: the may, thrust high in triumph and carried with loud cheering to the crowd, was first admired, then planted in the middle of the last remaining patch of standing flax. Seen from afar, the may looked like a twofold cross entwined with green stalks of flax. Colored candles had been fastened to a ring that lay over the four arms of the cross, and around it was braided a small crown of bluebottles and herbs. On the stem of the cross, among the flax stalks, hung blood-red poppies, white daisies, forget-me-nots, and blazing yellow water lilies—the girls had gone searching for and picked all the wild flowers, and the may stood, a spray of blossoms splashed with flecks of red, blue, white, and yellow, resplendent above the last corner of unharvested flax. The harvesters had progressed so far that only a little patch was left upright, the size of a table top. The work was at an end; now the feasting would begin.

Vermeulen's people stopped for a while and stood leaning on the handles of their hoes with the quiet curiosity of calm spectators who, knowing what is supposed to happen, watch to see how the game will end.

The hedgemakers were dressing the last flax, while the womenfolk formed a line and, singing arm in arm, walked away from the field toward the farmstead. The other harvesters sat at their ease around the may, waiting.

"Where are they going?" Schellebelle asked in happy excitement, and she looked around impatiently for Louis to come. "Is it starting now?"

"They're going to fetch the wife," Paulientje said. Sure enough, the crowd came back in a long line, singing and shouting, holding the farmer's wife in the middle by each arm. They marched in rhythm, and where the melody required it, all together they kicked their legs high and swung their heads down to the beat of the song:

And the hands were going
   plik-plok-plak!
And the feet were going
   trik-trok-trak!
He was a man of many years

his poor legs hanging slack
  from his back!

The two ends of the row bent toward each other on
the spot. Arms loose, now they closed the ring, hand
in hand. Letting the farmer's wife in the middle, they
milled about in a circle with a slow dragging song, a
stately beginning:

And flax as growing up so soon!
  Na-ve-va! Na-ve-va!

The farmer's wife stood waiting patiently, as
though at a compulsory ceremony, until she had
listened to all the lines of the harvest song. Then
Sobrie himself showed up with sugared gin, a whole
basket full of bottles. The circle opened to let the
farmer near his wife and, turning, shuffled over to
the patch of standing flax with the may in it.

All at once it was completely still, everyone held
their breath—the farmer's wife stepped forward and
with a simple movement harvested the may. And at
the same moment, the noise burst out: a resounding
hurrah, as vigorous as their throats could shout it,
three times in a row:

"Did we harvest the may?"
"Ye-e-es!"

At that, the milling shifted into the slow train of
another melody, the opening of the flax dance

proper:

> It's harvest here, it's harvest there:
> Harvest comes but once a year!

The farmer made the rounds with the first bottle while his wife remained standing with the weight of the one and only may in her arms.

Just before evening fall or thereabouts, Louis went out and walked slowly along the fields. The intensest heat had now cooled off, and the flaming sunlight shone aslant across the land from the west. The houses, trees, and everything that could be seen in the fields stood as though in the radius of a crystal prism, rimmed with the color lines of the rainbow. A close film lay over the whole distance, as if everything had lost its natural solidity; the houses appeared light and diaphanous, like the air itself, shimmering under the magic glow of the marvelously quiet afternoon, so ethereal yet easy to distinguish against the bleached blue of the high heavens. As he walked, Louis heard from far away the rise and fall of a fleeting song. The sound swished through the general silence, was extinguished at one swoop like a passing puff of wind, and then came back again like a ray of light weaving through the distance. Every existing thing seemed unreal to him, as if seen in a dream, and he tried to fathom with his sober mind the reason for the successive opposition of sound and silence, their connection across the crystal-clear, vividly colored, wide-open landscape. The extreme heat had somewhat drugged Louis' senses. It was like coming out of a dead sleep: things appeared so shadowy where he walked; he himself and the surroundings were floating and would melt and evaporate—just idle wisps of cloud in the sky. The song came echoing to him again, borne on a gust of wind, a breath of air. He could not yet make out the words, but the sound was utter loveliness, the tones turning and gliding so gently and simply in the inaccessible distance. Louis remembered now what Schellebelle had told him before noon with her laughing glance. Feeling a sudden anticipation, he struck out along the side road to the heights, although not walking any faster. As he drew near, he looked up and saw the reddish-blonde girl waving at him, with no trace of shyness, not holding herself back, excitement in her eyes and a beautiful sweep of her arm urging him to hurry.

"Here!" she shouted, "you're late! They've started!"

Louis walked to the lowest end of the beetfield, where he had the whole flaxfield open before him, and sat down on the grass edging. The harvesters were divided into equal groups and stood lined up on each side as on a dance floor. A couple of girls stepped forward and, sweetly now, through the stillness, came the opening of the quadrille:

À vous Marie,
À vous Marianne.

And all the other girls and women stepped forward, dancing, with measured step and feet lifted high. Likewise the men, and as the two rows crossed each boy emerged holding a girl's hand. They held each other by the fingertips, arm raised above each other's head, and every boy led his girl forward with a smart flourish, singing:

> Rectory
> Bring 'em by,
> You alone—
> Ah! sweet love, go 'way from me!

At the next crossover, the girls came together again while the boys quickly fell back. But a new row of girls stepped forward prettily and sang:

> Turn around.
> Welcome round.
> On the town
> With me alone—
> Ah! sweet love, again turn 'round.

Their eyes beckoned, the movement of their arms signaled a tempting invitation. They now came forward one by one, and with a whirl they each took hold of their partners again, the couples turning in a lively reel to the beat of the song.

Seen from afar, the dancing went so simply and peacefully, while the singing sounded so clear through the pure air, whispering as it were, in order not to shatter the fragility of the spread calm. The warm light of early evening enveloped it in a peculiar intimacy, the sun glowing on the hedgerows of flax that stood like gilt curtains to mark off the stage where that wondrously unreal game was being played.

Grown men and beardless boys were dancing; women and girls were dancing; many an old bag of bones threw a caper, not falling behind in the least, kicking their legs out from under their short skirts, nimble and graceful as young maidens. No one at all looked tired and worn out; no one felt how warm it was. The crowd of harvesters made up an odd little troop of people, and the flaxfield itself was barely more than a pale gray patch on the floor of the wide valley; but left entirely to their own enjoyment, they thought of nothing else, unaware of what existed beyond the field and lived farther around them—or that an end would come, a stop to their rejoicing. Intoxication filled their every thought and movement; the whole area reaching as high as the sky, as far as the stretching curve of the horizon, was charged with their exultation, expressed in song and gesture.

They relaxed awhile after this prelude—boys and girls clustered together on the smooth ground, drinking from the bottle that was continually passed around. But the rest was broken up fairly soon, the young folk all standing ready once more, eager to go on with the show. The older ones explained the pattern, humming the melody, and separated the boys from the girls, each to their place. They arranged it with great deliberation, giving orders and assigning everyone a position. The signal was then given for the second dance.

The girls moved toward the boys all in a row, hands on their hips and swaying, and the round dance started, a traditional rite. In measured step, with a natural swing of the body and arms, the rows turned, the couples changing and regrouping and coming apart again after each meeting, while everyone sang in rhythm to the movement. The old women wailed the loudest, with the intention of keeping the whole thing in good order. Everyone knew where to go and what to do, performing without falter, without roughness or unrestrained fervor, in courteous and graceful turns. They stood two by two, divided into foursomes, in double rows, changing from group to group in continual to-and-fro, each boy leading his girl through the crossover of the dance-game, arms arched over their heads, hand in hand or tips of the fingers touching.

At a signal, the formations slackened, couples parting—girls from their lovers—lightly falling back with graceful bows, heads nodding, and curtsies, in time to a song that spun on and on:

Tear not my apron, Trientje dear,
It's my best one—have a care.
If you tear it, then you'll sew it,
If you're angry, then you'll rue it—
Your lover's leaving? Shed no tear.

As the rows come closer again, the girls gaze flirtatiously and hold their aprons open by the tips like little tables . . . But the seductive smile, which seems meant as an invitation, is feigned: barely has the girl touched the boy's fingers with a haughty gesture than she skips away out of his grasp, light as a doe, and stands once more at a distance on the far side, smirking. The song now sounds like an oracle spouting wisdom:

> Who's e'er afraid of the burr
> Into the woods can't go.
> Whose maidenhead is sure
> Along with the boys won't go.

Suddenly, the girls go back on their resolve: they come forward in unison, prettily kicking their legs outward, in a dainty step in measure to the new melody:

> A solo, little lady—
> Stand aside;
> Look at me
>   Little lady!

The boys mimic the girls, standing straight across from them with their hands on their hips:

> My vis-à-vis,
> Come to me;

Look at me
  My Molly!

The eyes send a challenge, the lips smile flattery.
They can no longer deny one another, and their
lament rises in unanimous song:

Oh! such suffering
Oh! such suffering
The men have got!

And the boys repeat like an echo:

Oh! such suffering
The women've got!

The round starts up again, while they push back
and forth:

Aren't we allowed then
To give a little kiss—
We'd all be lechers here, you see!

And then with a devilish jump, at a given signal
they fly against one other, forming a dense, tangled
clump, a cluster, a whirling mass shouting over and
over again:

      Around, around, the round is here!
      Around, around, the round is here!

> Around, around, the round
> Of pleasure!

The words get lost in unrestrained noise and mad leaping. And when the furor has spent itself, the round dance starts up again as calmly as the start, following another pattern. A single voice strikes up the opening song in the tone of a genial tale:

> Pepperball ran into me
> His beard as white as flax.
> Who the devil would have thought
> That Pepperball was back?

All the while during the sporting, the farmer goes around with the bottle. The harvesters drink and dance on and on, and now that evening has fallen and it grows dark all around, the playing keeps on as if never coming to an end. But the drink takes effect, and when they once again reach

> oily-oil in it!

it reverberates without respect for the evening, so peaceful, so filled with solemnity—their shouting a challenge, wanting to profane the stillness. They bragged of the fun, punch-drunk with wantonness. The harvesters will not give up yet—they will dance and rave until they drop.

Later the exuberant, boundless joy rises so high that it is no longer expressed in words, and then everything is lost in the concerted, resonant shouting, with long-drawn-out meaningless tones: a thundering *oaeee!* without end.

Then the bell in the farmyard rings its message: the harvest pudding is ready. The news is greeted with unanimous cheering; the harvesters lift up the may, light the candles, and the crowd spreads itself out, arm in arm, across the whole width of the flaxfield. The farmer lets himself be dragged along in the middle. The shining may up front, the group starts a new song for leave-taking:

Ah Rosalie, my prettiest little friend!
I'm the one who loves you truly without end:
If only you would let me have one kiss!
You stand forever in my longing's bliss!

The tiny candle flames flicker amid the clustered flowers wavering up ahead, and the crowd follows with sturdy step and vanishes in the evening shadows. The singing becomes indistinct in the distance, fading away, even as they beat their clogs together in time:

The farmer took his cane,
The clock struck nine again,
He made his final round!
And the hands were going
    plik, plok, plak!
And the feet were going
    trik, trok, trak!

He was a man of many years
  His poor legs hanging slack
    from his back!

Shortly afterward, you could hear nothing except for a whoop now and then and some stray jabbering from where Sobrie's farm stood hidden in the dark.

Vermeulen's laborers had waited on the field all along, throughout the whole course of the country festival. Only now did Louis get up and join them, seemingly calm and content.

"The flax's . . . harvested," he said with a quiet laugh under his breath. "Come on, friends, it's about that time. Let's go."

"Wouldn't you say that there's a change in the weather, Poortere?" he asked as they walked off.

The old groom looked inquiringly at the sky.

"The stars are out . . . but the wind's shifted, and it's sultry on the horizon."

"The heat was too strong."

"It was unbearable today."

"That wasn't heat, but fire!" some added here and there.

"I guess it'd be best if tomorrow we start harvesting too," Louis said.

"A thunderstorm can very likely come after such heat," Huybrechts, a hired man, claimed. The others said nothing, but no one looked up surprised or wondered at the young farmer's sudden decision. And Louis himself did not consider for a moment that there could be a hindrance. Having witnessed that one celebration, his head was so filled with it that he thought, since it was now over at Sobrie's, they too were entitled to demand their right—immediately—and have their share in the general excitement of the flax festival without delay.

"Schellebelle," he said, "would you go over and ask the people at Sobrie's for tomorrow? You're not afraid, are you?"

"Me afraid?" the girl reacted, jumping up. "Should the whole crowd come? I'm off already! For tomorrow morning, right?"

"The whole crowd. We'll fall to it at three tomorrow morning."

"Should I say it was you who asked?"

"Say it was me," Louis ordered, resolutely.

Happy as a bird set free, in three leaps the girl was up and away across the field and lost in the darkness. Louis returned home with the others.

"What in the world keeps you out so late?" the farmer's wife shouted at them from the gate. "Here I am sitting with my food and look, it's black as hell and past nine!"

"We worked to get it all done, Mother," Louis said, "and then we stood and watched awhile: it was harvest home at Sobrie's." And, with another word:

"We'll go to it also, Mother, tomorrow morning: there's a storm brewing in the sky—I asked the whole crowd—they're coming here from Sobrie's."

The farmer's wife was glad in her heart, her son's intention coinciding with her husband's own decision. Early in the evening, Vermeulen had declared that he feared a thunderstorm: the blue mud flats were giving off damp; the peacock had sat on the barn all evening, screeching for rain; and the farmer had noticed how the ducks plopped and tumbled into the moat, how the frogs were making such a thorough racket—and so he had decided to go ahead with the flax. So it was that Louis, with his bold stand and personal arrangements, did not immediately make the storm that threatened outside break loose in the house.

"Who's taking care of getting the people, Louis?" the farmer's wife asked.

"I sent Schellebelle, Mother."

"Then we won't be seeing that silly freak again for the next half hour," the woman said. "Just clear her portion away, Sophie. Schellebelle's sure to get her bellyful of harvest pudding over there. And you young folks, get yourselves to bed now, quick—it'll be an early day tomorrow if the weather's good."

It was already late when Schellebelle came home again; she saw no lights on. "Quiet!" she called to the dogs and opened the house door carefully. She found everything empty and cleared away and hurried to bed—without a thought for the evening meal, having tasted harvest pudding for the first time in her life. She felt her cheeks aglow, and long after she lay under the blankets, the noise and commotion, the wild swarm of drunken harvesters with their clamor and shouting hammered and milled through her head, as if she were still on the go with that crazy bunch. She could see the wild dancing in the yard under the linden trees and the long table with the huge tureens full of harvest pudding. The pleasure, come so unexpectedly, had overwhelmed her. But all the fun she had seen and experienced was nothing compared to the prospect of what lay in store for her: it would be happening here tomorrow . . . with Louis nearby!!! Her longing and her intense eagerness were becoming reality now, and the girl could see no end to her happiness.

III

With the breaking of the first morning light, Louis was already up and searching the sky. He crossed the yard, then went out of the gate over the bridge and a short way down the lane to see if anyone was coming. The air was mild—not a trace of rain or storm. The white ducklings paddled around and beat their wings on the moat water; the ganders gave their grating cry in the morning stillness. In the chicken house, the roosters too were already awake, crowing bravely and undaunted in the dark of their sleeping space close to the hens. The farm dogs were still asleep, and it was perfectly quiet in the stable. Damp ground fog hovered over the earth in a blue vapor, a curtain that closed off the distance, enshrouding the nearby trees and making their green tops look like shapeless banks of clouds. The stench of retting water fouled the air. Louis sharpened his hearing toward the east, where he thought he had picked out a voice. The clock on the village tower struck two—muffled chimes thudding in the silence, feebly, as from a well.

After that, Louis was not in doubt any longer: the sound of voices was unmistakably coming closer—he heard cackling and calls rising in the distance, and at the end of the lane, he made out a clustered mass darker than the fog. He then went to the quarters where his people slept and in a loud voice shouted the farmhands and maids awake. The farmer's wife and her housekeeper were busily at work inside; Vermeulen himself came barefoot down the attic stairs and stepped into his clogs outside. You did not have to ask who had arrived: there stood the harvesters—though tired from work and celebrating far into the night—fresh again, prattling cheerfully, ready to start in once more. They were there in full strength: the hedgemakers—Houttekiet, Schaefel, Plancke, Wulleman, and Palinck; the harvesters—the girls and boys, even Wantje Krake, that old bag of bones, and the women with small children in their arms—the whole crowd gathered in the yard, their antics disturbing the rare calm of the morning hour. They chattered among themselves about the weather, about the fun they had had yesterday, not holding themselves in check when Vermeulen, his usual grumpy self after waking, came by to keep an eye on things. The farmer's wife called out for coffee, and the crowd stormed into the kitchen, quickly wolfing down breakfast in the dim light. After that, they hurriedly left the farmstead. The girls went first, arm in arm, talking loudly in the lane, knocking their clogs together to imitate the sound of quails. The women and grown men followed slowly, walking in a friendly knot, all at the same pace, exuberant and full of spirit, eager to get down to work and enjoy the fun.

While Louis was setting out with the bottles of gin, he already heard the first phrases of the harvest song drifting from afar, and when he appeared at the flaxfield, the harvesters were joining in the round dance. He felt something loosening in his heart, the song sounding more his own now that he knew he was the foreman of the group. It was just like when he was still a child, and after long anticipation he had watched the dawn of the morning of the fair—he observed the dancing now with the same emotion with which he had then looked at the merry-go-round revolving at the fairgrounds, and it promised him the same delights, but much more intensely so. The excitement made his whole body tremble. He waved the bottles in the air triumphantly and hollered aloud:

"Are we harvesting Vermeulen's flaxfield?"

"Ye-e-es!!" the concerted shout of joy came in answer.

The round dance took up again with greater energy, and the "oily-oil in it!" rang out louder.

They fell to work vigorously after drinking the sugared gin. Louis himself, who only had to be there to keep an eye on the harvesting, jumped into line and managed, too, to hold his own. And so they worked for quite some time in the coolness of the early morning, enveloped in blue veils of mist, alone in the general silence of the world. Fresh dew dripped from the stalks, and every time the harvesters swung their handfuls up under their arms, they spattered the wetness against each other's bodies in heavy drops. The flax reached above their knees, and the work became more a diversion when, sprinkling the dew intentionally, it sprayed over their heads like a cool rain. The men's shirts and pants—still sweaty from yesterday—were soon drenched; the girls stood laughing, their wet skirts clinging to their legs and the light clothes on their bodies stuck to their skin. The drops lay like pearls in their disheveled hair, and the water glistened all over their blushing faces as if they had crawled fresh out of the bath. They made it into a little game: who could sprinkle the farthest and the most with the wet tuft. They aimed their swings to catch each other in the face, all the while harvesting ever more quickly and competitively, so as to keep the sport livelier. The girls gave Louis his share of it: apparently, they were out to get him—he stood sopping wet and had to keep his guard up left and right to hold the roguish things at a distance.

But the sun rose stately above the crest of the horizon; it began to glitter through the blue fog, with as many rays of light as drops trickling from the flax. A flood of purest red surged from the east down across the valley; for a while, veils of gold turned and twisted in confusion, reds and blues in a mishmash, losing their color and finally vanishing, until the distance was eventually swept clear. And one two three, the warmth, which was starting to burn, had sucked up all the moisture. The heat came flaming from the sky as fiercely as the day before. As the sun climbed higher, the damp clothes dried on the bodies of the harvesters and the flax they were handling grew parched, just like the soil beneath their bare feet. The coolness of the dewdrops gradually gave way to beads of sweat.

"I don't trust it," Houttekiet remarked. "It's going to start burning again too strong. There's not a breath of wind."

The sky remained eyebright. The sun's living fire beat down from the roof of the heavens, and before half the morning was gone, the harvesters, standing bent over their work, found it hard to draw a breath.

Louis and the others took no break, working on and conversing with those next to them or for all to hear, while the birds carried on above their heads. Jokes went around, they teased each other, and there was talk about harvesting in the old days, comparing the fun then and now. Then old Wantje lifted her head:

"Wet with dew at morn, wet with sweat at noon . . . and wet with rain at night."

But the others mocked the bent crone's words:

"It can't rain, I've given my orders!" Louis shouted in reckless defiance.

"It'd finish off the harvest!"

"And so much for our fun!"

"The worst of it is," Houttekiet put in, "the weather often stays unsettled after a thunderstorm."

"Sure, there's a lot of fine flax out there, and it's stayed standing all summer, but that's not saying it'll get inside while it's green—it could just as soon turn black before it's stacked," Plancke claimed philosophically.

"Damn, that'd be some luck, and all our fun spoiled!" So it came from all sides.

"It can't rain," the farmer's son shouted once more. "The sky's dried up!"

The noon bell rang sooner than anyone was expecting it. The harvesters walked hurriedly to the farm to eat and afterward whiled away the noon hour as they pleased—scuffling, or napping somewhere in the hay.

It was during the noon break that Vermeulen noticed the weather was starting to change. He walked away, turned and looked in all directions, and shook his head. Going back inside the house, he growled something under his breath and kept stamping around the kitchen, moving from one window to the other.

"I think we're getting a thunderstorm," he told his wife who, oppressed by the fierce heat, stood puffing by the hearth, pouring boiling water into the coffeepot.

"If it could just wait until we've finished harvesting!" she ventured to say.

"Wait," Vermeulen snarled. "If it had to wait, you'd go a lifetime without a storm: it's always bad for somebody."

"It'll blow over yet," she hoped. "It'd be such a pity otherwise, now that the flax's almost in and it's been spared all summer."

She went outside in turn to look and see what there was to be apprehensive about. But from where she stood in the doorway, Barbele did not see the gathering towers of thunderclouds rising up on the eastern horizon, did not become aware of the harm that was beginning to menace from that direction, and so she returned inside, reassured.

The harvesters first saw it when they came out onto the open field again: the black monstrous clouds were piling up defiantly, the dark mass obscuring the whole sky. But even so, they danced and sang the harvest song as loud as ever, as though confident there was nothing to fear. After the dance, they went back to work and did not watch what was happening overhead. Louis was busy too, gathering intently alongside the maids, who were chattering and laughing as hard as they could—when Vermeulen appeared on the path and came over to look at the harvesters. He examined the handfuls lying spread on the ground and walked among the positioned hedgerows. He picked out a few stalks, felt them, looked at the flax close up, rubbed off the bast between his fingers, and pulled to test the strength of the fibers.

He was not pleased with Louis' helping with the work, and before going away he said curtly:

"If it starts to rain, stop the harvest at once."

Louis, just straightening himself up to even out a handful of flax, looked at his father, surprised. As the young man stood there, his face bright red and sweaty, with excitement in his flashing glance, he was like a light-hearted fighter who knows no fear, who recklessly goes his own way, who has it in his power to bend everything to his will.

"Rain!" he exclaimed. "Who's talking about rain? It's not allowed to rain before we've had our celebration! I mean it! We'll bring in the flax undamaged, Father," he added in a mild tone. He thought nothing in the world was capable of interfering with the intended fun of their fast-approaching flax festival.

"Right, men?" he laughed when Vermeulen was gone. "It's not allowed to rain?"

"It's not allowed to rain!" they shouted. And in way of confirming the defiant shout, they struck up a song:

And the little flax
Growing up so soon . . .

Vermeulen heard it as he walked past his wheatfields. Meanwhile, with increasing rapidity, mountains of clouds came together from all directions. They floated on the sunny side, shining with rounded cheeks, like downy silver wool; they sailed and rolled as white as light sprays of foam. They resembled smoothed mounds of fresh snow, with gaps where the joyous blue of the heavens shone through. The highest clouds hovered in a sky of untouched purity, following their own paths undisturbed. Heavier ones drifted lower down in the opposite direction, like laden airships, in a brilliance of white, blue, and fiery gold. And way below sat the bulky, gray mountains of clouds, like heaped stones—the whole awesome mass swelling and expanding, peaking to towers of thunderheads that threatened to swallow the sun with their dragonlike maws. The destructive menace seemed to rise up out of the earth: it was spewed forth from somewhere beyond the horizon, a new bank continually rolling in from the distance, heavy as lead, formidable in its great expanse. Around and around stretched the circle where the high-reaching towers settled. Up there, in space, the wind had to be blowing violently. It lifted all the monstrous clouds, driving and turning them around, smashing them together into smithereens. Before its breath, the airships flew with sails taut as inflated bladders. It heaved their weight upward, hoisting them one above the other like a miller piles his sacks—and then dashed the whole lot down again in a heap. It thrust straight up sheer high towers and drove them into each other like horned heads ramming. And it let them slide apart and blow away, reforming in brilliant colors whipped to a boiling foam.

But the gusting and buffeting in the higher regions of the sky went on soundlessly, without a noise, and down here you were not aware of the great upheaval in the dome of the heavens. Not a leaf stirred. The wind held its breath under the oppressive, heavy-laden heat—everything seemed in fearful expectation of what was sure to come and was on its way. High up, all the chaos merged into immense

blocks, anchored shapes too cumbrous now to roll or
move. The sun's rays thrust their spears through
narrow gaps, until heavier masses were hauled in,
and the mountainous clouds formed new tops
soaring upward, filling all the breaches; the sun itself
remained hidden, concealed behind the thick
curtain, and the whole world lay obscured under the
gray hood that threatened to cover over and smother
everything. Would, suddenly, evening come, would it
now turn dark? Across the whole expanse of the sky,
with its yawning depths below and white-peaked
upswellings, there was not a single gap left where the
day's brightness could seep through. Every living
thing outside was seized by fear and terror. The birds
fled in entire droves, screeching in alarm. A dull
rumble thudded out of the darkness in the west, as if
the hounds of heaven were growling, and the sky
shook all over like a heavy cart that comes
lumbering on clumsy wheels. The trees themselves
seemed motionless and dark, as if waiting for
judgment, and a breath rushed over the whole sea of
grain, flax, and potatoes, making the stalks and
foliage quiver. And what would become of those
stands of fragile crops?

The harvesters held still and looked at one
another. Over there, people were running like
fugitives off the field toward home, leaving
everything behind. The girls were silent; they held
their fluttering hair down in the back and turned to
the men, with fear in their eyes, to find out what
they should do. The wind came on, you could see it

coming—driving the sand off the roads wherever it passed. It rolled down the slope, shaking trees and shrubs of alder, wheeling through fields of grain and flax, sweeping on to the thicket of oak, which it rode through with a dull sigh and raced up the further slope. Then, all around, everything was still once more, and the anxious waiting resumed for what now inevitably had to come.

The harvesters started up work again, since the young farmer gave no sign of leaving the field; he himself worked on and would not believe that the hurricane overhead was ready to break. He harvested without looking up and encouraged the girls, who were getting jumpy, laughing at their skittish alarm.

"Are you afraid of the thunder?" he scoffed. "It's just some noise! Siska, sing a song!"

No sooner had he finished than the sky—before it was expected—was rent from end to end, and fire flashed out as from the mouth of an oven. At the same time, a tremendous thunderclap cracked and crashed and trailed off, growling roughly, through the clouds. A fresh gust of wind brought the first drops of rain. They flashed down slantwise, heavy as marbles. That was just the beginning. A second bolt of lightning, followed instantly by a heavier crack of thunder, rumbled across the sky. Then the water came pouring down in sheets, rushing in streaming spurts like a river, so violently that it cut hissing through the air, foaming over the ground. After that came hailstones by the tons, thick as grits and white, drumming and dancing like bouncing beads against the dry, hardened ground.

The girls were shrieking now, giving out loud cries, and raced to the thicket at a clip, their skirts thrown over their heads as hoods. They found cover there under the close branches of the oaks, brushed the water from their clothes, and nestled deep in the ferns and moss. The men, too, could not take it any longer. They dropped everything, sped away from the flaxfield head over heels, and reached the foliage at the edge of the trees, where they witnessed the destruction taking place before their eyes. The wind tumbled through the wood, crashed and soughed. The falling water splashed, rushing, spraying thick jets with clouds of drizzle that whipped along the ground and filled the atmosphere with a hazy mist. The sky slammed open and shut repeatedly: swift lightning hurled time after time like the throw of a golden dart. Jolting peals of thunder shook alike with heavy rumbles and droning, so that the universe quaked at each new blow.

The stillness and the beautiful course of the smooth summer days had gone on so long and the furious turbulence came so unexpectedly that everyone stood looking at it, shaken and undone. The flax which had grown and ripened for all that time, without deformity and undisturbed in the peaceful, caressing air, was now caught on the very last day—mangled, battered, and flung around, defenseless before the might of a wind that suddenly seemed crazed and enraged, as if wanting to lay it entirely to waste. In half an hour's time, all the fair splendor of summer was thrashed to pieces and strewn, without a hand being lifted that could prevent the catastrophe. All at once, the harvesters' excitement cooled—so deeply did they feel the pity of it, silently lamenting the farmer's bad luck. The men stood with their vests over their heads and shoulders, their bare arms crossed, gazing steadily into the distance. With each new gust of wind and whenever streams of rain hissed down with fresh violence, the flax beaten to the ground left and right, a general sound of wailing, a drawn-out oooh!, came from the group. Louis alone neither cursed nor complained; he remained cheerful and kept up his spirit. The disaster affected him worse than the others, but he saw through the situation and argued on the bright side:

"It'll be a little harder to harvest, but we'll get it in undamaged all the same," he said. "It'd be worse if it still had another month to grow in the field. There's no worry now about its rotting."

"You don't have it in yet!" one of the hands pointed out.

"Go on, it won't keep raining. The air'll be cleared tomorrow," Louis insisted. "We'll have good weather again."

The horror of the terrible squall awakened admiration in him rather than compassion or regret. He stood motionless and watched the violence with wide-open eyes, paying more attention to the thunderclaps than to the devastated crops. He saw the whole valley, from above to below, the whole atmosphere filled with peaks of clouds and drizzle. He followed the hurling lightning flashes in the distance, and he watched, trembling with fear because of that dreadful grandeur, how the cruel, monstrous clouds came in from different directions, how they sailed toward each other and smashed to fragments. He took pleasure in it: it thrilled him to see clusters of them split open and torn to shreds, rolling and wheeling in boiling eddies, surging up again in fresh towering pillars and standing upright as before, to build toward a new collision. To him, the resounding thunderclaps and erratic shaking were a delight. Never before had he seen from so close up the unleashing of the ubiquitous elements in their reckless violence; his eyes were unwavering, his nostrils quivered, and he breathed in and out with difficulty. He felt a new and glorious pleasure deep inside: he had seen something great and grand, something that made everything on the face of the earth seem an accidental trifle and of little account, himself and all men with their fancies and intentions, opinions and arrangements—farms and fields, goods and pride. The entire human dominion now appeared a poor little enterprise: everything sticking up anywhere from the flat ground lay in terror before the ferocious barking of the hounds of heaven. Louis knew that he alone had no fear, let everything hail down around him—he felt himself standing outside of it. Rather, it awakened his satisfaction, seeing that the prospects for all those

tough, determined farmers, their perfect expectations
of a good yield, had at one stroke miscarried and
come to nothing; seeing that all the property, all the
wealth and finery in which people had set the whole
of their pride, as if they themselves had created
them—all these things were wrecked, beaten by one
sweeping breath of strong wind, pulverized and
befouled, broken and brought low. . . . Louis longed
for only one thing more that was still missing: a
spark from that heavenly fire ought to come
shooting down onto the straw roof of some
farmstead or other, so that a huge bonfire—brightness, flames, and smoke—something of the wonder
of that beautiful storm would remain afterward on
the earth as evidence of all that raging and tempest
in the sky. That would be something to see from up
here! And he already imagined everyone running,
the shouting and horrible confusion among the
men—the commotion in the valley otherwise so
calm.

Snakes of lightning still bored tunnels in the
clouds, but the thudding and the crackling followed
at greater intervals after each flash. A fresh wind
arose, blowing in the opposite direction, making
gaps and great bright areas in the sky. The
turbulence gradually stilled, the rain diminished to a
calm rustle, plashing the canopy of leaves on the
trees; there was a gentle sighing now in the cleared
air, and streams of water glistened like threads of
glass in the glint of sun. Thunder rolled on in the
distance—exhaustion seemed to have set in, a respite

from the force of the elements: the danger had passed, and the men gathered to talk. The shy girls felt ashamed of their timidity, and none wanted to admit she had been afraid. They began to laugh and tease each other where they sat under the hoods of their skirts, protected against the rain but with tresses of hair stuck to their wet faces, drenched in their underwear and staying hidden as deeply as possible among the ferns. Louis enjoyed watching them sitting there, bashful and huddled together, not daring to move, and he heartily joined in the teasing.

Then Krako, the lame stablehand, came limping across the flaxfield. He stood there with a sack apron over his head, peering out to see where the crowd of harvesters had gone. When he heard the noise and shouting from the edge of the wood and made out the men in the thicket, he called out from afar:

"The farmer says you can't come in soon enough!"

"Say we're sitting here nice and dry!" Louis shouted back.

But when they heard this and saw a chance to disappear, the girls jumped up in a wink, and before Louis could hold any of them back, they all fled, wet as they were, without a thought to their sad state. With underskirts or shifts sticking to their legs, skirts up covering their shoulders and bodies, they ran in a flock, squealing in shyness—afraid of but wanting to be pursued. They splashed on with bare feet through the wet clover, down the fields, straight to the farm.

"Hurrah! Here we come!" Louis yelled. All the

harvesters were now caught up in the chase. Here and there, one of the fleeing does was overtaken, gripped at the waist by two strong arms, tumbled upside down, and spun around. Cawing like frightened magpies, the group sped on. They plunged through mud puddles and pools; they leaped across ditches full to overflowing that carried the bubbling, light water away—and smeared and splattered above their ears, red with flurry, the girls reached the farm, the young men right behind, and fled into the open barn, allowing themselves to be caught and pawed, and there they remained to fool around.

It mortified Louis that he was not allowed to join them there to take part in the fun and the dalliance. Now at last, he felt sorry the harvest and the work in the field had been interrupted by the storm. He was nagged and obsessed by desire, having grown attached to what he had been living with and could no longer do without: the smiling glances of roguish, challenging eyes; the blushing faces, fresh as the morning dew; the lithe, firmly shaped bodies, bursting with ripeness and health; the delicateness of slender limbs, the pert swing of the hips above springy thighs; the mystery of flowering youth, delineating everywhere trim figures under scant, light clothes. . . . He knew them all, those lovely girls, and passion went reeling to his head, drunkenly, while he—the respectable farmer's son—was forced to stifle his displeasure in solitary, there in the damp close kitchen, and sit staring outside. In his imagination, he enjoyed himself in their fast, carefree activity and catlike games, all the while ridden by the desire to grasp and grapple in the center of the press. His mother and the housekeeper sat wailing and moaning about the calamitous destruction, but for him there was only his petty anxiety: what would happen with the harvest and the flax festival, upon which all his longing was fixed. He had not the least fear, as yet, that that single rainstorm could spoil the show.

"No one can leave the farm!" he had ordered. In his mind, he intended to resume work as quickly as possible, and what difference if the stuff was a little bit wet?

Vermeulen stood like a man of oak, his head against the windowframe, sullenly staring outside. His tawny face looked gloomy, with his eyebrows lowered. The slit of his mouth, a single line amid the stubble on his unshaven lips, was turned down at either end and continued in two straight wrinkles that ran up along his cheeks, from the corners of his eyes to his chin, cutting deeply into his darkened skin. When Louis came in, the farmer had not moved a finger to ask what had happened to the flax. He remained standing, looking at the spewing and bubbling that seethed at the surface of the black cesspool water with the splash of each raindrop. His fixed stare followed the spillage from the straw awning in front of the window. And when the rain seemed light enough to him and the sky to be clearing more and more, he pulled on his shoes, took his walking stick from the room, and went out the door to inspect the crops.

A strange mist, a fresh blueness hung over the whole region. Color was brightened, everything seemed more sharply outlined and drawn against the deep field of vision. The air was clean and beneficial to the lungs, like a cool drink. Dust had been washed from the leaves and greenery, and the foliage shone in lush coloring. Runnels were cut in the sand on the roads, and the rainwater rippled in the ditches alongside and gurgled through the drainpipes at every crossing. In the joyous blue of the sky's expanse, the clouds sat fluted and ruffled like white feathers, quieted and calm. The sun looked like gold, and above the low ploughland, vapors with the strong smell of damp vegetation rose from the soaking ground. Peace seemed restored everywhere, and viewed superficially, there was little to be seen of the dreadful destruction; it was as if the thunderstorm had been merely a threat, turned away in time and swept elsewhere, without leaving any bad effects behind.

The first thing that struck Vermeulen, however, was the spaciousness of the whole countryside—there was nothing left standing to obstruct a general overview of the fields, just like after the harvest. His corn, which at noon had still reached half as high as a man, now lay leveled as smooth as a bowling lane; the stalks had been driven flat against the ground, all in the same direction, never to rise again. The potato field had suffered as much damage from the wind and the hail, and the ground clover had been broken up and flung around helter-skelter. The farmer walked on farther past his clover patch toward his vast wheatfields, and everything there too lay flattened by the wind, beaten by the rain and hail that had descended upon it, until the fine, healthy stalks, which had stood swaying so supplely in the light summer wind, succumbed; snapped in their slender length, they were strewn along the ground, lifeless, without movement. The undulant oats with their bells had been hit as well, demolished. But Vermeulen's real anxiety, his greatest fear, was to see how the flax had held up.

"If only it's fallen evenly and gets dry weather," the farmer speculated, and he walked over to find out the answer. He was startled by what his eyes saw immediately he reached the heights and had the stretch before him. He had not expected it to be that bad! Here on the crest, the wind had whirled and churned, wreaking havoc like a raging fool. The stalks lay scattered left and right like a tousled mop of hair. Not one stem remained sound. All of it lay crookedly and mashed flat, as if the storm's anger, the hurricane's blind violence, had left its special mark behind just here on the velvety green fleece that had stood swaying delicately the whole summer long, smooth as silk, without upheaval. It was a total ruin now, from top to bottom—the smooth green surface transformed into a wild, surging ocean with rough seas.

Vermeulen walked along the outer edges, stepping

between the hedgerows that had been blown down. He did not sigh or make an outcry of any kind. Not a muscle of his face moved, though he stood there all by himself. But anger and frustration rumbled inside. His powerlessness against the violence of the heavens humiliated his proud heart; yet he did not want to admit to his impotence, preferring to swallow back his displeasure, even though he felt deeply shaken by the catastrophe. Wherever he turned his eyes, there was complete destruction; it surely seemed like a punishment, as if the whole glorious summer palace—that beautiful, long row of days—had been toppled and crushed all at once by the tempest, as if what had needed such a long time to mature had been smashed to bits with a single blow. A frugal farmer, Vermeulen felt how pitiable the incalculable damage, all that work lost, and he cursed that stupid accident whose necessity no one understood and which could bring no benefit to anybody.

He turned back along the paths that led to the low ground and found his other oatfield virtually unscathed, protected by its advantageous position and kept safe from the wind. And the farmer who had not uttered a sound when surveying the extent of his bad luck now let fly a curse: the oats' undamaged condition would show him in the wrong before the hired folk, before the whole world, and only prove that his plan had been unwise. Back home, he asked his wife straight off:

"Why didn't you send the harvesters home?"

She pushed the blame on Louis and said:

"It could be dry tomorrow, and then we could go on . . ."

"It won't dry out in even a week," he snapped harshly.

Louis said: "Is it that bad?"

"It's lying flat."

"If only we'd sold it," his wife ventured.

The farmer raised his eyebrows.

"We ourselves," he said, "can bear the loss just as well as the dealer."

With that, he kicked off his wet shoes, flung them wherever they would go, and stepped into his clogs. He was on the way outside to give his own orders for what he wanted to see done, but he bumped into two buyers in the doorway, old acquaintances who got down to business without delay. They were still full of the mass destruction and were wet themselves through as well, having been caught in the downpour.

"Still any flax for sale?" the dealer named Baekeland asked.

"Yes," Vermeulen said. "How come you're passing through here so late? I like to sell to people I know."

The reason they gave was that they had been working Walloon country and were just now coming back this way.

"How many hundreds have you got standing, farmer?"

"Standing? I've got nothing left 'standing,' it's 'lying.' Everything still for sale is 'lying'—flat," he snapped at them.

One of the buyers laughed, the other nodded gravely and said:

"That we can guess, farmer. How much for what you've got 'lying'?"

"Have you seen the flax?"

"We're just coming from there."

"A hundred for a hundred."

"If it'd been like it was this morning," Baekeland remarked, "your flaxfield would've been worth something, and I'd even have offered a third more. And I'd still be willing to if the flax were stacked dry."

"Take it or leave it," Vermeulen said.

"Done then, if you guarantee it'll be delivered with its color still green."

"You think I'd let the flax go bad?" Vermeulen shouted.

"Do you know if it won't rain for the next two weeks solid?" the buyer asked. "It could rot on the field! Are you willing to risk that, farmer?"

"That's some way to do business. The flax's lying there—if you want, buy it!"

"I'll give you eighty francs. How much is there?"

"Forty hundreds."

"Done then?"

"Ninety."

The buyer shook his head: no. "It'll be hard to harvest, and the risk's too high. I'll give you eighty."

"Good luck!" Vermeulen grumbled, and he slapped his hand in the open palm Baekeland stretched out to him.

"To be delivered when I ask for it," the buyer stipulated. "Payment on delivery."

"We know each other," Vermeulen said. And by a simple agreement, the important deal was struck, without anything signed or put into writing.

"We sold one day too late," the farmer's wife concluded when the men had left.

"Don't go on about it," said the farmer.

Louis came back in after the matter was settled. Learning of the sale and the price, he pretended indifference and said not a word about it.

IV

The next morning woke with a quiet laugh, clearness hanging over the land from the first like a white blossom. Everything had turned peaceful again, nature having taken on its calm, immovable appearance once more. A hazy silver mist wound across the undulating lines of the fields and covered the destruction of the crops with a light veil. Translucent nearby, the mist shrouded what lay in the distance, over which was spread an air of tranquility. The cuckoo called, the lark soared singing to the heavens, and the swallows paddled through the pure blue of the windless sky. The glittering sun rose in all its power, flooding a newly created world with light in a radiance of brilliant colors. The morning seemed the start of a fresh sequence of stable summer days.

Vermeulen had lain sleepless all night. The sudden change in the weather, with the destruction of his crops, had taken him down a peg. The whole scheme had turned out wrong—with the damage and then the loss of what had been spared all summer and so very nearly converted into cash. It made him irritable to stand staring like an idiot at what had been knocked from his paws so unexpectedly; he cursed the fact that he had to knuckle under to an alien force that had come riding over his head, destroying his finished work at one stroke. It was not so much the damage as that damned flaxfield, which had now cost him all that bad blood and, the very day of the harvest, made him realize his wrong move.

And that it had to coincide exactly with the offering and sale of Legijn's farm, which already had been announced for a month, helped make his fretful mood ever worse. In this at least he could carry out his authority, force matters according to his will—but ever since that row with his wife, Vermeulen had been unable to make peace with himself. His stubbornness compelled him to act on his decision, but his uneasiness deep inside and his dawdling made him bitter and bad tempered. In a nervous state, he was up before daybreak. The dog blocking his way through the door got an angry kick, and when he saw Louis crossing the yard, he shouted at him in a rusty voice:

"The harvesters can pick up the flax that's been harvested and spread it open to air out! The hedges have to be turned inside out! The women can move the potatoes and clear away the straw in the barn to make room . . . the harvesters can leave at noon—we'll go on when it's dry!"

"Mind your own business, farmer," Louis muttered between his teeth. "We started it, and we'll finish it.

The flax can dry better when it's harvested and made into hedges than when it's lying on the ground, like now."

And not for a moment did it come into the boy's mind to change his plan in any way, that it was possible to interrupt the work or send the harvesters away.

"Father's going off, so I'm the farmer here. Today we harvest and . . . tomorrow we celebrate, devil take it—I'm doing what I want now!"

Vermeulen, meanwhile, sat at the desk in the best room, calculating, gauging his own intentions for one last time. He spread open the circular, counted the lots and copied the numbers, sketching the plan in his notebook, as he did so losing himself in the worries of preparation. It was definite now. His decision was made, and he thought it unnecessary to bandy words about it anymore with his wife. By midmorning he stood washed and shaved, his blue smock over his cloth tail coat, his white shirt collar cracking fresh, and his hat on. He took his heavy walking stick from the clock case, and with the latch of the front door in his hand, he said peremptorily:

"I'm going!"

"God be with you, farmer," his wife said calmly, without asking what was on his mind or what he intended to do at the sale. She supposed Vermeulen was going there for the amusement, since such an auction always attracted many curiosity-seekers, and now especially, with nothing to do in the fields after the rain. He might possibly buy an adjacent plot of ground or meadow, if it were going for a good price. She had surely talked him out of that other thing, for there had not been another word about it since, as if he felt ashamed because of the foolishness of such an idea—on that matter, then, she ought not be uneasy anymore.

Louis was already gone, having left early for the field with the crowd, cheerful and fearless, knowing he was boss, the master of his actions. He felt indifferent to what his father might do at the auction, for he was much too happy to be released from that severe overseer who, out of sheer obstinacy, was always, and only, an obstacle, wanting everything his way.

"Come on, friends! I'm in charge today, and you've got me to deal with! Too bad the farmer's not staying away for a few days—the flax'd be harvested before he got back."

Everyone felt tremendous relief at being free of their surly employer. Good cheer shone from each face; you could hear it in the noisy sound of the voices, the clear laughter. From the way the people moved and behaved you could tell another boss was on the job; with real enjoyment, the harvesters fell to work. Louis felt exultant because of the trust of his workfolk; he came off well as lord and master amid that swarming throng of boys and girls who were so fond of him and regarded him as one of their own. It delighted him to revive the fun, to let himself go among the younger ones. It seemed as if he had been whisked away from all distress; for his benefit, the day had begun like a fair, and he now let his eyes have their fill of what tempted him most. He could no longer contain his merriment—it overpowered him, like a thirst he had to quench, making him give in to an urge he had never satisfied. His love of life broke to the surface, his heart was expansive—for the first time, he felt freedom at one with his happiness.

Among all that femininity, he did not know where to turn his eyes first, how to begin to satisfy his passion. The fresh bloom of their healthy faces, the laughter of their shining eyes and white teeth, the full round shapes of their young supple bodies, alluring under the light cotton—everything aroused his lust, his longing to wrap all those treasures in his arms at once, no matter what, and possess them. He was their superior, above them in rank, but for all that, he stood before them a poor beggar coming to implore a favor—for with their teasing eyes they looked him over, frank and challenging, conscious of the allure of their beauty, the secret temptation of their youth they carried with them as a prize . . . and which neither his money and property nor his high rank could outweigh. He felt shy, clumsy, neither experienced nor bold enough to take what he wanted. And they knew it, the tricksters; they understood the seductive power of their womanly figures, of their calculated gestures, of their irresistible offer of love, with its sidelong glances and gleaming smiles. Beneath their seeming innocence, they concealed the refined art of coquetry and seduction. They did their utmost to excite and confuse the handsome young man, but were always on their guard, ready to jump away, deft and nimble, when he dared to lunge, and mock him for his forwardness. They kept their intention hidden behind exuberant tomfoolery: their voices chirped above the warbling of the birds; they hopped and skipped over the ground like frisky grasshoppers . . . Louis' perceptions became bewildered by it: one was blonde, the other brown-haired; Schellebelle was reddish gold—he found something peculiar to each of them, something that gave out a special charm. It struck him all according to the moment: a blush spreading suddenly across the milk-white down of their faces like a purple flood; a glance from blue or brown eyes, now looking at him roguishly and then with such depth and tenderness that he shuddered, as if happiness itself had overtaken him at that very instant. But when he wanted to seize it, it had already fled from him, and he sat there like an awkward child again, hankering after things he was not allowed to touch.

And he then felt himself the farmer's son who must maintain authority. It awoke in him again that what he was doing was not right; he wanted to tread on other people's ground, where he did not belong. For all their familiarity, he guessed more than he could notice how the schemers were in league together, playing their little game with the son of the manor, appeasing him with a delicate hint of a smile, polishing him off with a false look of love.

Louis then sensed how far he stood outside their world: the friendliness they extended him was a mere semblance—they could not hide that their deeper affection, their full abandon, went out to somebody of their own class. What did they expect of him? What could he give them? Listen how that mockingbird over there, way at the end of the line, was singing a little song as if deliberately to tease the farmer's son about his shyness:

> I quiver like the grass
> When e'er a girl she throws a glance,
> And yet I see them coming, going!
> If there was but a single lass
> Who for my love would now but ask,
> She'd have me for the taking!

There he stood, surrounded by unrestrained and teasing girls, their inferior for all his authority and elevated position—filled with regret because his very rank held him back, while a boy who had nothing at all had only to take his pick of any one of those tantalizing sunflowers and, without scruples or second thoughts, be allowed to make love. He, the gentleman farmer, envied those fellows: they could quite simply give rein to their passions, whereas he himself felt all too keenly how he was merely being tolerated. Fun and games, nothing more. For his part, too, he could not take it in any other way, nor was he supposed to; he admitted he only did it out of levity—because he felt drawn in their direction, and it was in his nature to look for the cheerfulness he could not find elsewhere. The girls played along, slyly letting him carry on, since they could certainly afford to throw off a little something from their abundance of free loving and were never quite satisfied enough with their own fun and games—*that* was really why the farmer's son was allowed his share. Louis knew, however, things would go wrong for him if he dared go a step further, that the lowliest of the working girls would rebuff the "gentleman" and send him off to a rich farmer's daughter, an equal match. After teasing Louis in the field, they would group together in their own circle in the evening, when work was over, and make great fun of the coward they had taken advantage of. Once they were among themselves, beyond his control, he remained an outsider, of another species, of a higher rank. He knew that then not a single one in the whole group thought any more about him. Even Schellebelle with her playful heart, he suspected, was not capable of fixing her affection on him exclusively and for any length of time.

While outwardly he joined in the merriment of the high-spirited crowd, once again the knowledge came over him in a fit of self-torture that he did not belong there, that his playing was not genuine. He now realized clearly there had to be something else that would make him happy—but the world everywhere was strange to him, whatever he thought about, except for the life there on the flaxfield . . . he did not know any wealthy farmer's daughter of his own class. Sobrie's were homely wretches; Poortere's, foolish with pride; Cannaert's, silly idiots for whom he felt nothing—not a single farmer's daughter in the whole region was worth his looking at. He could give neither form nor shape to what he was seeking; wherever he would lay hold of it, it fled before him, leaving his longing unsatisfied. And Schellebelle did not come into consideration at all. Her freshness and her pretty innocence had attracted him—he had set his heart on the girl just to have someone to whom he could pour out his feelings of affection, which weighed on him as such a burden. He wanted pleasure, a good time—nothing more. But his father kept an eye on everything he did; his mother too had already warned him to be discreet and behave more strictly with the workfolk. The two of them were grown old and sedate and found all their fulfillment and happiness in being farmer and farmer's wife. He, on the other hand, was yielding more and more to what had entered him unawares and wanted to come out, without his being able as yet to figure where it had to lead. And when he tried to make it clear to himself in words, once again he said: he wanted to proclaim his youth and now was the time; others were doing it and he would, too, without second thoughts or deliberation—beyond all consideration of good and evil. Why else had he hungered so, longing for the days that had now arrived?

He had in all simplicity envisioned the flax festival as the ultimate pleasure he could experience of

whatever he was now looking for—for he had seen
the same desire blossoming in the girls and boys and
had himself become lost in it with them. Why was it
that now, in the midst of the enjoyment, at the
height of the wonderful activity, he did not find what
he had expected? Why had it not turned out as in
May, when he had not depended on it and his
happiness was undisturbed and beyond doubt,
bright and full? Yesterday's rain had brought
vexation, and now this bad mood came bursting
over him like an angry squall, here in the middle of
the open field, while fun was bubbling up all over
the place. How had that secret urge got into him?
What was this incessant restlessness, always dazzling
him with unknown, dreamy delights? How had it
started? In the spring, all at once, like a flower
opening! But the flower had lost its bloom,
unblemished pleasure having changed to constant
introspection and deep brooding. Louis was aware
now that he lacked an object for his affection and
felt there was no aim to his longing; he had to have
something in his life, something that would hold
true and satisfy him completely . . . he saw
happiness slipping from his hands, and melancholy
over his loneliness flooded his thoughts. To whom
could he go with his affection? On what creature
should he focus his desire? He grieved for the pure
days of his childhood when he was content with his
mother's caresses, when he walked across the fields
holding on to his father's hand, babbling merrily . . .
when the look in his father's eyes caused him utter

happiness. . . . How things had changed since that splendid time! And now he was gnawed by doubt about what might chance to happen, about the precariousness of his decision if his father came and prevented what had become his only comfort. What would he do if Schellebelle was sent away or forbidden to speak to him anymore? He cared for her with all his heart but at the same time was ashamed of the seriousness of his inclination. He could rebel and have his way, carrying on with the girl in secret . . . but his sense of decency recoiled at the idea of doing such a thing. Louis was not afraid of his father, but he imagined his mother's look at the slightest hint of dishonesty and knew he would not be able to suffer her disapproval without losing all respect for himself. She had fostered a deep sense of moral worth in him, an ingrained disposition that until now had kept his strongly sensuous nature under control. He was aware he could not indulge himself without damage to his honor and respect, and he did not want to play the hypocrite or pretend to be what he was not.

Lately, he felt his passion seething more powerfully, an urge awakening in him just to turn loose what he held in restraint with such difficulty. But his strict and solid role as the prominent farmer's son kept him shy and diffident, as if he were a child, and in the midst of play, carried along by his bravado, his uncertainty remained—his fear, ever on the alert, of losing control. And now that things had progressed so far, he had become conscious of his enormous change in heart and followed the steadily growing disorder that dominated his thoughts. Right here, in the enjoyment of what he had desired for so long, it seemed to him a pitiful disillusionment. At the height of the fun, while the maids were cavorting lustily and their happy chattering rang in his ears—here in the full glitter of morning—he stood spinning black thoughts, reliving the melancholy stillness of a summer evening long ago. The memory welled up from deep inside, with no discernible cause, apropos of nothing; he did not know what had been wonderful about that night or why it had come into his mind. But he felt the atmosphere again with his whole being: he smelled the fragrance of the air, and he distinctly heard the singer, hidden somewhere behind an alder brake, holding forth. The song had struck him then as a lament, as lovesickness itself—a cry in the midst of silence, the despair of unsatisfied longing, the disenchantment of someone who has known it all. Louis now applied the feeling to his own plight, out of an unconscious need, a desire to enjoy the sadness that seemed mingled with his happiness. He still remembered the whole rhymed story of "Love Betrayed," and he repeated the sad refrain in his thoughts, as if he himself had been the singer:

> For her eyes of blue
> Deceived me too.
> I loved her with my heart, my all.
> I called her my angel, called her my soul.
> Is she gone forever then?

My own divine Magdalen!

Louis felt his situation was even worse than the betrayed lover's, for the angel he loved was gone without his ever having seen her . . .

And suddenly he was seized by unruly arms and pulled into the circle, dragged along into the dance.

The flax as growing up so soon,
Tops and bottoms we must prune!
  Na-ve-va! Na-ve-va!

With that, the gloom vanished from his mind: there was no longer time to think. He saw the black cloud of his displeasure passing, and at once the sun was shining again across the whole surface of the field, which had been darkened by his outlook—the carefree youth shook off all those serious reflections, letting himself go in the whirl of hilarity that sprayed open like a fountain. This was the harvest, and he ought to enjoy now, fast and free, what he had been yearning for all along. Yesterday's storm had almost put a stop to the goings-on, but the fear was past now. In his rash overconfidence, Louis had permitted the harvest to continue against his father's orders. What harm could it do? Look how the day came blowing in from the east with a mild, light wind. The sky was clear, with white clouds drifting lazily onward in the joyous blue. The damp from the rain was still on the crops, and the smell of lush greenery penetrated everywhere. The view across the valley was much freer now that the grainfields and fodder lay matted.

It became perfectly glorious to be outside in the refreshing coolness after the fearful heat of yesterday's storm. Louis felt his eagerness bursting forth again among the splendor of fresh colors. Everyone who was young surely experienced it the way he did, growing drunk with recklessness—like the wild rider gripping an untamed steed with his legs, galloping up into the mountains, like the intoxicated glutton wanting to guzzle his insatiable thirst, sucking down the air in cool draughts, seeing no end to his bliss.

"What do I care?" the grumbling ran on his mind. He shook off doubt and hesitation as if they were nothing. "I'm here for myself—in this life young and free! One day at a time, take all it can give—whatever's right in your grasp: celebrate the flax festival first thing now and have fun, come what may!" He paid no attention, did not so much as hear it, when Poortere remarked soberly to his sidekick:

"I don't trust this early clearing. If only there's no change so we don't get a rainstorm!"

But the cry of the troop of harvesters drowned out that timorous consideration:

"Are we finishing Vermeulen's flax?"

"Ye-e-es!"

The girls squawked, shrilly, waving their arms and straw hats high. The men repeated the call, their resounding whoop a challenge to whatever would dampen their high spirits. Vermeulen was not there,

and neither Louis nor anyone else bore in mind that
the farmer's orders and stern word stood opposed to
their rash action. Now that they had begun, they
wanted to go on without delay. The sun shone
bright; its light fell across the whole countryside like
a burst of laughter, prompting the harvesters to sing
lustily. The danger of new rain and the prospect of
the end drawing near spurred them on; and now and
then, in between the talking and singing, Louis
experienced a new pleasure—it rushed through his
mind in a flash: he was the proud leader, for the first
time carrying things out his own way, willing to stir
up might against might.

Krako came limping with two full kegs of beer, and
the harvesters drank it in huge draughts, in one gulp
without stopping. After that, they got back into line,
in a long row across the whole field, and set heartily
to work. Their hands seized as much as they could of
the flax already ripped from the soil at the roots.
With their bodies bent forward, they held their eyes
fixed on the edge of the field where the flax ended,
coming up against the wheat. The space behind
them increased continually: a white stretch of
stubble, as hard and smooth as a threshing
floor—the place where the flax festival would be
celebrated.

And yet none of the harvesters noticed how the
light milkiness in the sky had begun to congeal, until
the entire expanse and the sun itself melted away
behind a veil that dulled the intense glare.

After the noon break, when the opening dances

and harvest songs were done, the sky was already completely thick, with a light drizzle falling. But the harvesters were so far gone, they were not bothered by a little wetness. The wind veered to the west, and the mist then changed into an angry, splashing shower.

V

Vermeulen was in a good mood when he walked off, thrusting with his walking stick—as he always was once he had settled some matter; after mature deliberation and long of two minds, he had to make the important move at last. The ground plan and the papers with his calculations were in his pocket, and everything was ready and clear in his mind—all hesitation was now gone.

The offering and sale of Legijn's farm and lands was to go on from nine in the morning onward, which gave Vermeulen still time to look over the layout of the whole property. He marched along like a shrewd operator who intends to pull off an underhand deal without letting on, feeling pleased at the thought of seeing the farmers' eyes and their expressions when the news thundered unexpectedly in their ears. The major reason for his action, the urgency to get his son out of the way, was and remained the primary motive, though relegated now to the background. For at that moment, Vermeulen saw himself in contrast to the other farmers of the region: he was a man in his pride, satisfied, pleased with the opportunity to show how he, rolling in his riches, does not have to think twice about snapping up whatever is to his advantage, whether convenient for him or, simply, something to his liking. And deeper in his nature, too, there was still the businesslike pennypincher, weighing and measuring everything, certainly willing to do something extravagant in order to follow through his intentions, but without allowing himself to spend a cent more than he has to.

"Who'd really be interested in it? Let's see . . . Sobrie has land nearby, also Verstraete and Bovin, a couple of scratch farmers—they won't speak up. A buyer, a serious bidder who'd try for the whole thing? A man like that'd have to come from outside . . ."

Vermeulen walked over and took a look at the land, comparing the lots, and the condition of the crops caught his eye immediately.

"The old misers," he growled, "they've arranged it so well, there's no damage to their crops from the storm. They've saved on manure because they're afraid of the wind and the rain—look how thin that wheat is!"

Legijn and his sister were known as two stingy wretches. They had never enjoyed any comfort, always working and slaving away, living like laborers, with one ambition only: the prospect of retiring in their old age. Vermeulen shrugged his shoulders at the sight of sheaved straw that seemed gnawed on by rats.

"The last bit of fat's been squeezed out long ago, and the farmer who takes over won't find much health to the soil," he figured. The story had spread through the area that Legijn's grazing cows stood propped up by two wooden poles in their stalls, otherwise they would keel over from weakness. "And it's sure ain't with them oats that they'll grow udders like saddlebags," Vermeulen grinned inwardly. "But that's not wholly to my disadvantage—those who don't know it shy away from a run-down signboard: it scares off the buyers."

There stood the farmhouse, with its steep tiled roof and the small spire above the stepped gables.

"It could be a good setup," he thought, "once the mess has been cleaned up a little. I'm curious to see the condition of the goods and belongings."

Vermeulen made out a crowd of people in the yard: farmers from the district as well as outsiders, all the more because, so opportunely, there was no work to be done on the land after yesterday's rain. The prospective buyers walked around, in and out of the stable, through the barn and pens. They laughed, they mocked, they told jokes. Cannaert stirred the swill in the pigs' trough; Sobrie prodded a bareboned cow in the flanks to see if it really stood firm on its legs.

"Whoever takes over here," Vermeulen jeered, "he'll find it barren ground for a new business!"

He walked around, nonchalant, and when Veroken said to him, "Well, Vermeulen, so you've just come for a look too?" he replied pleasantly, "I sure am, and it's certainly worth seeing!"

The village policeman rang a bell to bring the bidders together—the notary had arrived, they could begin.

He read out the procedure: first, each lot separately would be offered for sale, but after that round, interested buyers were free to make a call for all the fields *in cumulo*. Next, the buildings, the farmhouse and dependencies, would be offered. The taking over of belongings—crops, animals, and tools—would be done privately, at face value. Occupancy was set following Christmas Day.

Individual lots were bid for by farmers who had land lying adjacent to them, as Vermeulen had foreseen. A few were withdrawn for lack of interest. Both the notary and the village policeman tried in vain to put some spirit in the sale—the farmers stood stiff, their faces tense and serious, whoever made a bid speaking unheatedly, without agitation. Vermeulen was silent all the while, until the notary had read out everything and declared that the sales would now be "thrown together." And he still kept silent when all was quiet and no one spoke up. He put in his bid at the very last moment:

"Fifty thousand francs."

After that, no one opened his mouth. At the first session, the land fell to: Johannes Lodewijk Vermeulen. The farmhouse with all the buildings went to the same bidder for the sum of: twenty-five thousand francs.

No one had dared outbid Vermeulen, but the

farmers' dismay was great.

"Who's it for? What's he going to do with it? Is he going to leave his farm?" There were whispers on all sides, muttering and muffled groans, but no one dared pose the question directly to Vermeulen.

Since there was no work pressing, and since they were together anyway, they might as well waste the whole day—not one of them showed an inclination to go home. The farmers were thirsty, and there was nothing to be had here in the farmyard: Legijn stood there miserable, like a scruffy dog, his body trembling with emotion, while the old, shortwinded sister was unaware of what was happening around her. Now that the weight was off his mind, Vermeulen suddenly seemed to have become a different man. With a regal sweep of his arm, he invited everyone to come with him to the village: he wanted to wet the coming sale! At the nearest tavern, he stood them to a round of beers. Little by little, however, he realized that here was a chance to do himself a favor. He would trick the other farmers and get them on his side.

In the Sint-Eloy, he ordered a bottle of wine for each man there. The proprietress served them their drinks in the back room for the occasion, the farmers seating themselves at the round table. They clicked their glasses one by one, drinking to Vermeulen's health and the success of the sale. Flattered by the honor they did him, Vermeulen complacently stretched out his legs: it tickled his arrogance, gratified him to see how he, the great farmer, could act their superior. Pride dripped from his every word. No matter, the farmers became cheery by and by, chatting away worse than on Sunday night when it's time to go home. When they had bragged and lied to each other and talked their drivel long enough, Vermeulen said to himself: "Those guys are making a holiday out of it"—but he had had his fill, and he left.

"Look, it's raining!" he cried out, surprised, when he stepped outside.

"The weather's changed," some yokel who had come with him said.

"Well, it's Bovin!" Vermeulen shouted, turning around, and as he walked on he grumbled: "Now our harvest's going to rot in the field, when it was almost in the barn! . . ."

"The only thing left was bringing it in, Vermeulen," Bovin laughed. "But 'there's many a slip 'twixt cup and lip.' A farmer's a sad craftsman, he only gets what's given to him." And the small farmer went on with another few words: "Hey, Vermeulen! You've gotten yourself a real good deal there . . ."

"Yes I have, Bovin. It's for my son, in the event of his marriage."

"He's getting married?"

"Not 'getting married' . . . in the event of his marriage—and since I've no intention of making room myself, if I buy that farm, then he can clear out whenever he pleases."

"That's a good trick for someone who's got the

cash on hand and can do it."

Bovin stayed behind under a tree, and Vermeulen took a shortcut through the rain, heading home over a slippery path of mud. He was a little drunk and felt only pleasure from the coolness of the rain. The wine had set him aglow, and his legs slid out from under him now and then, so that he had to watch himself in order not to lose his balance. With the heavy walking stick, he knocked away the wet stalks of grain hanging across the narrow paths at his feet. His face was flushed with friendliness; he talked to himself, repeating what the farmers had said to him and what he had made them believe. He felt now as strong as a thousand men and thoroughly happy. He had done what he wanted, and everything had turned out according to his plan. He was in a wonderful mood. What did a little further damage matter to him now? Yesterday was nothing and was already forgotten! "It's lying there under God's sky," he murmured. "There's nothing to be done! But when there's something we can do, hold on!—that's all there is to it!"

The rain fell like fine, bright droplets of dust: on every leaf of grass at the edge of the drainage ditch, on stalks of grain, on the spreading willows along the road—sprinkles of water clustered everywhere, tiny pearls suspended on the verge of trickling, crystal-clear. There was a steady dripping and flowing from leaf to leaf, splashing to the ground, but so quietly, so without force that you could not hear it.

"You'd get wet after a while anyhow," Vermeulen thought. "The ground's slippery as soap. Or maybe I'm drunk?" He trudged laboriously uphill along the narrow path, between the alder brake and a plot of rye high as a man, the small wet spikes sprinkling water in his face. He slid backward, stumbled over the uneven ground, teetered through the sticky mud as if he were walking in rice pudding, skidded haphazardly, then stamped through the puddles with his heavy boots, without looking up. Suddenly irritated, Vermeulen worked himself into a pitch and threatened a blackbird with his stick—that damn water-whistler!—because it seemed to him as if the bird was enjoying the rain, with its crazy warbling, making fun of people for good measure. Abruptly, the opening of the harvest song sounded in Vermeulen's ears. It jolted him like an unexpected thunderclap, made him stand stock-still, confused, dumbfounded, listening. Was this a dream or could it be true?

"Four o'clock . . . vespers . . ."

The farmer shook his head. He recognized the voices, the wild harvest-singing of his workfolk.

"Ha, we'll see!" he snarled, and moved more quickly in his fury.

On the left side of his path rose the high edge of a wheatfield, blocking Vermeulen's view. Up yonder at the bend he would be able to see his flaxfield. In his haste and blind excitement, he missed his step and slipped, ending up with his right leg in the ditch while his left hand splashed in the mud. Vermeulen picked himself up, cursing, and stumbled up the path, without taking a look at his filthy clothes or wiping off his hand.

Brazen, direct, with no hesitancy, the song echoed full-throated:

> Thanks to our host
> For everything sweet,
> To all of us a happy treat!
> Na-ve-va!
> Na-ve-va!

The noise grated in Vermeulen's ears. It seemed a deliberate challenge, an open rebellion against his authority. At the bend in the path, he had a clear view of the flaxfield . . . and there was the whole crowd of harvesters, soaking wet and dancing in a frenzy.

The farmer stopped as if nailed to the ground. He felt a blow in his heart, and his blood froze. Something came shooting into his legs, and his blazing anger flared up and stuck in his craw. He wanted to run toward them, cursing, roaring, but he stayed still, nothing coming from his throat except a dull growl.

After the round dance was done, every one of the drunken harvesters fell onto a girl's neck, and Louis, that big lug, held that red-haired slut around the hips, just like the meanest of them, and there they all stood, wrestling and squirming, their bodies pressing, trying to push one another to the ground.

Romping there on the bare field, openly for all to see
. . . against the farmer's orders! What business did
they have on that flaxfield in the rain?

Vermeulen jumped forward. He did not yell or
shout, but hot anger possessed him to bring his
controlling authority to bear. He strode ahead,
stretching his legs as far as he could, gripping his
walking stick in his balled fist. He did not know what
he was going to do or how this fury would
explode—he was not thinking about it. He was in a
turmoil from a shock to his senses. He felt a power
driving him onward and allowed himself to be
worked up in a transport of indignation. He still held
back whatever it was that was boiling inside, but he
would be unleashing it in a hurry.

Were they stupid or had they gone crazy?
Wantonly destroying the flax! Had he not forbidden
it? Who dared act against his will? Or was it to bait
the "old man"? Was Louis trying to play the boss
and carry out his plan with his own hands? Ha!!!

They could see the farmer coming toward them
now—all covered in mud, with the eyes of a raging
bull. In a flash, the couples let go their hold, and
silence fell. Fearfully, they jumped into line, so as to
strike a pose, just like children caught in a forbidden
game; and because they could think of nothing
better, they set furiously to work. They stooped,
bodies bent, not daring to lift their heads, letting the
farmer draw near, waiting for what had to happen.

"Who told you to bring in the harvest?"

Louis stood closest, at the end of the line. He knew

his father was just a step away—he could hear the breath blowing through his nostrils—but he did not look up and went on working in a rush. The dancing and playing had made him impudent, unafraid, and now the young farmer doggedly held to his own, stiff-necked against the sudden counterblow that came to interrupt the fun. He had half expected something would happen. It stirred up in him a mixture of fear and pleasure, and his only concern at that moment of tension was whether the harvesters would stand firm against the farmer without his prompting. They went on working and kept silent, as he did.

Vermeulen, however, sensed at once that they were making a fool of him, that this was a prearranged game. He felt provoked beyond belief and exploded at last.

"Beat it!" he bellowed. "Off my field!" But the sound of his shouting was without effect, the words fading away—an insignificant noise, like the hollering of a cowherd. His threat had not even startled the birds—you could hear their warbling in the silence that followed, and nothing else except the short *rrrit* each time a handful of flax was gathered and its roots pulled from the ground.

What was going to happen? Everything important on earth seemed concentrated here at this one spot; the blackbirds cackling lightheartedly in the thicket and the people at work elsewhere remained on the outside—it was as if they did not belong to the same world. Each breath seemed like the heavy, rattling blow of a hammer thudding in the brain. The harvesters knew something had to happen. The young farmer had given the order for the work, and now the old man stood there opposite with his counterorder—what should they do? What did it matter to them? All interest was fixed on Louis, but no one dared look up. Only Schellebelle had risked it: she had stared at the farmer in an irresistible flood of fear and had at once tried to cry out her terror to prevent the misfortune that threatened Louis. But that terror itself held the girl trapped, choking the scream in her throat. Her legs trembled under her body, her fingers were clenched convulsively around a handful of flax. In the silence, there seemed no end to the waiting . . .

Vermeulen, though, never paused. He had seen through his son's mean intent at a glance, recognizing willful rebelliousness in that bent posture. It lasted the space of a lightning flash, stabbing him like the sting of a venomous bee. The farmer did not hesitate for a moment. The searing dart shot to his head from his chest. A spasm of the arm. And there was no holding back or thinking as Vermeulen loosened his sinews and lashed out with all his might. He swung the heavy walking stick treacherously through the air, without cursing or shouting, the deed faster than the telling—and caught Louis in the neck with a heavy blow. The young man fell forward, his face to the earth, without uttering a sound.

Shock and horror rose in a shriek from the crowd,

and after the shriek total confusion. The women sprang forward, wailing and groaning. The girls fled, hands held high, calling for help. The men in the first few moments stood appalled, arms dangling at their sides, staring in bewilderment.

Vermeulen felt the stick's elastic resistance in the recoil of his arm, in the strength of a solid stroke that cuts into the back of a fat ox. Yet his anger had subsided with the blow itself—at the very instant his complete authority was again secured, he realized the disgracefulness of his fury. He stood ashamed before his workfolk, and did not savor the expected pleasure in maintaining his paternal rights. And so he still feigned wrath and anger—holding his stick ready, without even knowing whom to lift it against, for no one was looking back at the farmer, no one was paying him the slightest attention. All care was for the fallen youth, lying lifeless, who had suffered so treacherous a punishment: the whole crowd gathered around him, the women bringing dripping wet aprons they had soaked in the ditch water to bathe Louis' head. Vermeulen now hesitated whether he still should run the harvesters off the field—something had happened all at once to change his mind, something he had not anticipated. He was the winner. He had recovered his control. He held on, squeezing his power in his fists. He gnashed his teeth. . . . But something had been broken, something lost, more valuable than all the rest, which until a moment ago he still had not understood: only now did he realize how useless and unnecessary his commanding authority might be from now on. For the time being, he kept an angry face, like a mask he was not permitted to put aside.

The harvesters picked the boy up in their arms, his body gone slack and fallen limp as a rag, carrying him off the field. The whole crowd abandoned the flax now, quietly and of its own accord, without the farmer having to threaten or demand. Vermeulen stayed on alone. In that short time, the face of the world had changed: the rain, the flax, the land, the sky were just trifling matters now—a man had been struck down!

The procession moved off—they knew where they had to go with their burden. Farmhands catching sight of the strange parade all left their work and ran across the fields and pastures to the house. . . . Vermeulen alone did not know where he ought to go. The lord and master remained standing on his flaxfield, his teeth chattering. He did not notice it was raining and would be growing dark. The storm's destruction was still evinced by the unharvested flax lying in confused tangles, strewn and scattered like the roiling waves of rough waters frozen all of a sudden in full turbulence. A fine drizzle came sprinkling down now, drenching the stalks, which were left undisturbed by the wind. Vermeulen was insensible to all of it—there was only one thing: the terrible uncertainty over the consequences of what he had done and what was in store for him. He suddenly felt cast down from the heights: he dared not go home. "Louis is dead!" The reproach drummed on incessantly in his mind. He watched the people hurrying toward the house, realizing that every concern and all interest were for the murdered youth, but he knew already that such curiosity would turn in a backlash from the victim to the murderer. He could hear people's voices, how they would say it, that very evening. "His father beat him to death!"

Vermeulen could not, would not believe that such a dreadful happening could come about in so short a time, from so small a cause—a blow with his stick, a sweep of his arm. But the terrible curse reverberated through the land, and he pictured the alarm on the faces of the people who would look at him from now on with fearful curiosity. There he stood all alone, the evildoer, without aid or comfort, facing all mankind. And that isolation further hardened his heart. He would not give in, he swallowed his regret, even if God and men were against him. If he forbade a thing, he would be respected, and by his son too, even if that son was twenty years old! And whoever did otherwise, he would . . . kill him! . . .

The words sounded like malicious joking, grim nonsense, for Vermeulen knew all too well that the times were out of joint, and deep inside him was the great, urgent wish that no more tomorrows would dawn over what he had done this day in his senseless rage. He had to go away from this place haunted by Cain, the murderer in the Bible. In his imagination, the age-old figures and bearded faces from the Scriptures, in whom he had friendly confidence, rose up before him, their eyes starting

open and their thin arms threatening. The dreadful
sufferings of Job and the bark of the prophets crying
for revenge roared in his ears, shaking him like a
vision of destruction on Judgment Day.

One of them shouted hoarsely:

"Woe unto the world and the inhabitants who
dwell therein!"

And then many voices rose up together, like the
noise of some great commotion.

"In the anger of the Lord of Hosts is the earth
afflicted, and the people shall be as food for the
flames: and a man shall spare not his brother.

"And thou shalt have no fellowship, not even with
those in mourning; for thou hast corrupted thy land,
thou hast slain thy people. And in eternity shall not
the name be called of the seed of the wicked.

"And I shall fight thee with a hand outstretched
and with a strong arm and in a raging anger, yea
with wrath and in a great fire."

Then a single voice rose in the fearful silence and
above all the others cried out in cruel prophecy:

"A people that is unbeknownst to thee must
devour the fruits of thy land and all thy labor. . . .
Then shall that land have pleasure in its rest, all the
days of its desolation!"

Vermeulen wanted to keep calm, assuring himself
that what he thought he was hearing were his own
voice and his own imaginary words. But there in the
rain, in that evening landscape, he felt such terror in
his heart and such despair, he ran off the field to
escape his fear. He turned and wandered around the

farm, purposely taking roundabout paths. Farmer Vermeulen, always conscious of his authority, who used to come into his yard with heavy footsteps, along the lane, across the bridge, and through the gate as under a triumphal arch—this Vermeulen now envied the people who freely entered the gate, unburdened by guilt, while he looked for a fordable place, over the embankment, to get into the house unnoticed from behind. But everything was so well locked and secured against a break-in by prowlers that he was forced to go in through the gate after all. He wanted to throw away his stick first, then realized that was useless—it could avail him nothing, now that the blow had been struck.

"Barbele!" The name stabbed through his mind like the thrust of a knife. The idea that he would stand before her as a murderer. "Murderer!" The word horrified him, it was still so new, so strange . . .

Vermeulen slipped past the barn gate and, stepping across his yard, recovered awareness of his self-esteem; he was the farmer; what he had done was his right as a strict father—he would have a few words ready for anyone who wanted to talk to him about it. With that, he mustered his courage and boldly marched inside. But he felt his heart pounding all the while: he knew with what looks his people would stare at him—just like you eye a stranger who happens by at an awkward moment.

As soon as he opened the door, everyone in the kitchen moved out of the way and went outside, shuffling off, silent and timid. The farmer first put his stick back in the clock case, then took off his hat and smock and tailcoat, pulled off his boots, and in his shirt-sleeves, went to his place by the corner of the hearth—to wait for what would happen next. He could hear the sound of stocking feet in the further room, Barbele's moans and sobs, her cries: "My boy, ah my poor boy!" The groans at once roused Vermeulen's distaste and made him hard-hearted—any regret for what he had done was gone: he felt no connection with the young man he had so pitilessly struck down.

"My boy!" Vermeulen jeered under his breath. "Nice boy, badgering his father! Good thing I put a stop to it!" He saw now that the storm had not yet blown over, that there would have to be more noise and new mishaps if she made it hard for him with . . . "her boy."

He stirred up his anger to push aside his compassion, to deny the emotion that made his heart thump. Yet anguish awoke deep inside him, and a terrible curiosity. He brought up the question ceaselessly, gnawed by uncertainty, he had to know: Was Louis dead or still alive? Or was he about to die?

Sofie, the housekeeper, came through the kitchen with tears in her eyes, but he dared not, he would not speak to her. She carried a small bowl of water outside, came to fetch something from the sideboard right next to him, went back into the room, all without looking at the farmer. Then Mielke, the stableboy, came in through the front door, his mouth already open in his haste to give the news he brought with him, but seeing the farmer sitting there startled him, and he held back his words. He remained standing by the door until another maid came out of the room, and then Vermeulen heard the boy whisper: "He's coming right away!" The farmer guessed where the message came from, and it was at once a great relief to him.

"He's not dead!" he thought. "He's still living! It'll be just a faint." The catastrophe he had feared was inescapable was softened somewhat, and so too the shock that had almost crushed him. He regained his composure, now that it seemed he had not committed murder after all. The objects in the kitchen no longer appeared so strange to his sight. Everything returned to its context within the hours of the day and the passage of time. It was getting toward evening and darkness was coming on. Vermeulen seated himself more firmly in his chair and stretched out his legs again at full length, as he was wont to do.

"It'll all come to nothing," he thought. But the evening did not turn out like other ones after all: the usual things did not take place. Supper time was drawing near and nothing was prepared, everything neglected. Silence weighed heavy on the kitchen. The maids walked barefoot back and forth, while the dismal wailing in the room kept on. The farmer strained his ears to catch any sound, any sign of life deeper down, from the bed . . . but there was no sigh, no breathing to be heard. The housekeeper now came back into the kitchen. She went to fetch bread and meat—she was going to remedy the situation after all and get something ready in a hurry for supper, since the workfolk still had to eat. Vermeulen felt reassured to an extent when he saw that the course of life had not come to a halt, that everything was going on as usual. He wanted to leave at the prospect of having to sit there shamefaced in sight of that whole gaping crowd, but he resisted the urge: he could not let himself flee from his own kitchen. It was too late anyway, the household and the harvesters were there already, as if prepared to stand around and wait, now that they were being served their supper during off hours.

They came in hesitantly, without a sound—they knew all too well something extremely serious was going on in the house. Quietly, they slid onto the bench between the table and the wall, kept their eyes on their plates, and ate without saying a word. Jan the groom, Ivo, the faithful Poortere, that wrinkled workman with his bald head, Free, Bultinck, Vromant, all the old, familiar hands, even the poor hirelings, obedient and simple—they had done their regular job today and had now come to sup on their well-earned food, looking forward to the rest as their reward—an untroubled rest, a peaceful, sound sleep. . . . Why was Vermeulen not allowed to look forward to rest, too? He ventured to look at the poor workers since they themselves, ashamed and hesitant, hemmed in by fear, kept their eyes lowered, not daring to stare at the farmer. Nearly their whole lives long, they had been coming to the same place in the kitchen for their sustenance, faring better there than in their own homes, and now they held themselves back, acting clumsy, as if they had done something wrong yet were nevertheless allowed to sit down, out of indulgence. But Vermeulen saw through their timid performance, guessing the sly thoughts they held secret in their minds—how they, as Christian men, had their opinions about his case too, which they would quietly share among themselves on their way home. He peered furtively at the maids, sitting with their backs to him and eating hungrily, heads bent over the table. He tried to find the redheaded slut who had turned his son's head. She was not there. "She doesn't dare come in my sight," he thought, "but she'll pay for it, just as soon as this business is straightened out! That's for sure!"

The workfolk got up as soon as they were done, mumbled the usual goodnights by the door, and left.

Then it was silent once more, inside, outside, and this time for good. Not a word, not a sound could be heard in the yard. Vermeulen was unnerved by the stillness—its solemnity gave an awesomeness to the situation that made him uneasy, increasing his anxiety and exposing him, in cruel uncertainty, to all kinds of guesswork. Vermeulen, who was uncomfortable and thrown off balance when the least incident disturbed the normal course of daily work; who had a horror of ceremony, any important occasion that touched him deeply and made him face up to life; who only wanted to follow the regular routine, wearing his workaday clothes, his own master—he cursed the misfortune all the more now because he had brought it on himself through his own doing. Because of him, time had taken on a new aspect, one which did not resemble that of yesterday and the days before, passing so calmly, so quietly. It would depend on the change in circumstances now whether "time," for him, would ever truly recover its ordinary features—whether things would yet again be in accord with his nature, the hours of the day take their usual course. Something had gone amiss with the steady movement of the finely adjusted clockwork: all thoughts and concerns were no longer given over to what beset man, to the common matters of existence at large; they were centered on a single subject, and *that* one excluded all others, bringing everything to a standstill. No one had felt concern about the young lad when he was walking among the living, bright and cheerful, but now that he was struck down, no longer taking part in the routine of everyday business, the whole neighborhood was thrown off balance, everyone preoccupied with him. Vermeulen saw the days to come . . . and himself standing there like a stone statue, the stupid cause, having brought harm simply by defending his own rights.

The hoofbeats of a horse plodded along the soggy ground outside, and shortly afterward the footsteps of the booted rider sounded on the stoop by the front door.

"Who's that coming this time of night?" The farmer immediately recognized the doctor. He walked in and was about to speak to Vermeulen when a maid, without comment, motioned him into the room.

"What's the old guy to me?" the farmer grumbled. But he sat there all in a pique, eagerly waiting to be told and be released from his anxious doubt. He was jealous of the doctor, who would know his son's condition sooner than he would himself. Vermeulen, who had never placed any trust in medical help, felt so small and pitiful now, a nobody in the hands of the man who would render the verdict on Louis' fate, deciding on life or death! He listened. The examination lasted a long time. Nothing except some mumbling, a quiet word, and an even quieter reply from Barbele. No screams, no complaints, no sighs from the patient.

When the doctor came out of the room, Vermeulen was once again sitting self-assured and surly, like a man carved from oak, not wanting to know a thing, not caring about what was happening. He looked up only when the doctor stood right next to him and made as if to speak, throwing him a scornful glance that tried to say: "What do you want with me? Make it short, the matter doesn't interest me." But the doctor remained calm and resolute; his voice sounded completely normal, like someone talking about the weather.

"Vermeulen," the old gentleman said, "your son is in danger. Your wife has seen to it that he will be given the last rites, and she has done the proper thing. I shall start by letting his blood, and ice must be made ready for his head. He may regain consciousness. We shall have to wait." And before he left, he said to the maid who had come with him out of the room:

"Send someone for leeches, and place three on the back of his neck."

Vermeulen had not batted an eye, but long after the doctor was gone, everything that was said repeated itself in judgment in his head, word for word. Barbele was sobbing ever more loudly in the room. All at once, sadness welled up in Vermeulen, like a river overflowing, and the headstrong farmer had to force himself not to collapse and give way. Then, at the same moment, the wild scene of the workfolk on the flaxfield came before his eyes, and his indignation restored his calm, chased the flood upstream, and killed the emotion—he remained firm. His face drawn taut, he sat there like a stone with his head tucked down and tousled hair bristling on his scalp, like a man who has done what he wanted to do, just because he wanted to do it. He forced the conviction on himself that a father had to maintain respect for his authority, and he had struck his son because Louis was rebellious. His attitude, the sweep of his arm when he had lashed out, he regarded as the gesture of a wrathful Moses. . . . Nevertheless, he had not expected that the blow would shake him so deeply to his very heart. Even with the full knowledge that he was in the right, he could not ward off the accusation or bury the reproach that rose in his mind: he felt he was the murderer of his own son; he knew the contempt of all men weighed upon him; and he had to wrestle with his compassion as well—for only now when this rival, this degenerate son whom he could not stand was cut down, did he become aware that he had murdered his own pride, his own blood. The lad who had wanted to defy his father lay like a fallen rag, and yet he surely had not meant it so harmfully and deserved so heavy a punishment. The father now admired the reflection of his own nature in his son's reckless pride. The boy had had to pay for his first attempt to become a man, struck treacherously as though by lightning, and Vermeulen imagined his son whimpering like a child and pleading mercy for his life. . . . He saw him crawling on the ground and falling. . . . The farmer was frightened at last by his own ruthlessness . . . wanting to stop his arm from swinging after the blow had been struck. There he was, the excitable idiot who had acted in a fit of frenzied rage, the old, dull father, nearly senile, doomed and ripe for death—a fool, looking on his atrocious deed, without a tear coming to soften the hardness of his heart. The train of his thoughts was disturbed—he was being dragged left and right, his heart and mind tormented, and he suffered from his own bullheaded obstinacy.

From outside in the evening air came the clear ring of a bell—the priest approaching the farmhouse to administer the last rites. Vermeulen anticipated what was going to happen, and a tremendous surge of emotion beat through his veins. He had not thought about it yet. That, too, he had to endure, and there were many more cruel, unusual things for him to expect. He realized he was already known for his crime throughout the entire region—the villagers had spread the news everywhere. And how would it end? How should he behave at the funeral? He saw himself walking behind the body, head bare, bent, broken, the old farmer . . . or did he want to hold himself straight and look people square in the eye? In his imagination, Vermeulen followed the funeral procession: the villagers stuck their heads together; he heard them whisper as they watched him pass through the street, and he could read their thoughts on their faces: Vermeulen himself had one foot in the grave and had pushed his son into it because he was envious of the young man! But he understood, too, that he would never know another hour of peace—it was over for Vermeulen!

The ringing of the bell came to a stop at the door. The farmer waited until the last moment, still uncertain of what he would do. He was standing now before the Most High—the supreme Lord Himself, who "holdeth all the ends of the earth in His hands; He who beholdeth the heights of the mountains. He who driveth wind and weather and giveth growth and ruleth the course of the sun . . ." Now or never, Vermeulen had to yield himself and acknowledge his meekness in the face of the Revered One. Hardly had he seen the white surplice shining behind the door, even before the priest's tall figure was entirely inside the house, than the farmer was kneeling, head bowed and hands folded. His emotions overpowered him. He experienced the same pounding of the heart and the same fear in his throat as that other time, many years ago, when his own mother had received the last rites and he had knelt there as well, apprehensive and anxious before the Lord God, who filled the house with His awesome presence. Now, too, the feeling of veneration for the Greatest and Most High ran through him, and he gave himself up submissively as a humble nobody, ready to do penance. Mechanically, he mumbled a prayer, but his mind was not on the meaning of the words he was saying. He kneeled down, a servant, confessing his crime before God Almighty—in his chastened attitude alone lay his admission of guilt and complete surrender.

Vermeulen did not know how long he had been kneeling there. He stood up when the priest came back out of the room and did not dare sit down in his presence. The priest drew near and said carefully:

"Louis has received the holy oil. Send for me at once if he regains consciousness, so I can hear his confession and administer the sacraments. We must all pray for him now, that God grant him grace and not allow his condition to worsen."

Vermeulen nodded in agreement. His lips pressed together, his chin began to quiver; he swallowed the saliva caught in his throat and with a thick finger brushed the tears from his eyes. The priest waited a moment, wanting to say something more or waiting for a word from the farmer; but that word did not come, and the priest, too, thought it better to keep silent. He motioned to the sexton, and because the sick man had been unable to receive Our Lord, the bell now rang on their way back as it had when they were coming.

Vermeulen was seated again, and from where he sat he followed the ding of the bell across the evening landscape. He knew every inch of the route, and from the ringing he traced both priest and sexton step by step, just as well as if he were seeing them with his own eyes walking the roads in broad daylight. The hush of night already reigned in the farmer's kitchen. The devotional candle sputtering in the room, charcoal rustling in the hearth, and the authoritative ticking of the clock, these alone were alive in the house—every other sound was of the dead. Barbele and the housekeeper sat in the room, praying of course; they would keep watch the whole night long.

"When my mother lay dying, I watched at her bedside, too, and felt the sadness of the hours dragging by," Vermeulen thought. But then it had been a resigned expectation of something that had to come; now he had to suffer in terrible uncertainty.

All the rest of the people had gone to bed—those living outside the inner circle of the household slept as they did on other nights, when nothing had happened at the farm. Vermeulen decided to follow suit and go upstairs; but he wanted to try it without making the slightest noise, slinking off like a thief. For the first time in all his years as a farmer, he failed to draw up the weights in the clock and lock the door. Things that at other times he always did, become innate needs through long habit, he now left undone.

There was, in any case, general confusion in the house, and he lacked the heart still to keep the old order going. It was immaterial to him from now on whether the clock would tick the next morning or not.

He avoided making the steps creak however much he could, opened the door of his bedroom with extreme caution, and as he lay down, loosed a sigh from the bottom of his heart. But as soon as he had closed his eyes, he saw the harvesters dancing wantonly like wild foals and heard their songs bruited across the field. His anger flared up again. He knew he would strike the blow and wanted to hold back his arm this time; but he was urged on by a strange power, and the blow fell. The images were distinct in his mind in the darkness and still of the night. As if from a height, he viewed in perspective and recognized the worth of everything that concerns a man; he saw through the context of all human endeavors and understood how useless and vain were the things one strives for. The whole display was spread before his eyes like an open landscape. He had never had the time to think of these things in the past, having been absorbed by the press of circumstances. Now that the course of his life was brought to a halt, it all seemed clear to him, each thing having its own value. He brooded over the entire pattern of his plans, the efforts and pursuits of his whole existence . . . adding up to nothing—an unexpected happening had confounded all his calculations and given them a new turn.

"For a long time," he thought, "I'd been considering something to maintain my control . . . yesterday I found it at last: I bought a farm—I'd gotten what I wanted . . . but right away I made all my efforts useless, striking my boy down when there was no need for me to fear him anymore." Vermeulen saw the mocking grin on his face—it was scoffing at his own self—and he understood that an evil spirit had led him astray. . . . He felt how useless his earlier imagined fear had been, murmuring in self-pity as he realized the absurdity of his notion of authority, for everything hangs from a single thread, with the balance ever changing. It was suddenly so clear to him: someone lay in agony in the room-for-show, peace had been violated, and all things were now out of their accustomed order. His awareness that a man was suffering in his house prevented Vermeulen, like everyone else, from sleeping; he was losing his rest over it, all his senses were focused directly on it, everything except that one thought was insignificant. He understood for the first time that his son constituted the main reason for his own life. Only yesterday, Louis had been in good health and Vermeulen had slept peacefully. But now his son was lying in pain, perhaps dying, and likewise there was no rest for the farmer. He did not think about

sleep, listening to identify every noise—he could hear
people coming and going, doors opening, a chair
being moved . . . yet only one thing really existed in
the whole house, beside which all the rest was
forgotten: Louis! Louis was lying in that room and all
thoughts were straining toward it.

Vermeulen experienced a longing desire to see his
son, to be by that bed himself. He did not know who
would prevent him, but neither could he figure how
he would get to Louis' bed! Why had he never
yielded to the promptings of his heart? Why had he
never dared show himself to people as he really was?
What was always coming between his inner nature
and his outward behavior? Why must he always be
the severe master, unable or unwilling to let his
family see anything of his warm indulgence? Why
was he not like Barbele? Life, after all, seemed to be
merely the simple consumption of things throughout
a succession of similar days, the turning of time
above the heads of men. . . . All the rest was pretense
and feigned blindness by those who refuse to realize
what is actually there . . .

With the bright dawning of a new summer
morning, Vermeulen had to admit that he had slept
after all. Upon awakening,he became conscious once
more of the frightful breach of his existence, and he
reproached himself as a coward for having slept
while Louis lay doomed to death and everyone else
in the house had abandoned sleep, filled with
anxiety. The start of the new day brought him no joy
or pleasure; he was overcome by sadness and a

heavy despondency. He got up, and the instant he reached the first step of the attic stairs, he immediately found that everything he had understood so clearly in his solitude was receding. And he knew at once that his status and his shyness of others would force him again to put on his usual face and appearance—he would remain hard on himself and his household.

The aroma of coffee floated upstairs. Coming down, he sensed that no one had slept—they had kept watch without him. He, the only one who properly ought to have held vigil, had slept while others suffered through his fault. . . . Vermeulen realized then that the morning was not starting out just like the day before—he least of all felt any inclination to get things stirring with his presence. He did not think about making his usual rounds.

His determination to go directly to the room, to Louis' bedside, had already weakened—shame held him back. He anticipated endless vexation and anguish but took his place by the hearth nevertheless. Farmhands and maids began running around in an unusual way again—no one was thinking about work and everyday business. The farmer sat there toying with his intention to risk the big step; he entered a tremendous fight with his own nature and disposition, but without reaching any decision. He was distracted, staring in front of him dull and listless, now looking at the core of flames in the hearth, then at his clenched, useless fists. Having to sit there, left to torment himself in the presence of

people coming and going, was an agony for him. Yet
he did not dare go away: for where could he hide? He
wished he were ill himself and bedridden, bearing all
of Louis' suffering, if only he could be free of shame.

Barbele had already come into the kitchen a few
times, leaving—perhaps intentionally?—the door to
the room ajar. She had been outside as well and had
just come back when Vermeulen made up his mind
and decided to go into the room. He would definitely
do it at the next opportunity. He had seen the sorrow
and resignation on his wife's face; but also how she
denied her own grief, remaining calm yet filled with
sorrow and anxiety . . .

Vermeulen waited for a chance until noon, and
then, while Barbele was in the storehouse and the
housekeeper was pumping the churn, he got up from
his chair and went—unafraid, like a man staking his
claim—where Louis lay.

He did not dare look at the head of the bed. His
eyes remained focused on the little table, cleared of
account books and papers, where now bottles stood
and black leeches swam around in a glass of water.
There was a bowl of cracked ice, looking so strange
in the midst of the summer heat, and on the large
table, the crucifix with its consecrated branch
between the burning candles.

Vermeulen was calm now and reassured. He had
gained a victory over himself and made his stand.
His decision was firm: there would be no going away.

Everything had the look of a room for the
dying—you could breathe in the smell of death with

the fumes of the burning candles. The farmer tried to overcome his horror, and gradually he ventured a glance at the head of the bed. He looked for his son's face in the hollow of the pillow; it lay covered, deep in the whiteness of the sheets. A heavy shock rocked his whole frame at the sight of the face, pale as a corpse's, with its closed mouth and bloodless lips. He understood at last what had happened, and he held his eyes on the features of the poor boy who lay there lifeless, doomed, never to rise again.

Barbele had been watching her husband, coming to look in her stocking feet. But out of respect, she went silently back to the kitchen to leave the farmer alone with his son.

Vermeulen now felt he was where he ought to be, wanting nothing more than to be left here quietly and to wait. . . . Dry-eyed and sober, he went over what had happened, unable to fathom the reason for his action. Thoughts that had never visited him before assaulted his mind; here he could give himself over completely to reflection and see matters as they were, without flinching.

He had been sitting there—half an hour or half an eternity, he did not know—when the door was pushed open softly, and Vermeulen received a new blow that threw his whole mind into confusion all over again. He was not prepared for it; he had not even considered that they would be coming, that they still existed—and yet there they were! their identical figures in identical black clothes, ignorance and fearful expectation on their slow faces and in their great, anxious eyes. Unsteady in what they had to do, occupied solely with their carriage and the affected gestures used to express a mourning they did not feel deeply; afraid of coming close to their father—there stood the two boarding-school girls, wearing false expressions like empty-headed little geese, fresh home from school because an accident had happened to their brother. They approached the bed in silence. When they saw Louis lying there, unrecognizable, lifeless, with his eyes closed, they thought for sure that he was dead or about to die, and at that same moment they began to cry from the bottom of their hearts. But first, they each took out a white handkerchief, having been taught that even in sorrow one must behave.

It provoked the farmer's disgust. "Looks like a lesson they learned, the way they're copying each other," he thought. And he was seized with the desire to thunder against their tempered grief, just to shake up that tame weeping and sheepishness, to shout that *he* had done it! That he had severed the tendons in Louis' neck with his walking stick . . . and that he would do it to him again, and to them, too, if they dared rebel against his authority!

But he said nothing and remained seated—he was afraid of his own roughness, and it was not fitting to disturb the holy silence in the room.

Their mother led the two girls away from the bed, and a triple sobbing rose up in the kitchen.

The priest came again that same afternoon, and seeing no change, no improvement in Louis' condition, had to return with nothing accomplished. The doctor came, too, the man disturbing with a rough hand what Vermeulen, out of respect, had not dared to look at: he threw back the blankets, turned over and manhandled the limp body. The farmer, who did not hold with tender treatment himself and crashed impatiently through everything, felt his heart contract, held his breath, and could not watch what was being done to his son. Ivo the groom and the housekeeper had to come help the doctor. Vermeulen expected a scream any second, a struggle, some sign of life, but after the workover Louis lay there quietly as before. The housekeeper took the bowl of blood away, and Ivo filled the bladder with fresh ice to put on the patient's head. Then they all left, and the farmer remained by the bed, alone.

And so the slow course of the long day dragged on toward yet another night. Not once had the clock sounded, not at noon, not for vespers, not in the evening—all life, all noise was subdued around the farmstead as though it were a prolonged Good Friday. The horses remained in the stables, the hands bringing the animals only the necessary fodder. The harvesters had been let go, and the regulars walked aimlessly here and there, looking for something to do. They spoke very softly and made no noise; footsteps on the front-door stoop were muffled by the straw scattered there on purpose. The workfolk came barefoot into the house to eat and left again just as quietly. Passing by along the boarded pathway, they peered over their shoulders at the windows of the room where they knew the farmer sat keeping watch by his son. No one said a word about what had happened; grave concern and compassion was on every face.

"How's it going now?" was the usual question, asked repeatedly. And the answer remained unchanged: "Still the same, no improvement, no gain."

Schellebelle, like the others, carried on in grim silence. She ventured into the house only if she knew the farmer was in the room. Whenever she had the chance, the girl crawled into a corner of the stables and sat there staring into the dark. She only dared vent her great sadness at night in her bed, deep under the covers, weeping from her heart. An unconscious sense of honor moved her to hide her sorrow, for she had no right to show distress; she was tortured by shame and guilt, knowing herself to be the cause of the accident. Sophie had been alluding to her when she had declared yesterday: "What did I predict? Such foolishness comes to a bad end." After that especially, Schellebelle remained reserved with the old maid and did not reveal what was going on in her heart. She would not, could not allow herself to think about the disruption of her own happiness and the collapse of that uncontrollable delight in which she had wallowed drunkenly—her own pain counted for nothing. But when she found herself alone somewhere, she said softly:

"Louis! Louis! It's my fault! Louis, your father should've killed me! Louis, it was because of me! . . ."

She remembered now the way she had acted: how she had made eyes at him, looking at him and laughing, putting all of herself into it—cunning, sly, and crafty, she had used all her feminine charms and tried to catch him. How wild and rash she had been, letting everyone see she desired him and wanted to seduce him! But that was because she found him so supremely attentive, she couldn't help it—and now it had cost him his life and his happiness . . . suddenly it was all over! Her thoughts turned again and again to the flaxfield, and she saw it happening: they were standing there just after the dance and embracing each other so tightly—with his face against hers, he was forcing her down to the ground, and she let him kiss her . . . then, unexpectedly, the farmer appeared, and she sensed the danger at once! She was afraid of Vermeulen; she shuddered at the possibility of meeting him—she would never dare come under his gaze again. It was such a pity for his wife—so cruel to see how she cried day and night, and Louise and Anna . . . Schellebelle felt a burning shame and remorse consuming her.

For the first time in her life, the girl was having to learn that other things existed in this world besides laughter and fun. Only yesterday it was so fixed in her mind: nothing but unending joy lay in full prospect, happy days from one season to the next. Her own dream and what she discovered everywhere, in everything—what the other girls had taught her all the wonderful summer long, was this: one pure, everlasting love, without trouble, without impediment. She saw love all over. Love was her sunshine and her warmth, the cause and root of life itself. In her disillusionment, stunned by the calamity, the girl all at once felt how defenseless, how poor and miserable her standing was among people who were entire strangers to her! Her own young body, which she had been so proud of and pleased with—for his sake, since he had revealed it to her—counted for nothing anymore, serving only for work. Everything was reduced now to its stark value, and nothing mattered to her. Pleasure in itself, pleasure in her pursuits, pleasure in fun, sunshine, and the sweet summer days—nothing in all that could still cheer her heart. Louis would no longer be near where she was working, that clever fellow with his exuberant, mischievous eyes and his graceful figure. She would miss him everywhere; fields and pastures would be dead from now on, holding no attraction for her.

More and more, against her will, her thoughts kept returning to what she had lost, the past acquiring an exquisiteness which tortured her all the more now that the joy was gone. Her happiness! She was reliving it in a thousand ways; it had enveloped her on all sides—to the left and right, and above her in a sky that was filled with it. Louis had been present everywhere, in everything; she could see the soft gleam of his eyes and the flash of his smile wherever she looked. The whole summer with him had been an unconcealed feast; each day had meant a step further into fresh happiness; again and again, new

appetites had been awakened. And on the highest
rung, when she was about to enjoy her deepest wish,
on the very day of the long-awaited flax festival, her
happiness had collapsed and gone under in misery.
Why hadn't she ever been afraid it could happen?
No, without any such suspicion, she had just kept on
indulging herself, laughing and chattering,
wallowing and dallying—she had gone around with
him as with a . . . like someone who . . . with her. . . .
She did not dare pronounce the word, for he lay
there suffering and would perhaps die. Not wanting
to think about it anymore, she had to push it aside,
but: the open door to the stables; the little place
behind the barn, in the corner by the elder tree; the
field, the thicket, the flax—the sheen of her great
happiness remained everywhere she looked: she had
waited for him *just there,* jubilant at his appearance . . .
and the memory of that fond delight, mingled with
despair, wrenched her heart. From now on, it would
be all the same to her: she had to forget everything;
she would have to endure the housekeeper's hatred
and the farmer's anger; she would have to watch in
shame the farmer's wife's suffering while concealing
her own sorrow. She thought at first of running
away, but she could not allow herself to! She felt
rooted there, grown a part of things, and would not
be able to live anywhere else; better to put up with
the worst of everything than leave—she was willing
to grovel and beg so as to be allowed to stay. The
secret of her love would lie buried in her heart
forever! She would hide it, keep it hidden, but never

abandon it! She wanted to store it, sealed like a treasure her whole life long, to think of and worry over always.

The calamity had come too suddenly and too unexpectedly, and too much attention was taken up with the sick man lying between life and death to pay any mind to the affairs of a mere maid. No one noticed Schellebelle. All eyes were directed at the windows of the best room, everyone anxiously waiting for the outcome of the grave situation.

But there was no change. Vermeulen still sat at his son's bedside. He stayed there the way he had at first stayed in the kitchen—not daring to leave. And now he could catch all the noises from the kitchen; he listened to them and would have preferred to be with people instead of sitting there, stuck. But *life,* the little spark of life he had to watch over did not permit him to leave. He remained where he was. On the fourth day, he had yet to touch any food—he had refused with a mute gesture and continued refusing.

His wife let him be. Without openly humoring him, she pretended not to know how he stole into the cellar at night, coming like a thief to get his food; but she intentionally left provisions within his reach. She herself stayed in the kitchen, resuming her work and leaving Louis' care entirely to the farmer. She very rarely came to the bedside and then never by herself, only with the doctor or the priest. She no longer wept.

Whatever the doctor ordered, Vermeulen carried

out precisely, with patience and care. He moistened
Louis' lips every hour with a little feather dipped in
wine. Whenever it melted, he filled the bladder with
fresh ice. Beyond that, he kept staring at his son and
followed his breathing. It was the only sign of life he
could observe. Once he had risked lifting the
patient's arm, but it had weighed heavy as lead in
his hand and fell back limp on the covers. In his
despair, he had asked the doctor's opinion but had
got nothing from him except a critical raise of the
eyebrows and doubt expressed in these few words:
"Wait, rest, a great deal of rest."

Vermeulen had patience enough, so long as he
might hope for some improvement, some alleviation.
And as for rest, he was on the alert: not a single
noise penetrated the room. The hours crept by slowly,
steadily, with no relief. The tenuous silence and the
enforced tranquility permeated Vermeulen's heart—a
calmness and resignation unknown before held him
now in its sway. He surveyed all of life's ups and
downs, pondering what he had done and what he
ought to have done. . . . Chewing over his thoughts
by himself again and again, he achieved exact
insight into a number of matters, sensing some
relation between their causes and effects. Many of
the things to which he had attached importance in
the past, much of what had seemed to him the very
basis of living, he now regarded as of little
significance. It was as if a haze of dreams lay spread
over every surface, inviting his gaze to see deeper
within. The whole aspect of the room, even the air in

it, had changed: the sun came shining through the windows; the writing desk was still standing there, the books, the walking stick with its white-iron trowel, the strongbox—everything was in its usual place, but their meaning and their interconnection were no longer the same. The old Vermeulen used to come here in the past to arrange his affairs leisurely, in seclusion—but now that the young Vermeulen had been moved in, the farmer occupied the subordinate position. The master farmer himself sat like a tenant visiting his landlord—like a stranger waiting while others decide his fate. The tables were turned.

The young man, lively, strong, impudent—lay felled like a tree. When his son was healthy and walking around, Vermeulen had dreaded him like death itself, opposing Louis as an enemy, a rival, someone he had to crush with his utmost efforts—but now that his mindless act had brought him a victory he had already won in another way, the farmer realized how fleeting and without value was the control he had so anxiously been pursuing. . . . He had regarded all the property and possessions as his very own—as were the clothes on his back. The total authority over the farm, over all that belonged to it, depended on his will, and so he had supposed that everything, being a part of himself, would stand or fall with him. Blinded by pride, he had not seen how reckless and arrogant it is to want to move the immovable, to have the vanity to set yourself before the imperishable—trying to stem the tide of nature's

law and sail against it. He understood now that what
people call "private property" is given, for use only,
to the man who happens along, passes by . . . and
fades away—taking possession, yielding it up to his
successor . . . of no importance in the sweep of time.
His great folly had been his wanting to direct the
course of life against eternal laws, and he realized to
his shame how a higher scheme above him had
prevailed—everything had been wheeling and
spinning over his head, and he himself had given his
own plans a new turn in an ill-considered moment.
His victory and triumph had become his
punishment—in striking down his enemy, he had
struck down himself. And now he stood there, a
doomed man, weary of life, ashamed of his crime,
miserable, his reason clouded by confusion, all
because he, who was himself going to die, had
crushed the flower of life in his own flesh and blood.
All he could do was sit and keen over himself and his
poor boy, who so undeservedly had to pay for his
father's arrogance. At times, Vermeulen gave up
completely, sitting there senseless and staring. His
farm and his lands, his standing with the farmers of
the region, his authority and his wealth no longer
mattered. Sitting on the chair in the room was
enough for him; he had found rest there and the
opportunity to penetrate more deeply below the
surface of everyday business. The only things that
still concerned him were his son's breathing behind
the curtains of the elegant bed and the fear, the
anxious doubts, that the breathing might stop at

any moment—that it would be over . . .

Breathing remained the one sign of life, and it was the farmer's only hope. It came regularly, quietly, like someone sleeping. But it got no better or worse—no change from the first day.

"Is he suffering, the way he's lying there?" Vermeulen asked, and the doctor had reassured him. But the distrustful farmer did not believe it anyhow, convinced the old man was just guessing, that he knew no more about it than he did himself.

Sometime in the stillness of the lonely afternoons, when Vermeulen heard no sound from the world outside, he would approach the bed, draw the hangings aside, and stand gazing for hours, insatiable, at the face of death. Louis . . . he did not seem to be the same anymore. This was not the Louis who was running across the yard just a few days ago, brazen, with strength in his body—a fine young man! Now he was lying there, his features calm, with a pallor over his face, his eyes closed as in quiet attention. A sweet smile around his mouth suggested bliss, like someone in the transports of a happy dream. Vermeulen would linger, filled with awe and veneration, overcome by fear, and he asked himself: had the mind perhaps left the body and the soul been taken up into the clouds? . . . Then his attention would suddenly turn to the spot in the back of the neck, all bruised and disfigured, where the leeches had been sucking—and he became horrified. He would dip the feather in the small wine bottle and moisten his son's pale lips. Vermeulen had never before done anything with such grave ceremony, taking so many pains. His great labors in the open field, where monstrous clouds vast as continents rolled on high above his head while he stood with his work in the sight of the whole countryside—even *that* seemed only child's play to him compared with what he had to do now. Then he would sit again in the silence, listening with the same attentive humility, and count the sounds the woodworm made . . .

And so it happened that he recognized the voice of old Poortere, talking to his wife in the kitchen. He was shaken as though by a sudden seizure when he heard Barbele say: "Go ask the farmer about it . . ."

Vermeulen held his breath, his eyes fixed right on the door and fear in his heart, waiting for what was going to happen. At last, the door of the room was opened warily, and there stood Poortere, the aging workman, a miserable wreck: barefoot in worn-out pants, shirt open across his hairy chest, sleeves pushed up, and knobbed, bony hands hanging down from his arms. He held back, not daring to set foot in the room he was never at other times allowed to enter and which affected him as would a solemn shrine. With fearful eyes, like a criminal, he stood before the farmer, next to the bed of the stricken son. What he wanted to say stuck in his throat and left him tongue-tied . . .

Vermeulen looked at the disheveled wretch, and he too could not get out a word. Finally, the man ventured to give a reason for his obtrusive entrance:

"Farmer," he said, stammering, "they sent me to

ask, the farmhands did, what's to be done today? . . ."

Vermeulen remained silent.

"It's been drying for six days now," Poortere continued. "Shouldn't we go ahead with the flax?"

Vermeulen did not move, but two large tears fell from his eyes. He clenched his jaw so that his teeth gnashed audibly. The shabby hired man, decrepit and poor, stood with the words stuck in his throat, his eyes watering. Vermeulen was startled by the sudden question—the entire landscape all at once lay before his eyes, spread out in a vision of sunshine. But at the same moment, a great despondency came over him as regards the immutability of everything. A haze whirled around him like a storm of ashes. He could not see beyond the boundless despair that was weighing on him—a feeling of impotence he had never known pressing him down. Anxiety was on his face, and you could see the childish bafflement in his eyes. While thinking, his chin began to nod. He made an awkward gesture of resignation, of helpless supplication, at the man—he shook his heavy head, like someone pleading for mercy, and he sobbed out at last:

"Poortere, I can't . . . go away from here, old man! Just do . . . whatever, it's all right. I don't know . . . I've got to stay here."

Poortere stood bewildered, his head bowed. Fat tears rolled down his cheeks and plashed on the ground in front of his bare feet; his thin shoulderblades hunched up; his lips trembled—but no sound came. People were sobbing in the kitchen, too, and loudly—utter despair suddenly broke loose throughout the whole house. Vermeulen heard it, darkness swam before his eyes, and he felt everything crack deep inside. He pushed his face into the covers at the foot of the bed, thrashing around and snuffling horribly with each breath. For the first time, he let his grief pour out openly.

The fine life that had been waiting for the boy! The remaking, the continuation of Vermeulen's own existence . . . was disfigured, in ruins. He was about to die himself, he was next. But the boy had only just entered life . . . he needed so much to live! The sudden realization tormented him, and he suffered from the wretchedness of his cruel deed.

Then a hand pressed his shoulder, and when he looked up, Barbele was standing next to him. She had been crying, too, but her expression was serene, and she looked at Vermeulen kindheartedly:

"God must help us," she said, and calm submission and quiet trust spoke from the look in her tearful eyes. Vermeulen was touched. Following the primal urging of his crushed heart, he gripped her hand without thinking, without hesitation, and squeezed it in his weather-hardened fist. His chest tight, he implored:

"Barbele, Barbele, if only he could get well again!"

Vermeulen had called his wife by her name and in speaking it had humbly confessed his guilt. Conscious of his surrender, he abandoned himself to her tenderness, for he was helpless and in his great need had to find a refuge somewhere from the heavy gloom that burdened his soul. He was a broken man standing empty-handed, with all power fallen from him—a man who has destroyed his own happiness by nurturing arrogant plans. The beauty of the season, life in the open air, was over for him—he had hastened his last summer to its end—nothing awaited him now but the cold and dark. He would wander around a while more, but aimlessly, his mind gone, for the living farmer had already given up—his part was played out to the end. And because young Vermeulen, who was to succeed the old man and reign over the farm and its lands, because that lad lay fallen and doomed—Vermeulen had abdicated . . . leaving his authority to the aging farmhand.

"My turn's over," he thought. "I've got nothing more to do here. I feel the hand of God heavy upon me, and it has made me 'into a withered tree . . . I am become a snag in the teeth of the Lord God.'"

But then his tough hold on life rose up again in a convulsive start—he wanted to live, he wanted everything to be like before . . . he did not want to be old, he did not want to die, he wanted to live! to live! For he saw life everywhere. He was aware of it all around him and knew it would go on once he had given way—the mute trees, the crops, everything would continue to grow and move, recurring through the succession of days. He wanted his fields, his livestock, his land, and his crops—he wanted to remain a farmer! He wanted to stay as long as his farm would stand! He wanted to live as long as there was life in the world! He gnashed his teeth in fury over his helplessness—he could not budge the things that were immovable. And when he had exhausted his rage, despair came over him once more—an immense, infinite sadness, a shadowy disquiet that would smother him. The old farmer, the sinewy fighter, stood there like an innocent child—he looked everyone in the eye, pleading for someone or someplace to bring him peace and comfort, so that he might await his final exit calmly and resigned.

SUN & MOON CLASSICS